# Enforcer's Redemption

## A Redwood Pack Novel

By
CARRIE ANN RYAN

# Enforcer's Redemption

Adam Jamenson has suffered through the worst loss known to man. The only reason he lives day-to-day is to ensure the safety of his Pack. As the Enforcer of the Redwood Pack, it is his job to protect all in his path, though he was unable to protect the ones he held dear. The war with the Centrals is heating up and Adam must try and grit through it in order to survive. Though the broken man inside of him may not want to...

Bay Milton is a werewolf with a past. And a secret. She's met the Redwood's Enforcer only once, but it left a lasting effect. Now she needs to find him or everything he had thought he lost, may be lost again.

Together, they must struggle and find a way to fight their pasts and present in order to protect their future. But the Centrals have a plan that might make their path one of loss and destruction.

# Dedication

*To Lia Davis. Thank you for helping me keep it together with Adam. We needed you.*

# Acknowledgments

This book took almost everything I had in me to write and I couldn't have done it without my writing family. Thank you Lia Davis for being there for me with everything. Thanks to my Pack, you know who you are. You guys are so energetic about Adam, that it totally helps.

Thanks to my hubby for not laughing at me when I'm sobbing as I write. I know I looked a mess, but you stood strong. And thanks to my readers. You guys have been so supportive and vocal about wanting Adam's story. You're the reason I get to do this. Thank you.

# PROLOGUE

"**D**amn, it wasn't supposed to be this difficult." Caym cursed as he paced, his fists itched to punch something. He picked up the piece of paper he'd dropped on the floor earlier and saw red as rage coursed through him.

*Still no results. Target not acquired.*

Caym screamed and flexed his powers, the pulse of energy causing the paper to go up in flames. The heat burned, leaving trails of ash on his skin. Good. He needed the pain. He brushed a lock of hair out of his face and cursed again. Nothing was going as planned. Nothing.

A whimper sounded in the corner of the room, and Caym snarled. The wolf had failed him. Well, not exactly this wolf, but it was one of the hairy beasts. He always had such trouble figuring out which wolf was which. Not because it was hard, but because he really didn't give a damn. It was just unfortunate that this wolf had delivered the message. The man he'd sent out on his mission must have known Caym would be displeased and sent another wolf instead. That pissed Caym off even more.

It would be a shame to kill the messenger, but Caym loved to go against the grain, especially when blood and mayhem were involved.

They'd failed him. Again.

He'd known another of his kind resided on this plane the moment he'd set foot on that grassy circle the night the Centrals had called him and sacrificed two of their own. Still, he'd held the fact a fellow brethren lived on this plane closely to his chest in case he needed it. With the Centrals fucking up at every turn, first with the Willow girl, then with the trinity bond, he needed to step up his timeline and take control sooner rather than later.

Now, since that abomination, Josh, had killed Hector, there was only one wolf in his way—Corbin. Caym almost felt something for the sadistic bastard, but not enough to waylay his plans. No one was good enough for that.

But, back to the point—he couldn't find his brethren. All demons could find each other if needed; it was in their genetic code. Why was he having so much trouble finding this one?

Though he wouldn't dare to mention it aloud, he desperately needed this other demon to make his plans work. The trinity bond had severed his connection to the hell that he came from. Without that, he wouldn't be able to call forth his brothers to take over this world, but there was another here that could help him.

If only he could find the bastard.

He didn't know how the other could elude him, but he was beyond pissed. Caym didn't want to use the wolves any more than he needed to for his plan to work, but he might have to. This, after all, was the second time he'd been on this plane. He couldn't allow for failure. Not this time.

Caym turned to the whimpering wolf in the corner who clutched his arm. He looked closer and saw a bit of bone sticking out at an odd angle. Ah, oops, he supposed he'd gotten a bit rough earlier.

No worries. He'd make sure the wolf wouldn't feel any pain...after he felt just a bit more. Okay, a lot more.

Caym smiled, and tears fell down the other wolf's cheeks. "You've failed me. I asked for results, and all I get are six words that mean nothing to me."

"But...but I only gave you the note. I don't even know what it says." The wolf curled up into himself, sobbing harder.

Pity. He'd thought wolves were supposed to be strong. Though, he did like it when they begged.

"I don't care. I take it as a personal offense that you dared showed your presence here without results."

"Please...don't..."

Caym couldn't hear what the other wolf said under his pleas and moaning.

Whatever.

Suddenly, not in the mood to deal with the piece of garbage in front of him, he flicked his wrist, and demon fire erupted around the wolf. The other man screamed in pain, and Caym let himself smile a bit.

It was a good sound after all.

When the wolf was nothing but ashes, Caym stopped the fire. Nothing surrounding the scorch marks was burned due to the powers of his fire. A perk, if he did say so himself. Updating the upholstery of any home he was in was ever so bothersome.

Caym straightened his cuffs and tie then went back to his leather desk chair, sinking into the cushions. He'd have to take matters into his own hands, apparently. He needed to find this other demon, and the wolves weren't getting the job done.

And if the demon was shielding from him and didn't go along with Caym's plans, there would be hell to pay. After all, he was a demon; giving hell was his expertise.

# CHAPTER 1

Adam Jamenson watched as Jasper swept Willow around the dance floor, which the family had built outside their den, delight on both of their faces. A sharp and familiar pang pierced his heart, rattled around his ribs, and then settled in his stomach like a rotting, dead weight. He took a swig of his Jack on the rocks, the burn not quite dulling the ache that had haunted him for two decades.

God, he missed Anna.

He rubbed a hand through his shorn, dark brown hair, trying to release some of the tension he'd felt over the past eight months. Well, if he was honest, it'd been much longer than that, but the intensity had increased dramatically since... No, he couldn't and wouldn't think about that.

Not again. Not ever.

He drained the last of his glass and wondered if he should get up and pour himself another. What he needed right now was to get blinding drunk, but his family was watching him. They were always watching him, and with this being Willow's birthday party, the Pack was celebrating and trying to be happy.

Adam didn't want to be happy.

He wanted to be fucking drunk, that way the feel of the spindly fingers wrapped around his heart in a death grip would dissipate to a dull clench. His body felt on alert at all times, as if, at any moment, something would come in and attack, taking away anything else he thought he had.

It wasn't much, just a jumble of memories that wouldn't fade away.

He was the Enforcer of the Redwood Pack. As such, he felt the threats to the Pack deep in his soul and held the duty to protect his family. Sometimes, though, he felt as if he were failing at every turn.

Willow's laugh brought him out of his gloomy thoughts. She smiled, her face brightening as North took her from Jasper's arms, and they two-stepped to the change in music. He loved Willow like a sister and would do anything for her. He'd almost taken her into his home when she'd had a falling out with Jasper. She wouldn't have taken Anna's place, but maybe her laughter would have warmed up his tomb slightly.

Did he even want warmth?

"You don't want that other drink, man," Maddox grumbled as he took the seat next to Adam without invitation.

"Damn it. Stay out of my head."

"You know I don't read minds."

Adam held back a wince. Of all his brothers, Maddox was the one he did his best to avoid. As the Omega of the Pack, he could feel every emotion from its members, and Adam didn't want Maddox to be privy to some of his emotions. Or, rather, *any* of his emotions. He didn't even want to deal with them himself. But, Maddox knew everything. He'd seen the way Maddox looked after Anna's...death. He knew too much, and Adam didn't want to look his brother in his all-too-knowing gaze and see pity...or worse, understanding.

No one could understand.

He had been the first of his brothers to be mated. He'd met and fallen in love with Anna forty years before. He'd had twenty years with the love of his life and then had lost her and their unborn child. He gripped his glass tighter as the gaping wound bled just a bit more. Now, one by one, his brothers were finding their mates, in Reed's case *two* mates.

Adam was left to sit back and watch. Alone.

He didn't want to be around to watch the smiles on their faces, see the love radiating from their pores, watch the women grow full and ripe with their children.

Children.

He closed his eyes, the stinging increasing.

He didn't want to see Finn, Mel and Kade's son, and Brie, Jasper and Willow's daughter, toddle and grow up. That was the worst part. The part he couldn't ignore. They were the physical representations and proof of a mating bond so strong that the Redwoods had a chance of a future.

Adam had almost had that once...then the Centrals had taken it away from him.

"Tone it down, man. You're projecting enough emotion right now that everyone else can feel it as well." Maddox put his hand on Adam's shoulder, and Adam flinched.

"Don't touch me," he snapped. God, he sounded like an ass. "Please."

Maddox pulled his hand back, but he didn't move his gaze. Adam's gaze traced the jagged scar on the right side of his brother's face. He didn't know where he'd received it, but he knew it held more meaning than Adam knew.

"Adam, what's going on?"

"Like you don't know?" Adam growled. "Just leave me the fuck alone."

*"Stop lashing out at him, he's just trying to help," his wolf pleaded.*

Adam ignored him. His wolf had failed him when he needed him most. He didn't want to talk to the constant reminder of why he hadn't been there for Anna.

"No, I won't leave you the fuck alone. I don't know what happened, but something's changed. You were healing, Adam."

Adam snarled and stormed away from the party, ignoring the cautious and concerned looks boring holes into his back. Yeah, let them look at the deranged Enforcer. He was used to that.

"Adam, don't run from it. You're going to fuck up if you don't stop this." Maddox walked behind him, his voice low.

Adam stopped and turned, glaring at his younger brother. "What the fuck are you talking about?"

Maddox raised his chin, undaunted. "If you don't reign in those chaotic emotions of yours, you're going to fuck up, and the Pack will be the ones who pay the price"

Adam planted his feet on the ground and put his shoulders back, chest forward, shock radiating through him. "You don't think I can handle my Enforcer duties?"

Maddox shook his head. "I don't know. I don't think you'd purposely put anyone in harm's way, but you're not yourself. What happened when you were away, Adam? You were finally healing, smiling more. Laughing and hanging out with Willow. What changed?"

"Nothing."

8

Maddox frowned, disappointment on his face. "You need to trust someone, Adam."

"I trust my family." *Just not with everything. No, not this.*

"I just wish it were enough." Maddox sighed. "I'm here if you need me."

Adam nodded, unable to speak. He loved his family with everything he had...because they *were* everything he had.

"Adam? Maddox? Is everything okay?" Ellie Reyes, the Centrals' princess and newest Redwood Pack member, came up to them, Maddox's twin brother, North, on her heels.

Maddox stiffened at the duo's approach, and Adam raised a brow. It looked as though he wasn't the only one with secrets.

"We're fine," Maddox grumbled. "Just having a brotherly chat."

North tilted his head. "Anything I should know about?"

Adam shook his head. "Nothing. Just dumb shit."

Ellie looked at Maddox, her gaze unwavering. "If you're sure," she whispered, the scent of pain radiating off her like a thick blanket.

She still hadn't healed from her lifetime of torture at the hands of her brother, Corbin. Frankly, Adam didn't think she ever would. Though the female wolf was one of the strongest wolves he'd ever met. People just couldn't get over some things.

Case in point: him.

"Let's get back to the party then," North said after a few moments of awkward silence. "The folks already are getting antsy over the fact that you guys walked out. I don't want to make them think something was up." He said the last part as an unspoken question, but neither Maddox nor Adam bothered to answer him.

North sighed, sadness on his face for a moment before he schooled his features into the pleasant expression he always carried. "Shall we?" He held out an arm for Ellie, and she took it with one last look toward him and Maddox.

"We should go back, as well. I don't want to disappoint Mom and Dad," Maddox said, his body tense.

"Fine. Plus, we haven't seen Willow open her presents yet. God forbid we miss that," Adam said, a small smile threatening to form.

Maddox grinned full out. "I swear those women and their presents, but I think Finn and Brie will be the ones to open them. You know how much they like getting into things."

Adam smiled and walked back to the party with his brother, ignoring the pangs again. He'd never see his child grow up to break into presents. Never watch Anna celebrate another birthday with a smile on her face.

He'd lost his chance at happiness. He didn't want another.

\*\*\*\*

Bay Milton rubbed her eyes and looked at her GPS again. This was right, wasn't it? She pulled over to the side of the road, not wanting to veer off and get into a wreck because she wasn't paying attention. She pressed the top bottom on the screen to look at the next set of turns and frowned. Yep, she was going the right way, but it looked like she was out in the middle of nowhere.

On the other hand, it seemed like a perfect place to hide a werewolf den. It wasn't as if she could just input "Redwood Pack den" into the search function and hit go. No, she'd had to quietly ask around to find the coordinates.

Then, of course, she could feel the other wolves.

But, that was something she didn't want to think about quite yet.

Bay sighed, her body aching and radiating with tension. She looked out her window, hoping to see something confirming what she was about to do was a good idea. The tall trees seemed to reach up to the sky, touching the heavens but casting a shadow on the road in front of her.

Poetic justice at its best.

"What am I doing here?" she whispered to herself. She'd been doing fine on her own for so long she didn't need or want to rely on others, but this time it was different. This time she could taste the danger on her tongue, like a heavy metallic film she couldn't swallow.

As much as she wanted to turn back, she couldn't. They would find her. Though she didn't know who *they* were, she had a feeling. Dread threatened to choke her, and she took a deep breath, trying to calm her shaking body. It wouldn't do her any good to have a heart attack on the side of the road. No, she was a werewolf, dammit; she'd be fine. She just had to get through the next few hours, and she'd be fine.

Well, as fine as she could be in her situation.

Bay took a deep breath, straightened her shoulders, and pulled onto the road again. She could do this. She could. She'd been on the road for five days, taking the long way from Southern California to

11

Northern Washington. She'd backtracked a couple of times and gone in circles to lose any tails she might have. She wasn't sure if whoever wanted to cause her harm was actually following her, but they'd come eventually. She didn't want any harm to come to the people she was about to ask—no, beg—for help, nor did she want to get hurt herself.

That final thought might have long since proven futile. The Redwoods might shut their doors to her and leave her on her own. Or they'd take her in, and she'd have to be in the one place she didn't want to be.

With him.

She choked back a sob and made another turn. She needed to get a handle on her emotions before she got there. As it was, the Alpha might be able to tell she was coming soon. Only her special abilities had kept her escape from being discovered for this long.

She had to find him. He'd help her. He had to. If not...well, she didn't want to think about that. Damn it. She didn't want to see him, rely on him. She didn't want to look into those green eyes again and remember. The place at her neck thrummed, her body aching, but not only because of her long car ride anymore.

Damn. As much as she wanted to deny it, she couldn't. Well, that wasn't the only evidence...but that was another story altogether.

She took another turn and bit her lip as she felt the sentries posted at the gates to the den. Humans couldn't see the den, nor could they feel its presence. In fact, the warding caused humans to want to veer away from the den altogether. But she wasn't a human; she was Pack. The Redwoods just didn't know it yet.

The sentries, who had been visually hidden by their stealth, crept from the shadows, their eyes glowing gold with aggression, but confusion marred their faces. She couldn't blame them. Her wolf felt like Pack to them, but they'd never laid eyes on her. She pulled the car to a stop, rolled down her window, and held her hand out in a sign of peace.

"How can we help you, miss?" A tall man with gray eyes and brown hair came to her window, his posture on alert, ready to *deal* with her at any moment.

"I need to see the Jamensons." She couldn't state her true purpose, just like she couldn't name the real person she needed to see. The name wouldn't form on her tongue.

"Your name?"

"Bay Milton." As soon as she said it, she held back a wince. There was no hiding her identity now. She should have given a false name, but she hadn't thought ahead that far. Damn. The sentry would relay the information, and they might not let her in. But there was no turning back. She needed them. She might have grown up a lone wolf, but she'd become Pack in truth if it meant protection when she needed it most.

"Why do you need to see them?" He gave her a pointed look, and she met his gaze. She might be a lone wolf, but she was more powerful than either of them.

Her wolf growled, but she held it back. No need to antagonize the poor wolf. The sentry ducked his gaze and cleared his throat. He looked over the hood of her car at the other sentry, who gave a slight nod.

"The Alpha has let you through, but be warned, you harm our Pack, we'll take you out, even if you do smell like Pack."

She nodded, grateful that her scent had at least raised curiosity in the Alpha so she could be let through. One hurdle down, just a few more to go to find her fate.

Bay drove along the winding roads, knowing she wasn't alone. No, other sentries would follow her path and watch her. She was okay with that. She didn't want to cause harm to anyone here; she just needed help. She held back the bile that threatened to rise. She didn't like asking for help, practically never did it. But just this once, she'd let her pride die and beg if she had to.

She pulled up to what she assumed was the center of the den and parked. In the distance, it looked as if a party was going on. People were dancing and laughing. Children were playing, giggling when the adults tickled them or tossed them in the air. She clenched her jaw, forcing any tears that threatened to come to hold the pain back. She had to be tough, cool, collected for this. If she broke down and acted as if she were a helpless weakling, she wouldn't earn their respect and maybe their protection. She might not have grown up with wolves, but she at least knew that much about them.

She sat in the car and watched as three men prowled toward her, their power radiating off them in waves. They had to be part of the Jamenson family, though she knew there were probably others hidden in the shadows, their eyes on her.

The center one must be Edward, the Alpha. She'd done her research. He looked the same age as his sons but looked every bit the Alpha with his power and grace. His hair was cut short, and neat. His green eyes pierced her as she sat in her car, waiting for them to give permission to get out. He wasn't as big as the two sons who flanked him, but he was still a force to be reckoned with. To Edward's left was a man who looked just like him, but the man had longer hair. Bay let her wolf come to the surface so she could taste his power, the energy of leadership and protection washing over her. This must be Kade, the Heir and next in line to be Alpha.

Bay forced her gaze to Edwards's right and held back a gasp.

Adam.

It had been so long since she'd seen him; eight months to be exact. He was taller than the other two, at least six-five, and built. She swallowed, hard. She'd seen every inch of him. Licked it, too. His hands were fisted at his sides as he strode to her. She looked into his eyes and suppressed a shudder.

Such hatred.

Oh, yes, he remembered. He just didn't want to.

Well, too damn bad; he'd have to get over it for just a little while. This was about more than the two of them and a night they'd shared.

"Well, get out of the car, Bay Milton," Edward ordered. "You can tell us just how you came to have the scent of the Pack when I've never felt you before."

Steeling herself, she opened the door, grabbed onto the sides, and then hoisted herself to a standing position. She closed the door, put a hand on her aching back, then the other on the very noticeable bump protruding from her stomach.

Kade and Edward gasped, but she had eyes for only Adam. He paled but didn't say anything.

Bay forced herself not to shake or, worse, throw up, and opened her mouth. "Hello, Adam, I'm glad I found you. We have to talk."

15

# CHAPTER 2

Was he dying? Maybe he was already dead. It was the only reason Adam could think of for this to happen. Maybe it was a dream. Yeah, that sounded better, though it was more like a nightmare. His body felt heavy, as though someone had added weights to each of his nerve endings then punched him.

Bay stood there, red hair curling around her face and the mass tumbling down her back and over her shoulders. Her green eyes were bright with the fear she probably thought she'd hidden so well.

She looked so small standing there, though knew she was average height. He remembered her coming up to right below his shoulders when he'd held her...

*No. Stop it.* He couldn't think of that.

She'd been curvy before, her hips flaring out, making it easy to hold her when he'd pounded into her. Her breasts had been full and heavy in his hands.

But he wasn't staring at any of that. No, his gaze rested solely on her stomach and the evidence of her late pregnancy.

*Holy. Shit.*

16

This couldn't be happening. It had to be a mistake. She couldn't be pregnant. She couldn't be here, smelling of his Pack. No, she was supposed to be a faded dream...a nightmare. She wasn't supposed to come into his normal world. She was supposed to have been a fling. A nothing.

Maybe she was just here because she needed a shoulder to cry on and the baby was another wolf's. Because in order for that baby to be his, he'd have had to mated her.

Flashes of teeth on skin... sweat sliding across bodies... his cock deep inside... fuck.

Once again he told himself Bay Milton could not be here and pregnant because that could only mean one thing.

*"Mate?"* his wolf growled, his claws scraping along the inside of Adam's body.

He ignored the traitor. No, he'd had a mate. Anna. Oh, God, Anna. Fuck. What was he going to do? This stranger couldn't be his mate. He'd had his chance, and he didn't want this...this thing in front of him.

He couldn't speak. Couldn't move, didn't want to. He wanted Bay gone. Whatever problems she had couldn't be his. If he could have, he'd have willed her away. He was the Enforcer. He should be able to kick someone off his land if he desired it.

Why was his father letting this stranger into their den?

His father let out a breath beside him. "Well, this is unexpected. You smell of Pack, yet I do not know you, nor did I feel you come into our Pack with your bond." He leveled his gaze toward Bay, and she bared her throat for him.

At least she had the submissive thing going for her, considering she was apparently Pack. Fuck. He didn't want to think about her. Her simple presence felt like a betrayal to his Anna.

A chasm opened up inside him and threatened to swallow him whole. He fisted his hands again, his lungs seizing. He closed his eyes, Anna's long brown locks waving in his vision. He calmed a bit, soaking in her presence, if only in his mind. A flash of red surfaced, and bile rose in his throat.

No. Not her.

Edward cleared his throat. "Do you have an explanation for this?"

Adam risked a glance at his father. His Alpha wasn't talking to him, but to Bay. His emotions warred. On one hand, he wanted to thank the man for being on his side, yet on the other more frustrating hand, he wanted to stand up for Bay.

Something that wouldn't happen in a million years.

She was supposed to have been a one-night stand, a way to scratch an itch and fill a need. That was it. He didn't want her here in his space. In what had been, and still was Anna's space. The lone wolf in front of him didn't deserve it.

Because even though she smelled like Pack, she wasn't *his*. Not now, not ever.

Bay didn't meet Adam's gaze. "I need to talk to Adam, *alone*."

Still standing on the other side of their father, Kade finally spoke up. "I really don't care what you want. I don't know what's going on, but you're not taking Adam alone anywhere. Whatever you have to say to him, you can say to all of us."

Bay finally looked at Adam, her gaze pleading.

Ice filled his veins, and his heart echoed in an empty tomb. "I can handle it." His voice was deep, hoarse.

Why'd he say he could handle it? He didn't want to fucking handle it. He wanted this imposter off his land. She shouldn't be anywhere Anna could have been.

Kade looked over his shoulder and sighed. "Well, the rest of the family is coming over here. So if that's what you want, little brother, then get her out of here so she doesn't disturb the rest of the family."

Kade stomped over to the pregnant woman, anger radiating off him in waves. "If you touch so much as a hair on his head, I'll make sure you'll regret it."

Bay raised her chin, but being a lesser wolf than the Heir, she didn't meet his gaze. "I won't hurt him."

*Too late.*

Adam stormed toward her, rage filling him, suppressing the dread of talking to her, looking at her, being near her. How dare she come here? This wasn't her place. She didn't belong. He grabbed her arm and hauled her back to the car. She let out a wince, but he didn't stop. He opened the passenger door, stuffed her in, and slammed the door.

His wolf howled and threatened to break through his skin.

"Adam, stop it," Edward warned. "You touch that girl like you just did again, and you'll have to answer to me."

Adam glared.

"She's pregnant, and it looks like it may be your problem. I don't know what the hell is going on, but you need to fix it. But, I swear to God, if you hurt that woman, you'll have to answer to me."

Adam lowered his head, shamed. He hadn't meant to hurt her, but he couldn't stop himself from wanting her gone. He just needed her out of reach of his family and out of his sight. If she wasn't here, then it wasn't real.

19

"Handle this as best you can, but I'm coming to you later, son. I don't want to ruin Willow's day."

Adam nodded then got in her car. He drove off without looking at her, though she sat right next to him. He didn't apologize for manhandling her. He didn't know how to put it into words. Plus, if he spoke to her, she might speak back, and he couldn't deal with that right now.

The smell of Bay's fear filled the car, an iced-berry, sweet scent that enraged his wolf. Adam tightened his grip on the steering wheel, his knuckles going white. His wolf stopped growling and whimpered, bumping his head against Adam's body, as if reaching out toward Bay and her wolf.

Adam held back a curse. He'd been lying to himself for so long he was surprised he could even tell what his wolf wanted.

But Adam knew.

His wolf wanted Bay's wolf.

They'd both been feeling her and her wolf since that night, but Adam had ignored it, something he was good at. Or at least he had tried. His wolf had fought back, causing Adam to almost lose control a few times, but the man had overcome the wolf.

And now, just the scent of her fear, overpowering her sweet berry-mingled-with-ice scent...fuck.

He didn't want to think about her scent and the way it had seeped into his pores that night as her skin lay flush against his, or the way her fiery curls had caressed his body as she lay on top of him...

He pulled to a stop, thankfully, in front of his house, and closed his eyes. In the past twenty years since Anna had been ripped from him, he'd been with only a handful of women—three to be exact—before Bay.

And now he was in a car with a woman who could ruin that fragile hold he possessed on his sanity.

Adam looked up at the house and swallowed the bile that crept up his throat. This was Anna's house, which she'd decorated over and over again as their years together progressed. This is where she'd decorated their nursery...

He bit his tongue, tasting blood, the sharp sting forcing his tears back and causing his emotions to tighten.

He didn't want to take Bay inside so she could taint it with her foreignness. But he was the Enforcer, God damn it. He couldn't stick his head in the sand and ignore it anymore. Though he'd try if he could.

He got out of the car, his movements stiff, and glared down at her. Bay lowered her head, her body shaking, but he could sense the power within her, the power that told him she was stronger than she looked. His wolf liked that.

Damn it.

"Get out of the car, and follow me," he growled, and slammed the door. He stomped toward his house, ripped opened the front door, and paced his living room.

The house had long since lost Anna's scent, but on some days, he swore he could feel her presence. But not today. No, today he could only feel the presence of a little wolf who could destroy him.

He clenched his fists and paced around the room that he'd slowly started to make his own, at least as much as he could without deleting Anna from it entirely. The walls were a chocolate brown with a cream trim that kept the room from being too dark. He had thick cream drapes to block out the sun when he wanted to sit in darkness, which happened more often than not recently. Simple, clean cream-and-brown furniture filled the room, so it didn't look so empty. He had frames filled with random photos of landscapes that Cailin, his sister, had made him put on the walls. He didn't want any pictures of his family up there because, if he did, he'd have to remember that Anna's photo wouldn't be up there.

Couldn't be up there.

His house was a small, one-story three-bedroom home. He'd always planned to build on with the help of his contracting brothers, Jasper and Kade, but when Anna had been taken, he'd given up on his plans and his dreams. What had been the point to make more room when her laughter and their babies would be absent? His chest ached, and he rubbed the wound that wouldn't heal.

Bay's scent filled the room, and he bit back a growl. As much as he wanted her to leave, his wolf didn't want to scare her.

They stood in his living room—Anna's living room—and stared at each other. He clenched his jaw, thinking about what to say, how to start.

What were they supposed to talk about?

Bay rubbed a hand over her swollen belly, and Adam swallowed.

Oh, yeah, *that.*

"Why didn't you tell me?" he whispered, his voice raspy.

She met his gaze head-on and didn't flinch. "How could I?"

Adam snorted. "I don't know, maybe pick up a God damn phone?"

Bay took a deep breath, but he could see the telltale signs of her temper, temper he'd thought he'd imagined that night. Yep, she had been a fiery redhead before, and by the way, she narrowed her eyes at him, she hadn't lost it.

"Excuse me? Where was I supposed to call? You lit out of there so fast I thought something had stung you in the ass."

"Nice language for a pregnant lady."

"Fuck you."

He raised a brow but didn't speak. He didn't want her here but had no idea how to get her to leave.

"Adam…" She closed her eyes and shook her head as he tried not to think about his name on her lips.

"What, Bay? What is it you want to tell me, huh? Why are you even here?" His voice rose with every question, and he fought the urge to throw something. Not at her, particularly, but at *something*, just to release some of the tension.

"What is your problem?" Her voice was just as loud as his, and he could feel the anger rolling off her in waves.

God, he was acting like an ass and it wasn't her fault. The only thing she did was exist and show up, filling his life like she shouldn't. She wasn't Anna. If he liked her at all, it would be a disgrace to Anna's memory. But now, because he'd made a mistake, she was in his life and in his Pack, because as soon as he'd mate claimed her, she'd been enveloped in the Pack. Because he had mate claimed her, he was able to get her pregnant. It was the only way for wolves to have children—with their mates. He didn't know why his father hadn't felt her come into the Pack, but that was a discussion for another time.

"My problem?" He growled and stalked toward her, his hands clenched so hard he was afraid they'd pop a vein. "My problem is that you're not supposed to be here in *my* Pack. You were just a quick fuck when I was too drunk to know any better, and now you're standing here looking like you deserve something from me. Well, let me tell you, I didn't make any promises that night, and I'm sure as hell not making any now."

She flinched as if he'd slapped her, and his wolf howled. His body raged as he fought for control. If he changed right now, his wolf would be the one doing the comforting, not the man, which was opposite for most wolves. He didn't want to be nice.

No, the man wanted to bare his teeth and growl in anger.

He watched her throat as she swallowed. She lowered her voice and spoke slowly. "I'm here because I need your help. I don't want to be here. I know how much you precious Redwoods love your Pack. I may smell like you, but that doesn't make me want to be yours. I'm only here because this isn't just about me anymore."

She placed her palm on the swell of her belly, and Adam flinched at the not-so-subtle reminder of where this conversation was heading.

"Is it mine?"

She nodded, a sad expression on her face. "Yes, Adam. It's yours. I wouldn't be here if it weren't."

Adam swallowed and closed his eyes, pain ricocheting through him, followed by a terrible numbness. He'd known the baby was his the second he saw her get out of the car...but hearing her say it? His temple ached, his pulse skipping in a staccato beat that made him want to vomit.

He growled and walked away from her, unable to even be in her presence. She was the epitome of everything he didn't want, everything he'd once had and lost. He didn't want her here.

"Adam, you can't just walk away from this," she said from behind him, her voice stronger than he'd have given her credit for.

"Watch me, Bay."

"This isn't about you or me and the fact that we got too drunk and mated. Fate's a bitch. I know that. Don't get me started."

He turned around, his body shaking with his anger. "You're fucking kidding me, right? The poor-me routine? You're a little old to do that. I know how much Fate likes to fuck with us, so just drop that subject."

"Fine, but we need to talk."

"No, we don't. We're going to sit here and wait for my father to deal with you. I don't know why I said I could handle this, but I don't know what you want, but I can't do it. My father will have to deal with everything. I can't." God, he hated himself, but he was shaking. He needed Anna, not *her*.

"I have things to say before he gets here."

"You're not keeping anything from him. Whether you like it or not, he's your Alpha. You must obey him."

"You don't get to have it both ways, Adam." She walked toward him and stood so close her belly brushed him. He jumped back as if he'd been burned, and she winced. "You can't say you don't want me here and that I'm nothing and then, in the next breath, say that I have to listen to my Alpha. Either I'm Pack, or I'm not."

"Like I said, you may be Pack, but you won't have anything to do with me. We had a decent fuck, and now I'm done. I left without a look back, and I don't want to look at you again."

She threw up her hands and let out a breath. "I know you're an ass and think you're hurting me by saying that, but get over yourself. I'm here because someone is after me."

That brought him up short. "What do you mean?"

"Oh, now you're interested in what I have to say."

"Get on with it Bay, or I'll leave."

"Fine. Someone has been following me, and I can't protect myself and the baby. I'm just one wolf. I need help." Her expression told him that last part about needing help had been ripped from her, but Adam didn't really care if it hurt her to ask for help.

"So, you're telling me you may have led people who want to hurt you here, to *my* den? What the fuck were you thinking? You've endangered us all!"

"I was thinking that *our* Pack is supposed to be the strongest of them all, and I needed help." She stared at him, and he looked into her green eyes. "*Please.*"

He couldn't think, couldn't breathe. He needed to get out of there, now.

He growled and lifted his lip. "My father will be here soon to talk to you about this and the fact that you've hidden yourself from him. I don't know how the hell you did that, but you've got some explaining to do."

She lifted her chin but didn't meet his gaze. "I understand that, and I'll answer any question that can help me protect my baby."

He didn't comment on the fact that she'd said *her* baby. He couldn't even stomach the thought of it being...*theirs.*

"I'm leaving you here while I go deal with something." He walked toward the door then paused. "Don't even think of leaving. I can smell the enforcers, the men who work below me, surrounding us. They'll know if you try anything."

"So, now I'm a prisoner."

He turned toward her and glared. "Deal with it, Bay. You're not welcome here, and you're sure as hell not welcome in my home. Once we figure out what the hell is going on, you're gone."

With that, he stormed out of the house, slamming the door behind him. He staggered to a nearby bush and heaved, his stomach revolting at what he'd said, done, and what he'd have to do.

He'd left the Pack before to get some breathing room and had come back darker, shakier. And now his past was back to bite him in the ass.

What the hell was he going to do?

# CHAPTER 3

B ay walked on wobbly legs to the couch and awkwardly sank into the cushions, her body drenched in a cold sweat. She held her stomach and closed her eyes. The baby kicked softly, as if reassuring her she was doing the right thing.

She choked back a sob as the tears fell from her eyes. The baby turned and kicked again into her palm.

She rubbed softly and blinked away the tears. "I know, baby. I'm trying to stay strong for you. You're such a good baby already. You didn't let me get too sick, and you let me sleep. See? You're amazing." She spoke in soothing tones to her stomach and tried to calm down. She knew the stress wasn't good for the baby, and she had a feeling it would only get worse as time progressed.

Bay knew she'd shocked them when she got out of the car and they noticed her pregnancy. And if she were honest, the petty part of herself had wanted just that. She'd wanted to see the shocked look on the face of the man who'd claimed her as his mate and walked away without a backward glance.

But, as she sat here in his living room, she didn't feel any better. In fact, she felt worse. The things he'd said to her...

She shook her head then blinked away the tears. She couldn't show weakness by crying at the drop of a hat. Most people might have been able to blame it on the hormones—and yes, those contributed—but she didn't want them to know how much being rejected hurt. She had to be strong for both herself and her baby; even if she had to look like a cold bitch to do it.

She'd do anything for the life that grew inside of her, even face the man who hated her and wasn't afraid to let her know it. Why did he hate her so much? She hadn't done anything to him other than sleep with him when he'd come onto her. It didn't make any sense. What had she done?

Damn, she hated self-pity and wallowing. She'd been alone for so long that she was used to standing on her own. And no, she didn't want anyone to think that was a request for pity; it was just a fact. Her mother had been banned from the Talon Pack when Bay had been born, and since then, she'd lived without a Pack.

They'd forced her mother to choose—the Pack or her child. She'd chosen her child and lost everything for that.

Bay would never forgive the Talons and barely resisted the urge to blame the Redwoods, too, just for being a Pack. Yet, now she had to rely on them and their strength to protect her. Didn't that just grate?

She lifted herself off the couch with great effort and rubbed her back. She was a big as a blimp, or maybe a whale. Though most of her weight resided in her midsection, her ankles were swollen, her breasts had gained two cup sizes and ached from a mere touch, and her rings wouldn't fit on her fingers anymore. She'd cursed some days when she wished for a partner in this experience; someone to hold her hand, rub her feet, and tell her that everything would be okay.

But, no, like she'd wanted, she had no one. No friends, no family, and no mate. She may carry his mark beneath her skin on the juicy part of her shoulder where it met her neck, but that didn't make him her mate.

He'd left her.

Fate really sucked ass since it had decided to leave her with a man who could look at her the way he did *and* give them a baby on the first try. Her baby kicked her ribs, and she cradled her stomach and groaned.

"I'm sorry. I didn't mean I didn't want you. I love you so much. It's just that I didn't think I'd be in this situation." The kicking stopped, and she sighed.

*"He'll protect us, Bay. Stay strong,"* her wolf whispered.

"If only it were that easy." She walked around the room to inspect her prison. The room looked like it had been warm once but had long since grown cold and emotionless. No pictures of friends or family or actual paintings dotted the walls. They just held images of landscapes and random things. It wasn't unlike her own apartment. After all, she didn't have anyone in her life to take a picture of, and putting up pictures of herself on the walls seemed a bit narcissistic.

She traced her fingers along the dark mantel above the fireplace without thinking and gasped. Images of a brown-haired woman flashed through her mind. Bay fought to breathe, her body shaking, as she watched the woman tip her head back and laugh melodically while hanging two large stockings on the mantel then a smaller one right between them. Love

30

poured through the woman and into Bay, and she wanted to scream. Bay focused on the image as a man stepped into the vision and knelt to kiss the woman's flat belly. The man turned to the side. Bay froze then pulled herself forcefully from the memory.

Adam.

Oh, God.

She'd known he had a life before meeting her; she hadn't been that ignorant. But he'd been mated...

She stumbled to the couch and plopped down as the baby kicked. Adam had a mate and a baby. Or rather, *had* a mate. Since Adam had mated Bay that meant the laughing woman must have died.

No wonder Adam looked at her like he wanted her to shrivel up and die.

He'd lost the love of his life. No wolf wanted to move on after that and mate again. It was a nasty trick of Fate that a wolf could be mated again after such a loss. In their world, there were several potential mates that a wolf could find and identify by scent. The couple could choose to mate or part ways, depending on the need of the mating scent. But to have found another mate after losing the first one no matter how recently was cruel in every sense of the word.

Why would Adam want to be in her presence when she reminded him of all he'd lost?

And what about the baby that the woman had been pregnant with?

Was Adam already a father?

There was a stark absence of children's pictures, and her heart ached as she knew the truth. Whatever had happened to the laughing woman had also taken her baby.

Poor Adam.

That little spark of connection to Adam flared through their dull mating bond, and she snapped it close. No, he couldn't know she felt anything for him. That would only make it worse.

She looked down at her hands, spread her fingers, and cursed. She hated her so-called gift of psychometry. She could touch something and see the memories ingrained within it. Her powers though were sporadic, and though she'd been practicing for all of her forty years on earth, she still didn't have a handle on them. Visions would come out of nowhere, ripping her consciousness from her current time and throwing it into hazy images of the past.

She hated every bit of it.

What good was seeing someone else's past when she couldn't change it? No, she was instead stuck reliving what other people had felt, seen, and heard during key points in their lives—their happy moments *and* their sad ones.

She'd relived both life and death.

And now she was imprisoned in a home surrounded by painful memories of her mate's lost mate.

She cradled her belly and forced herself not to cry. It wouldn't do anyone any good, and she didn't want to appear weak, even if only for herself.

What the hell was she going to do?

\*\*\*\*

"How the hell do you mate someone and not know it?" North asked as he paced his living room while Maddox snorted beside him.

When Adam had regained his energy after leaving his house, he'd walked to his nearest brothers' home to see North. He'd needed space to think and decide what the hell he was going to do. The enforcers, the men who answered to him, were guarding her to make sure she didn't do anything that could harm the Pack. He hated, though, that he'd left her alone in his house, in Anna's house.

North's house was a smaller version of Adam's, having one less room, though attached to it was the Pack's clinic. So no matter how much privacy his brother might have wanted, he was never alone. As the Pack's doctor, he had to be on call for all the major and minor injuries the Pack might encounter. Now that Reed's mate, Hannah, had been brought in as the new Healer, North's duties had been downgraded a bit, though Adam couldn't tell how North was taking that. As the Pack's Healer, Hannah was magically connected to the den and could feel if someone was in pain. She could also Heal small wounds, and if she used her trinity bond with her two mates, Reed and Josh, she could Heal quite a bit more. She was also an accomplished witch and potion maker who made some of the drugs and medicines the Pack used. As werewolves, they couldn't use pain medication and other drugs, but the potions she made helped, though that was a bone of contention with his sister, Cailin, who had done the job previously. Now his sister felt a bit lost and had become the nanny to Kade and Melanie's son, Finn.

Maddox groaned, bringing Adam out of his thoughts, and held his head in his hands. Adam knew his own emotions were wailing in twists and turns, so his brother, the Omega, must be in as much pain as he was. Thank God, despite Mad's title, he wasn't touchy-feely with his feelings when it came to his brothers. Adam didn't want to talk about what was going on in his head with anyone, let alone someone who could share it.

"Well? Are you going to answer me?" North asked again, his normally smooth demeanor breaking to show his strain.

Adam glanced away, ashamed to tell North the truth.

"You've got to be fucking kidding me!" North yelled. "You knew all this time, didn't you? Ever since you left, oh, eight months ago? And I bet that's how far along Bay is, right? You *knew* you were mated before you left her, and you did *nothing*. You left your mate, Adam. Why?" North sank to his couch, a look of pure disbelief on his face

"That *woman* is not my mate," Adam growled, the taste of the lie bitter on his tongue. He could deny it all he wanted—oh, and he wanted to—but it didn't make it a truth.

Maddox growled and took a deep breath, the jagged scar that ran down his face darkening to a deep pink.

"Stop lying to yourself," the Omega said, anger and regret lacing his tone.

"I'm not lying to myself," Adam answered. "Just because she's here doesn't make her my mate."

"You marked her, didn't you?" North asked then shook his head. "No, wait. You don't have to answer that; of *course* you did. That's the only way she could smell of Pack, be pregnant, and have you up in arms like this."

Adam looked away, not wanting to speak. He closed his eyes and saw the flash of teeth, remembering the feel of her body beneath his as he sank his fangs into her shoulder when his cock drove into her pussy. He held back a shudder. Whether it was the result of revulsion or need, he didn't want to know.

There were two parts to a werewolf—the wolf and the man. That being so, the wolf and man had to *each* perform a task in order to create a mating bond. For the wolf to mate, the man had to mate-mark the juicy part of the potential mate's shoulder with his fangs while in human form. This released an enzyme not unlike that which turned humans into wolves, but the results were not as gruesome. No, this enzyme was pleasurable. Adam held back another groan. Both parties had to mark the other, and then their wolves would be mated. If one of the mated pair was not a wolf, then only the werewolf had to mark. For the man part of the werewolf pair, it was easier. There had to be only a sharing of fluids—the man releasing his seed within the woman. Or man, in his brother Reed's case, as he had done with one of his mates, Josh.

Together, the two parts of the whole would create an everlasting mate bond that would connect their souls. Some mates could sense one another and share their magic. When one of the wolves held a position of power, their mate would share it. So, whomever Adam mated—he swallowed hard—would hold the title of Enforcer's mate and would help protect the Pack if they desired; or they could stand by their mate and help them lead behind the scenes if they didn't like to fight—like Anna had done.

The icy shard drove deeper into the place where his heart had been at the thought of her name. Anna had been his mate—no, *was*, his mate. Not Bay. Never Bay.

"Adam, you have to talk to me. Sitting on your hands and brooding in silence won't work for you. Not this time." North bent so his forearms rested on his thighs and sighed. "We can't help you if you don't tell us what happened." Pity underlined his tone, and Adam wanted to vomit. He hated pity, though he should have been used to it by now. He'd lived with the pitying stares and undertones for twenty years.

And each time, it was as if they were reminding him of all he'd lost, chipping away just that much more at the place he'd once called his heart. He hated it, but he'd lived with it because they were his family and Pack. He did much for that reason.

Maddox stood and walked to a corner of the room, his body radiating his tension. North looked at his twin and sighed, but Maddox merely glared.

What was going on between the two of them?

Adam shook his head. He had too much to deal with right now, and he couldn't be looking into the workings of their twin issues. He sighed; he needed to get this over with.

"I left the den when Josh and Hannah came to stay," Adam began.

North and Maddox nodded since they had been there at the time to watch him walk away, something he desperately wanted to do right now.

Adam coughed and fisted his hands, his body shaking. "I just got in my truck and drove, not caring where I went. I just needed to get out, you know?"

The twins nodded in unison but didn't say anything.

"I finally ended up in a small town in southern California." He'd driven and tried not to think about anything, especially about the fact that his brothers were one-by-one finding their happiness and highlighting the fact that he had none. "I stayed in a grungy motel off the beaten path for a few days, running in the woods nearby as a wolf." He'd needed that. As a wolf, no one would look at him as if he'd lost something. Some days he'd almost hoped he'd change to a wolf and stay there, but he didn't want to give his wolf the satisfaction. After all, he still blamed the wolf for letting him down all those years before.

"Then one night I couldn't take it anymore and ended up in a bar, trying to drink away my troubles."

North gave a low whistle, and Adam nodded. They all knew it took over ten times the normal human alcohol intake for a wolf to get drunk. He'd bought and drunk a few bottles of tequila from the witch who ran the bar. He'd been lucky in finding one run by a paranormal, but he'd given it up to Fate. His mistake.

"Bay was the waitress," he grumbled. "She got off her shift, and I let her join me." He didn't remember why he'd asked her to join him. Maybe his wolf had had more control of him at the time than he thought. "One thing led to another, we got drunk, ended up in bed." His face burned as he told his brothers, but he needed to get it off his chest.

"And then you left?" North asked, and Adam was thankful he wouldn't have to go into any more detail of what had happened during the "in between".

"Then I left." Because he couldn't deal with the fact that he'd betrayed Anna, his love.

North shook his head, disgust warring with that pity on his face. "I can't believe your wolf let you do that? Doesn't it hurt?"

It hurt like a fiery hell, but Adam wouldn't tell him that. "I'm stronger than my wolf." His wolf whimpered, upset that they'd left Bay, then and now. Screw him. "I made a mistake."

Maddox coughed. "Well, that *mistake* is now pregnant with your child. What are you going to do about it?"

Adam grew cold. He'd had his chance at fatherhood and lost it. He didn't want another. "As far as I'm concerned, Bay and her baby are on their own."

37

North stood up and snorted. "I can't even look at you. Do you even hear the words coming out of your mouth?"

He did, but he needed to keep saying them to stay sane. "I lost everything I had, North. Bay is not what I want or what I need. She's here because she thinks she's being followed." Finally, he said what he'd come to say.

"Followed?" Maddox asked. "By who?"

"She didn't know."

"You think it was the Centrals?" North asked.

"I have no idea, but it's not my problem."

"Really, son?" his father asked as he walked in the room.

"Dad? What are you doing here?" Adam asked.

His Alpha raised a brow. "I could say the same to you. I felt you here instead of at your home where you should be, so I stopped by here."

"Dad—"

"Save it. I don't want to hear your excuses. That woman in your house is carrying your child and is your mate. I don't care if you don't agree, but that is the truth. I may not trust her because I don't know her, but I'm not turning my back on a woman who is in need. And the fact that you say she was followed? Yes, there is something we can do."

"That's why I want North and Maddox to help her."

His Alpha growled, releasing his strength. Magic shot through the room, sending tingles down his arms and filling his wolf with awe. He and his brothers staggered to their knees under the weight of their bond.

"You disappoint me, son. She is your responsibility, not the responsibility of others. I know you are hurting, but that is no excuse to do what you did or do what you were planning to do. She is your charge and yours alone. You are the Enforcer of this Pack, and you will deal with the consequences of your actions."

Adam felt like a scolded schoolboy but nodded then bared his throat.

"Good." His father released the magic, the room feeling like it was filled with oxygen again, and Adam stood. "Now that we have that settled, I want North to go over and check on Bay with Hannah. Bay looked like she needed someone to see how the pregnancy is progressing. While North is doing that, I want you to see if you can find anything about her, son. I still don't trust her, and that is a sad state of our times, but I don't want you leaving her side once you finish that, Adam."

Adam didn't say anything, rejecting the words his father spoke. He wanted nothing to do with this woman, yet it looked as if he had no choice. If Fate wanted something, it looked as if it would do anything to get it.

Damn it.

\*\*\*\*

Caym paced in his study. He still had no word from Samuel. Damn it. He'd shared his blood with the wolf so he could find the other demon. Samuel had gotten close. Close enough that Caym now new the other demon was a female.

But not just a normal demon female. No, this female was a half demon, one sired from a demon and human, witch or wolf.

Caym grinned, pleasure at his circumstances running through him. Oh, he had an idea of who this half-demon was. This could be good for him. Oh, so good for him. He needed to celebrate.

Caym strolled through the office and walked to Corbin's playroom. Screams echoed along the walls, followed by masculine laughter.

He opened the door and sighed with contentment. His lover was using a razor-edged whip against a female wolf that resembled Ellie, Corbin's sister. She'd do in a pinch, but nothing could replace the toy he'd lost.

Corbin turned as if he'd sensed Caym's presence. Corbin smiled, his almond skin carrying a layer of sweat from his exertions.

"What is it, my love?" Corbin asked as he walked toward him, forgetting about the woman bleeding behind him.

Caym held back a wince at the use of "my love." He hated emotions such as those but would endure them for the greater purpose.

"I think we're getting closer to our goal," he crooned, though he didn't mention the woman. No, only Samuel knew that. And when Caym was done with the wolf, he'd kill him, leaving no loose ends.

Corbin traced a finger along his jaw. "Good, the Redwoods deserve to burn."

"Oh, they will, they will. All in good time."

Because Caym had an ace up his sleeve. He just needed to find her.

# CHAPTER 4

B ay rotated her wrists so they would crack, an annoying habit, but one she couldn't stop. Her whole body felt under intense pressure and tension, and anything to help relieve it was welcome. She thought of Adam's face and cursed.

Okay, not *anything*.

He'd been gone for over two hours. For some reason she'd thought that things would move quicker. She'd never lived with a Pack, but she'd figured they'd want to get things done and not just sit around. Apparently, she'd been wrong. Or maybe they thought she was the enemy and making a pregnant woman wait around was a form of torture.

Though she was thirsty, she didn't help herself to anything. No, she sat in the living room and waited. Curiosity had almost gotten the better of her, and she'd thought about searching through the house, just to see how the man who'd mated her lived, but she hadn't been able to find the courage to do so. Not only would he have been able to scent her presence in his domain, she'd also have felt like she was snooping, and as a person who valued their privacy above almost everything, she couldn't do it.

She heard the footsteps outside before they reached the door. She inhaled their scents— not Adam—and she turned, ready to defend herself and her child if needed. The Alpha, Edward, walked through the door, a brow raised.

"I like the spunk," he quipped as he walked into the living room. He was followed by a man who looked so much like him he had to be his son.

She lowered her gaze, not wanting to offend the Alpha. Though she'd never grown up in a Pack, she'd heard horror stories of Alphas who'd beaten and even killed if they weren't shown proper respect and protocol at all times.

She didn't know the protocol though, one of her mother's failings. But Bay couldn't be too hard on her since her mother had been thrown out of the Talons brutally by their overpowering Alpha.

Bay took a deep breath, trying not to show her fear. Maybe wolves liked fear. God, why was she doing this again? She hated wolves, even though she was one. Her baby kicked, and she instinctively put her hand on her stomach.

*Oh, that's why.*

For her child.

"You don't need to fear me, little one," the Alpha said, and took a seat on the couch, looking quite comfortable in his son's home.

She nodded and stayed where she was, not sure what she was supposed to do. Damn, she hated being weak.

"Hello, Bay," the other man said, and gave a small smile filled with compassion. Damn. She hated compassion that bordered on pity just as much as being weak. "I'm North, Adam's brother, and also the Pack doctor."

She inhaled sharply, her body clenching. "You can't hurt my baby."

North's eyes darkened, and he growled. "What kind of wolf do you think I am that I would hurt an innocent child?"

She raised her chin, not bowing to the wolf's power. She was the same strength as Adam in terms of hierarchy now, even if he wouldn't acknowledge it. This North would have to bow to her if she wanted it, though she wouldn't, not unless she needed to.

"I don't know what kind of wolf you are," she finally said. All I know is that you've come into Adam's home where he's left me prisoner and claim you are a doctor. What am I supposed to think?"

North growled and opened his medical bag, grumbling under his breath about pregnant females and their lack of sense. Yeah, like that was helping his situation.

"I have to apologize for my son," Edward said, amusement on his face. "He usually has a better bedside manner than that."

Bay nodded, not knowing what the Alpha wanted her to stay.

"Why is she standing up as though preparing for you to attack her?" a woman said as she came into the room. Her brown curls danced around her face, and her dove gray eyes were warm and intelligent. She walked up to Bay and held out her hand. Bay clasped it, unsure. "I'm Hannah, the pack Healer, and you're Bay."

Warmth radiated from the woman as well as another energy...a witch. Bay smiled; she loved witches. They were warm, loving, and easy to get along with. At least the witches she'd known had been.

"Hello, Hannah."

"So, the boys are acting all big and bad and trying to scare you?"

Edward barked a laugh, and North scowled.

"Pretty much."

"Did they even tell you why they were here?" Bay shook her head, and Hannah turned to the men. "You didn't mention the fact that she's Pack and you were worried about the baby as well as her welfare?"

Edward blinked, unperturbed that a little curvy woman had scolded him while North gave a small smile.

"You're lucky Josh and Reed love you, or I'd take you off their hands. I like it when you're feisty," North teased.

Hannah laughed. "I love my two mates way too much, babe. But thanks for trying to flatter me."

"Two mates?" Bay blurted out then felt her cheeks heat.

Hannah turned and smiled. "Yep, I'm mated to Edward's son, Reed, and another man named Josh." She put her hand on her hip and cocked a brow. "Have a problem with that?"

Bay smiled, liking this woman already. "Not a one."

"Good, then we can be friends. That is, after I check you out to make sure you're okay."

Bay nodded, unease creeping up her spine. "I haven't been to a doctor," she whispered, shame joining all the others emotions she felt.

Hannah brushed a lock of hair from Bay's face and then forced her to sit on the armchair. "I understand. You didn't have a Pack or anyone to trust, right?" Bay nodded. "How were you supposed to help your baby if you didn't have someone to take care of you?" Hannah growled that last part, and Bay fell a

44

little in love with the woman. "It's no worries; we'll take care of you. I use my hands to Heal, so I'm going to put them on your belly, okay? It can be done through your clothes."

North cleared his throat. "I apologize for not making you feel comfortable when I first came in. I don't know who you are, and the situation is a bit explosive at the moment with Adam, but I shouldn't have taken that out on you. You're my patient, and I should act like it."

Bay gave a small smile. "Apology accepted. It's a little difficult for all of us."

North came up to her, his black medical bag in his hands. "If it's all right with you, as Hannah looks at the baby, I'll check on your stats. Is that okay?"

Bay nodded, not knowing how she felt about all of this. She didn't know these people, yet they were caring for her like she was family...or Pack. Her heart warmed. Was this what it meant to be Pack?

Hannah put her hands on Bay's belly, and warmth and magic infused into her. She hissed out a breath at the unfamiliar contact, and Hannah started to pull back. Bay put her hands around the other woman's wrists and shook her head.

"No, it's fine; I just wasn't expecting it."

Hannah nodded, then continued her Healing, her eyes closed and her body swaying as she did it. North took Bay's pulse, checked her lungs, and did other random tests.

Hannah pulled back, a smile on her face, but she had an odd look in her eyes that disappeared as quickly as it appeared. Oh, God, did she know?

"Your baby is fine. Do you want to know the sex?"

Bay shook her head. "No, not now."

"Okay, you're in your third trimester, so you're almost done baking."

"You're making me sound like a turkey."

"Well, you *will* pop," the witch teased.

"I declare you fit, Bay Milton," North said once he was done.

"How did you know my last name?" Bay asked, fear rising again.

"We know a lot of things, Bay. Plus, you told the guard at the front." Edward said.

Though she'd known that, Bay's pulse kicked up, and she looked for the nearest exit.

Hannah and North backed away and stood near their Alpha. Oh, so this was how it was going to go. Make her feel comfortable then interrogate her. She'd do it because she needed help to protect her baby, not because she felt like they had the right.

"What do you think you know?"

"Your name, the fact that you're Packless. Your mother was kicked out of the Talon Pack, and your father is unknown," Edward stated. "Am I missing anything else?"

"That's about it," she lied.

"Really? Then how is it I couldn't feel you come into the Pack when you mated my son?" His voice may have been low, but the power in his voice and the gold of his eyes told her she had to tread lightly.

"I don't know," she lied again.

"Don't lie, Bay Milton. You won't like the outcome."

She could die right here and make things easier for herself, but then her baby would die with her. And even if they took her baby, who would raise it? The man she'd mated with a cold heart who'd lived through an unbearable loss?

No, she couldn't do that. So, she would tell him part of it, and hope that was enough. It had to be enough.

46

"It could be because of my powers."

Edward shifted, alert. "You're not a witch."

"No, I'm not." She would never reveal what she was. For if she did, it was a death sentence. "But I do have psychometric powers."

"Really?" North asked, awe in his tone.

Bay nodded. "I can touch things and see memories. But they aren't consistent, and I can't make my powers do what they want. So in essence, they're quite useless."

Edward stared at her a long moment, then nodded. Relief filled her, and she sank back into the cushions.

"That could be it," he said smoothly. "Adam told us your problem, and we will decide tomorrow how to deal with it. For now, you will stay here."

She tried not to cling to the hope that sprang within her. "Am I a prisoner?"

"No. But you don't know the area, and the Pack doesn't know you. It would be...best if you stayed here." Edward raised a brow, and she understood. She didn't have to stay, but they couldn't protect her if she left. That was fine with her. She needed any help she could get.

"Since it is getting late, I'll show you to your room. I don't know when he'll be back," North said as he picked up the small suitcase she hadn't seen him bring in. Her suitcase. "I didn't see anything else in your car. Am I missing something?"

"No, but thanks for going through my things," she muttered.

"I need to make sure my family is safe, Bay," North whispered, and walked toward the back.

"Goodnight, Bay, we'll see you tomorrow," Hannah said as she hugged her. Bay didn't know what to do with so much touch...so much good, but she gave an awkward hug back.

Edward nodded, giving her a questioning gaze, and then walked Hannah out of the house. North cleared his throat, and Bay followed him to a room in the back of the house that had to be the master room. Dark greens and browns covered the walls and bedspread. A king-sized, four-poster bed dominated the room with a matching set of furniture off to the right. There were two doors on the other side that she assumed would be the bathroom and closet, but Bay couldn't keep her eyes off the bed.

"This is the where you'll be sleeping. For your own good, I wouldn't be looking around at anything else. Got it?"

"Why am I staying in Adam's room?"

"Because he doesn't have another bed." He turned to her and tilted his head. "He'll be sleeping on the couch."

She shook her head. "No, I can do that. I can't put him out."

North gave a dry laugh. "I think where you're sleeping is the least of your worries right now, Bay. Just sleep here; you're pregnant. Even Adam isn't heartless enough to make you sleep on the couch. I'll lock the door behind me. I don't know when Adam will be home. You're welcome to the kitchen, bed, and bathroom, nothing else." With that, he walked away, leaving Bay feeling more alone that she had before.

She walked to the bed and ran a hand over the smooth comforter.

"What am I doing here?" she whispered.

The baby rolled, and Bay closed her eyes. She'd do anything for the child growing within her, even be near the man who hated her. But how was she going to keep strong and remain who she was through it? Or did it even matter?

****

The sweet burn of rum scorched down his throat as Adam took another shot directly from the bottle. It landed in his stomach, doing a dance that threatened to force him to fall over, and then settled. He stared into the amber liquid and groaned.

Why had he thought drinking until he couldn't breathe was a good idea? Look how well it had turned out the last time he'd done it.

"Are you going to sit there and stare at it or pass it over?" Maddox drawled, his eyes a bit glossy from the amount he'd drunk.

After doing some digging in Bay's life and finding almost nothing, he'd come to Mad's home to ignore his current houseguest. North had called and told him he'd put her in Adam's bedroom and told him to deal with it. After all, Bay was pregnant, swollen, and in need of comfort, while Adam was just the ass who'd got her in the situation in the first place.

Now, his problem was sleeping in his bed. Thankfully, it wasn't the same bed he'd shared with Anna. He'd gotten rid of that in a moment of desperation to get rid of the thoughts, memories, and scents that came with looking at something she'd touched and where they'd made love countless times.

"Adam? Get your head out of your ass and hand me the bottle."

Adam slid it across the table, watching the contents slosh against the sides. Maddox gripped it, staring at it, but not drinking.

"I thought you wanted a drink," Adam slurred.

"Not really, I just wanted to cut you off."

A slow burn of rage crept over him, but the drunken haze made it too hard to care. "You're an ass."

"Pretty much." Mad stood and walked to the kitchen.

"Hey, why aren't you wobbling around? Didn't you have as much to drink as I did?"

Mad came back empty-handed and frowned. "No, I had about half what you did. I'm buzzed, not shit-faced drunk like you."

"Hey, that's not nice." His tongue felt heavy, and he could swear the room tilted to the left when he tried to blink.

Okay, maybe he had drunk a little too much.

*"You think?" his wolf growled.*

"Shut up."

"Uh, who are you talking to?" Mad asked.

"My wolf, he's an ass."

Mad shook his head then winced. Ha! His little brother didn't feel too good now, did he? "You're crazy. But we already knew this."

"No more crazy than you."

"True."

"Will you two shut up and let me sleep?" North asked from the couch where he'd passed out after two shots. His brother hadn't slept in a few nights and had been apparently exhausted.

"Why aren't you at home?" Maddox growled, a weird tension radiation from him that was too much for Adam to discern at his current intoxication level.

*Hey, I'm thinking in pretty big words.* Maybe he wasn't too drunk. He tried to stand and promptly fell on his ass, but he didn't feel much pain. He was numb from the booze.

Maddox didn't even laugh, just sighed. "What am I going to do with you?"

"Just let me die."

His brother growled, picked him up by his upper arms, and slammed him against the wall. That he felt, the pain shocking him slightly coherent.

"What the fuck, Mad?"

"I never want to hear that again. Do you hear me? I didn't let you die twenty years ago, and I won't let you die now. You may feel like a complete shit and want to hide from your problems, but you will not die. Do you understand? I won't let you do that. You have a second chance, Adam. Don't ruin it."

Adam growled. "I didn't want a second chance."

"Well, it's too late for that. You're going to have to man up and deal with it."

"What did she feel, Maddox?" He whispered the question he'd asked a hundred times, knowing Maddox wouldn't answer.

Because his brother was the Omega, he could feel all of the emotions of the Pack, meaning that when Anna had been kidnapped, beaten, and raped...Maddox had felt it all. Adam could only sense her presence, not her pain in truth.

Maddox dropped him to the floor, his eyes growing dark, his skin going pale. "You know I won't tell you that. Stop asking."

"Oh, I'm sorry; I didn't realize everyone would be here," Ellie said as she walked in, her dark hair in her face so she could hide. She'd been beaten and abused all her life at the hands of her brother, Corbin, the new Alpha of the Central Pack, and now she was here, part of the Redwoods. Adam still wasn't sure what he thought about that.

Maddox turned abruptly, his fists clenching. "What are you doing here?"

Ellie raised her chin. "North texted. He wanted me to come take him home."

North stood and shook his head. "Thanks, Ellie, I'm a little too tired to drive or walk right now, and I knew you'd be up."

Shadows passed over her eyes, and she nodded. "No problem, come on." She gave Maddox one last look then walked out of the house without another word.

North nodded toward both of them then staggered behind her, closing the door behind them.

Maddox stood and watched the closed door for a few moments before he shook his body, looking as though he were steeling himself. He turned and picked up Adam, bringing him to his feet.

"What was that about?" Adam asked, utterly confused about what was going on between the three of them.

"Nothing," Maddox bit out. "Come on, let's get you home."

"No, she's there."

"And I really don't give a fuck right now. You're going to have to deal with her sooner rather than later, and I don't want to deal with you."

Adam growled, but it came out weak.

"Whatever."

"It'll get better, Adam," his little brother whispered as he pulled him outside the house.

"It has to, right? I mean it couldn't get any worse." At least, he didn't think so, but he didn't want to find out.

# CHAPTER 5

A crash from the living room brought Bay out of a fitful sleep. She pulled herself to a sitting position, her belly getting in the way. Someone mumbled a curse, and she inhaled their scent.

Adam and Maddox.

A very drunk Adam and a slightly inebriated Maddox.

Oh, goody, just what she needed; a drunken wolf who probably didn't know she was in his bed and wanted her nowhere near him. Oh, what fun.

She pulled down the extra-large shirt she wore so it hit her mid-thigh even over her belly and waddled out to the living room, her ankles aching with each step. When she got out to the living room, she shook her head. Maddox had Adam draped over his shoulders and a sheepish expression on his face.

"Sorry, Bay. Didn't mean to wake you," Maddox said as he carried a very drunk Enforcer past her and into the bedroom.

"What happened?" It was like déjà vu. The first time she'd seen Adam he'd been drunk, and here he was again. Was this something he did often?

Maddox dropped Adam on the bed and shook his head. "Drank too much."

"I guessed that, but why?"

Maddox turned to her with so much emotion in his eyes that she almost staggered from the weight of it. All of that couldn't be just him. How on earth did he live like that as the Omega?

"He's had a long day," he said simply, and Bay under her breath.

He'd drank because he didn't want to deal with her. On one hand, she felt horrible and wanted to make him feel better. On the other, she wanted to kick his ass. How could drinking possibly help this situation? She was pregnant, on the run from...something, and he wanted to drown in a bottle.

The perfect soon-to-be father.

"I'm sorry, Bay," Maddox whispered, bringing her out of her thoughts.

"What? Why?"

"I wasn't thinking when I brought him to his bed. I should have just left him on the couch."

She looked into his eyes, unsure if she could believe him. She didn't know this man and had a feeling he didn't make mistakes like that. This wolf was up to something. What, she didn't know.

"I can move him."

She shook her head. "No, I'm the intruder. Let him have his bed."

Maddox tilted his head, gave her a look she couldn't decipher, and then nodded. "Okay, I'll leave him here then. Good night, Bay."

She murmured a good night, and he walked out, leaving her with her passed-out mate and the sudden urge to take care of him.

*"He needs us,"* her wolf whimpered.

"Shush, you," she whispered back. "He's a grown man who doesn't need us staring at him like a freaking stalker while he's sleeping."

Adam groaned from the bed and tried to take his shirt off, struggling in his current state. She caught a glimpse of tanned flesh and wanted to groan right with him. Damn, she was pregnant and ready to pop. She shouldn't be thinking dirty thoughts.

Especially not with the man currently trying to strip out of his clothes.

With a sigh, she waddled over to him and placed a hand on his arm, the heat radiating from him shocking her. She'd forgotten how hot his skin was.

"Adam, stop trying to take off your clothes. You're going to hurt yourself." Need filled her and she cursed. Her libido was picking a strange time to wake back up.

"Bay," he grumbled, and she froze.

She loved the sound of her name on his lips. Or rather, her wolf did. The woman desperately wanted *not* to like it. Damn mating bond.

She shook it off and chose to ignore it. This was not the time to be thinking such things. She helped him pull the rest of the shirt off his body then stopped and stared at the ridges on his abs and an urge came over her that begged her to touch him. The swirled tattoo on his arm looked as sexy as it had that night and she bit her tongue so she wouldn't lick it. With a sigh, she went to the foot of the bed and took off his work boots, placing them on the floor out of the way. Adam groaned and twisted on the bed so he looked even sexier and she fisted her hands. She wouldn't touch him. Because she couldn't touch him, for when she did, she'd want to touch him all over. And he didn't want that; nobody wanted that.

She would go to sleep on the couch. That's what she should do. In fact, that's what she would do. Adam wouldn't want her staring at him like a freaky stalker. He moaned again, and she brushed the hair from his forehead because she couldn't help herself. The tattoo on his right arm was just the way she remembered it. It covered from the shoulder to mid forearm. The tribal tattoos he said told of the time when wolves ran as wolves and man ran as man. Is that what he wanted? To be a man or a wolf and not the blend of both. Without thinking, she traced her fingertips along the tattoo, remembering how it tasted against her tongue.

She started to pull away so she could go sleep on the couch and try to forget the mate that didn't want her, but Adam pulled her to him, and she gasped. He nuzzled his face in her hair, and her stomach brushed against him, the baby kicking. He moved in this sleep until she was lying right beside him, stiff and frozen, not knowing what to do. He traced his fingers along her back, tendrils of sensation moving through her like a wave. When he brushed his lips against her forehead, she sighed and relaxed. Without thinking, she closed her eyes and let him hold her.

Bay knew he was thinking of his other mate and not her. He would never be thinking of her that way. And why would he? He'd had his mate and lost her, their baby too. Bay was just another example of what he'd lost, but she didn't want to think about that right now. She just wanted Adam. Damn the stupid hormones for making her want this and making it okay. She fell into his hold, loving the way his arms tightened around her. He held her head with one hand and her lower back with the other, her belly and their child lay nestled between them.

She really should get up and leave. She tried to get up, but then he pulled her closer, and she sighed. Maybe just for a few moments. The baby kicked again, and Adam groaned as if he'd felt it. Relieved at the movement, she turned to get out of bed and leave him there, but he pulled her back, letting her body spoon against his, his hand resting on her belly, shielding her. A tear slipped down her cheek without her permission.

Damn, she didn't want this. Yeah, she did want it, but she didn't want it like this. This wasn't real. This wasn't him. He was asleep and would regret it in the morning, just as much if not more, than she would. Oh, God, what was she getting into? He wanted his mate and not her. The baby rolled, and she closed her eyes, remembering the real reason she was there. They needed protection from those that followed her, and she couldn't do it on her own. The Redwoods would help her because of her bond with Adam. She needed to remain cold; detached because, if she warmed up and remembered the feeling she'd had that night with him she'd lose herself. And if she did that, she'd lose everything.

****

The scent of ice and berries filled Adams nose. He loved the way it made him feel at home, like he belonged. A warm body lay flush against him, and he smiled. His Anna. She'd come home. He rested his hands on the swell of her belly, feeling their child. He inhaled that ice and berries scent again as the fog lifted, and he froze.

His Anna did not smell of those things. No, his Anna smelled of oranges and cinnamon. He cracked open his eyes, ignoring the dull throb in his temples and behind his eyelids, and bit back a curse. Bay lay snuggled in his side, and his erection strained his jeans, rubbing against her. He stopped the movement of his hips and bit back another curse. Flashes of the night before came back to him. Images of Maddox dragging him back to his home and throwing him on the bed mixed with images of the red-haired stranger taking care of him.

She whimpered in her sleep, and instinctively he cradled her face with his hand to quiet her. She rubbed her cheek against his palm and quieted, her body sinking into his like it had a right to be there.

With a groan, he pulled away from her and got off the bed, careful not to jostle her or the baby. He regretted hurting her the day before when he'd pushed her into the car. Though she was a wolf and did not bruise easily, it was still no way to treat a woman, especially a pregnant one. Yeah, his father had threatened him, but that wasn't the only reason he felt like shit. He had fucking hurt a woman because he had been in a bad mood. There had been no call for that. Even if he didn't want Bay near him, he had no right to hurt her. No matter what happened in the coming months or years, he could do his best not to hurt the woman in his bed. He might not like her, want her, or want anything to do with her, but he wouldn't hurt her.

Or the child she carried.

His head ached from drinking too much the night before, and he slowly made his way to the kitchen for some coffee. He took out some gourmet beans that Willow had left a couple weeks before and ground them. Adam cursed and shut off the grinder, remembering that there was a woman in his bed sleeping, and the noise would wake her up. Thankfully, he didn't hear her stir, and the coffee was ground enough to be used. He started the pot and made his way to the living room. He sank onto the couch and held his head in his hands.

How the hell had it come to this? Just the day before he'd been a typical wolf, okay, not so typical, doing his job and living day to day. Now everything had changed, and he had no idea what to do about it.

He heard the other wolf coming to his door before they rang the bell. Seeing how he didn't want to wake Bay, he went to the door and let his brother's mate in. Willow smiled at him, her long brown hair framing her face making her seem more radiant than before. He'd never love her the way a mate would, but he loved her more than a sister. She was the reminder of everything good in their Pack because, even though she'd been through the worst pain imaginable in the worst circumstances imaginable, she was still the bright light of their Pack. She'd been kidnapped, tortured, and changed into a wolf at her near death. The Centrals had taken her from them and almost killed her, but Jasper and the rest of the Redwoods had saved her. She was stronger than the most alpha of Alphas.

"Hello, Adam," Willow whispered then she grinned, her brown eyes radiating the love and happiness she held for her mate, Jasper. "I heard you had a guest, and I wanted to make sure you two had eaten."

Adam grunted and held back a smile. Oh, she'd known the day before that Bay had come into their lives, but she'd done the polite thing and waited to meet the newest member of their Pack. Yeah, she'd waited all of twelve hours.

"Hello to you, too, Willow. Bay's still sleeping, so we have to be quiet." He winced when she gave him a knowing glance that held a mixture of happiness and sadness at this situation. Damn, how was he supposed to deal with reactions like this? He hated the pitying looks, but these new ones were sure to be the death of him. "And, no, we haven't had breakfast yet, but I did start some coffee."

Willow smiled and shuffled past him, her little body bouncing on the way. Before she'd met Jasper and joined their Pack, she had her own bakery and had been a very skinny little thing. A little too skinny in his opinion, but now that Jasper and the rest of the Jamensons were taking care of her, she'd put on a few pounds and gained some curves; something that all of them were happy about.

"I'm going to make you and your guest an omelet if that's okay." He noticed she didn't say mate or anything else about Bay, as if she were being very careful about not mentioning the fact that his drunken one-night stand had turned out to be a whole lot more.

He clenched his fists and ignored the headache coming on harder. His body ached, not just from too much rum, but from the fact that he was in turmoil. He was a grown-ass wolf, and yet he wanted to hide and run away from his problems. Preferably at the bottom of a bottle. However, on second thought, that hadn't worked out the way he'd wanted to last time. Maybe it was time to find a different way to hide from his problems.

"Willow, you didn't have to come over here," he grumbled as he walked into the kitchen and watched his brother's mate take over the room as if it were her own. "I'm a hundred years old. I think I know how to make my own breakfast."

"I know that, Adam, but I wanted to come and help." She smiled, and he shook his head. Willow had become one of his closest friends since she'd joined the Pack. In fact, when Jasper had almost fucked everything up, Adam had been the one to show his brother how not to be an ass and had offered to take Willow. Not to be his mate, but to care for her. The irony of his current situation and how he didn't want to take care of Bay wasn't lost on him.

"Sure, and to see Bay." She blushed and went back to flipping the omelet, and he smiled. "Don't think I don't know what's going on in that head of yours, Willow."

"You can't really blame me, Adam. And come on, I never did get to see what you got me for my birthday. Let this be it."

Adam let out a laugh, and the tension eased from him. He might be going into a shit storm, but he could always rely on his family to be by his side and give him what he needed. At least most of the time.

"Don't try to use that trick on me, dear Willow. But in any case, thank you for making breakfast."

Willow shrugged and plated two plates. "You already had the food over here from when I brought you some earlier this week. So it isn't like I needed to lug any heavy bags."

Adam smiled. "Yeah, like Jasper would've let you lift anything."

She blushed and poured herself a cup of coffee. "Well, that's true."

He took the coffee from her hands right before she placed it to her lips, and he tsked. "Are you still breast-feeding? I don't think you should be drinking coffee if you're doing that."

She growled at him, her eyes glowing gold in irritation. "Brie is with her father, and she's doing just fine thank you. I'm allowed to have at least some caffeine, you know. Since I'm a wolf, my metabolism burns it off quicker. So it won't hurt her."

Adam shook his head and took a sip of the coffee, watching her upper lip curl. "I don't think so. How am I to know how much caffeine you had before you even walked over here?"

"You are not the coffee king."

"True, but I don't want to have to deal with Jasper when he finds out."

"And to think I came over here to make you and your guest breakfast." She smiled when she said it, and he knew she was just teasing.

The scent of berries and ice filled the air, and Adam froze.

Willow turned and smiled, warmth radiating from her. "Hi, you must be Bay." She walked over to the other woman and pulled her into a hug. Bay looked startled but wrapped arms around the other woman and gave Willow an awkward pat on the back.

"Yes, I am. I mean, hi. Nice to meet you." Bay blushed and looked out of sorts. Adam had the sudden urge to help her but didn't know what to say. If he helped her, she might get the wrong idea and think it was okay to stay, and that was not the right thing to do. At least not from his perspective.

"I'm Willow, Jasper's mate," Willow said with a soothing tone. She'd once been the newbie in the Pack, and Adam guessed she knew what to do with a new member and all the awkwardness it entailed. "Jasper is the Beta, meaning he helps with the day-to-day things in the Pack and stands by Edward's and Kade's side."

Bay nodded, looking as though she was taking in all the information, yet not knowing what to do with it. Adam felt for her but didn't help. He couldn't help.

"That's nice. What do you do?" Bay asked as if she hadn't known what to say.

Willow smiled and gestured to the other woman to sit at the table. "I own the bakery in the den. I made you and Adam some breakfast because I know he's not that good with a spatula. Why don't I sit with you while you eat so we can talk?"

Bay shook her head. "Aren't you hungry?"

"I ate before I came. I have a six-month-old baby at home. Her name is Brie." Willow smiled like all was right with the world, and something sharp pierced Adam's chest. He rubbed his fist against it, trying to take out the ache, but it wouldn't go away. Damn.

Bay smiled for the first time, and Adam saw something warm melt that cold exterior. She blinked, and the warmth he thought he'd seen faded away. He didn't know what to think about this woman, but he really didn't want to think about her at all.

"Brie is a lovely name," Bay said, and sat down at the table. Willow sat next to her leaving Adam to sit on Bay's other side since the table was against the wall. He grumbled and sat next to her, ignoring the way she smiled and the way she made his cock harden.

It was just a natural reaction to sitting next to a woman that held a certain scent made for his wolf. That didn't mean he would do anything about it. He'd already done enough.

"Thank you," Willow said, her smile threatening to make the room seem a little too happy for him.

God, he sounded like a melodramatic ass. When had that happened?

"So what is it you do, Bay?" Willow asked, and then she nodded toward Adam with a glimpse of something in her eyes. God, she wanted him to get to know Bay and like it. Damn, he didn't want to. He couldn't, not with the fact he'd lose Anna all over again if he did. He grunted and started eating his food, not caring how it tasted. Even though the woman could make anything gourmet, he was afraid if he tried the taste what he was eating, all he would taste would be sawdust.

"Well, I was a waitress." He noticed they pointedly did not look toward him, and he was grateful.

"Really? I own the only restaurant and bakery in the den and could use the help."

Bay blinked, and Adam groaned. Damn, he didn't want Willow to show her that she could be useful here. Yeah, he sounded like an ass, but he didn't really fucking care right now.

"I don't think that will be necessary," Adams said, his voice low. As soon as the words came out, he wanted to take them back. Both women stared at him as if he'd hit them. Fuck, now he was officially an ass.

Bay raised her chin and gave a cool smile. "Adam is right. I don't think that will be necessary either. After all, I'm approaching my due date, and I shouldn't be on my feet that much. Plus the whole reason I'm here is not to settle in but to make sure my baby is safe."

Tension crept through Adam's shoulders again, and he wanted to reach out and brush the stray red curl behind Bay's ear. The mating urge rode him hard, harder than he'd expected. Yes, he'd already had her and marked her, but his wolf still wanted her. Wanted to show her that everything would be all right, and that they would work it out.

Willow's smile died, and she looked between the two of them with sorrow on her face. He hated that. Willow had been one of the only ones who hadn't shown pity toward him daily. She'd known he hated it without him saying anything about it. But now. Here she was, unable to hide her emotions. This redheaded stranger was ruining everything.

Bay gave a quick nod and started to eat her breakfast, mindlessly.

"It tastes delicious, Willow," Bay said, no emotion in her tone.

"Thank you, Bay," Willow said, sorrow in hers. "Well, I don't want to bother you guys any longer. I'm going to head out and go back to see Brie and Jasper. I left him alone with her, and I'm a little afraid to see what will happen to the house."

Adam gave a reluctant smile at the image of the big bad Beta and the little bitty baby. Oh, he knew who would win in the fight; he just felt bad for Jasper. Again, that ache entered his heart and threatened to rob him of his breath. He didn't want to think about babies, daddies, and all that came with that, but, apparently, he didn't want to think about a lot of things.

He stood up and walked Willow to the door. She placed her palm on his cheek, and he froze, not letting himself lean into it. He couldn't rely on her. She wasn't his, nor did he want her to be.

"Be careful, Adam," she whispered.

Adam gave a wry smile, knowing that no matter how low she whispered, the wolf in the room behind them would hear them. "You know me; I always am."

Willow lifted her brow and looked behind him. "Oh, I don't think that's the case, is it?"

He didn't say anything and kept control of the range of emotions plaguing him for he was afraid he might say something he'd regret.

Willow let out a sigh and shook her head, lowering her hand. "You can't just be careful with yourself anymore, Adam. It isn't just about you anymore."

He glared, not wanting to have this conversation. "Thank you for breakfast."

Willow bit her lip but didn't say anything. "Let us know if you need anything, Adam. You know we're here for you." A statement, not a question.

He nodded, afraid of what he might say.

With that, she walked past him to her car and drove off. He heard the sound of dishes clattering in the background, knowing Bay must be cleaning up after them, tossing away the uneaten food. Neither of them had been that hungry.

He closed his eyes and rested his head against the doorjamb. How the fuck had he gotten himself in this situation? Oh yeah, he'd given in and been an idiot. What the hell was he going to do about it?

# CHAPTER 6

**B**ay dried her hands on the towel and took a deep breath. She hadn't been expecting a conversation with Adam and his sister-in-law and a whole meal where she could sit awkwardly and not feel like she belonged when she'd woken up. In fact, she hadn't expected to sleep as long as she had. She'd wanted to wake up before Adam that way she wouldn't disturb him and start a fight she wasn't ready to have. But, apparently, she'd been more tired than she thought and had slept like the dead. She hadn't even woken when Adam had gotten up. She had no idea what he could be thinking at that very moment or what he had thought when he saw her sleeping next to him.

She closed her eyes and sighed. This was not at all like she'd planned. All she had wanted was to make sure she and her baby were protected. And here she was, feeling like she was out of place and unwanted, though as she thought about it, that's what she'd thought would happen. She didn't know these people, and they didn't know her. In fact, she was used to people not knowing her and, in return, not trusting them.

Damn, she hated this. She was thinking in circles, not getting anywhere. She squared her shoulders and waddled out to the living room. *Oh, yeah, that's the way to work it. Try to look fierce and know what you're doing and end up waddling.* In times like these, she hated being pregnant. The baby rolled, and she put her hands on her stomach, closing her eyes.

"Sorry, little one," she whispered. Damn, she was already a horrible mother. Thinking she didn't want to be pregnant. What would her baby think of her?

Bay sank into the cushions and inhaled the lingering cinnamon scent. She gave a small smile as she thought about the woman she'd met. Willow seemed like such a warm soul and had a strong spirit. She bit back a laugh at what she had thought when she'd first heard the woman's voice this morning. She'd been deep asleep when she heard Adam's rumbly voice and the softer one answering. Nervous, and only a little jealous, she had quickly gotten out of bed, got dressed, and ventured outside of the room to see who it had been. She had the lingering feeling it was someone close to Adam. And she'd been right. Willow was not only Adam's sister-in-law but a true friend to Adam, and frankly, that scared Bay a little too much. She didn't know the intricacies of their family, nor did she know everyone's past histories, but she knew she was missing something between Willow and Adam. Though she had been relieved to find out the woman was already mated, Bay had been worried the woman had been a past lover or, worse, the current one. Bay knew that had not been the case, thankfully.

But when Willow had spoken to her, Bay hadn't felt any jealousy on the woman's part. No, all she'd felt with happiness and a bit of sorrow wafting off her and maybe something else... acceptance?

Adam still stood at the front door, his head resting against the frame. He hadn't moved for ten minutes, not since Willow had left. Suddenly, he growled and stalked toward her. Bay tensed, her hand instinctively covering her belly.

Adam stopped short, a frown on his face. He tilted his head, just like a wolf would, his gaze studying her.

"I'm going to have to deal with you," he growled.

Annoyed, she lifted her lip, showing her canine, or what would have been a canine had she been in wolf form. Some instincts she couldn't ignore.

"I get it, okay?" she spit out, exasperated. "You don't like me, and I don't really like you." *Liar.* "But that doesn't really matter, does it? We're going to have to learn to deal with each other." She held up her hand when he wanted to speak. She needed to get these things out before they ended up internalizing everything and then combusting. "I'm not here for you to fall in love with me." He growled again, this time more menacing with a layer of hurt. They were already too connected if she could feel the intricacies of his feelings. She ignored it, like she ignored everything else. "I'm here because my baby needs help. I'm in trouble; I know this. Something's following me, but I don't know what. I can't stop it, and I can't protect myself and my baby without help. That's where you come in. I don't need you to hold my hand or say nice things. What I need is for you to be there to protect me. I know that's not something you want to do, but it's something I *need* you to do."

Adam glared at her and sat down on the coffee table, their knees brushing. "I'm sorry, Bay."

She blinked, not knowing what to do. Of all things he could've said, that had been the last thing on her mind. "For what?"

He shook his head and rubbed a hand on his face. "I'm sorry I'm being such an ass. I know you didn't ask for this, and I know this isn't your fault. But I can't help it. I'm just in a pissed-off mood, and there's nothing I can do about it."

Well, there sure was something he could do about it, but she didn't think he would do it.

"But, Bay, we're going to have to figure out what is stalking you. I don't think you're making that up. You wouldn't come here if you didn't have to be. I know that much."

She nodded, the words heavy on her tongue so she couldn't speak. Hope bled into her heart, but she tamped it down. No, she couldn't think like that. He was just saying he was sorry. He may have trusted that she wouldn't have come to town for any other reason, but that didn't mean he trusted her for anything else. And frankly, he shouldn't.

"I'm glad you believe me."

Adam nodded. "Good, then we got that out of the way. What I want to know is *why* someone would be following you."

She did her best not show any reaction to that remark. Yes, she had an idea why they would be following her, but she didn't want to tell Adam. No, she *couldn't* tell Adam.

"I don't know why, Adam."

Adam narrowed his gaze, and she raised her chin, not letting the Enforcer get beneath her skin. "Why is it I don't fully believe you, Bay?"

"Maybe because you're the Enforcer and you don't believe anybody who's not your own flesh and blood?"

70

She gave a wry grin and tried not to let her hands shake.

Adam gave out a surprising dry chuckle and shook his head. "I don't even tend to trust them when it comes to protecting my Pack."

"That's a really sad thing to say, Adam."

"Yeah, well, I'm the Enforcer. I don't get to choose family ties over their own well-being. I'll do what I have to protect them."

It sounded like a warning, and Bay sat straighter. "Understood."

"Do you know how to protect yourself?" Adam asked.

"I'm a wolf. I can fight," she said, her chin raised.

"But what about if you can't shift? Can you use a gun?"

She shook her head, feeling inadequate.

"Fine, let me show you." He stalked off, rummaged through something in the back, then came back with a gun she didn't know the name of and a clip.

He showed her how to load it and how to turn off the safety.

"You aim and shoot for now. You're a wolf, you'll be okay. But I will show you how to actually shoot and not blast your foot off later."

She nodded, thinking she hoped she would never have to use a gun.

"Tell me about your life before you came here," Adam ordered.

"You saw what my life was like that night." She didn't want to go into it and have him look down on the fact that she had nothing. He had everything—a Pack, a family, a home. She had nothing.

He shook his head, and then put his head in his hands, clearly not wanting to remember that night.

Too damn bad. She had to live with the consequences daily. In fact, the consequences were currently trying to play a nice song and dance number on her bladder. If they didn't finish this conversation soon, it might prove embarrassing.

"I remember you in the bar that night. I don't remember much else. And frankly I'd rather hear it from your lips."

She let out a sigh and shifted on the couch to try to get more comfortable. Well, at least as comfortable as she could get looking like a freaking beach ball. "I'm a lone wolf, Adam. I've always been that way. I don't have a Pack, and I don't have any responsibilities. No, wait, I mean had. I've never *had* responsibilities. I never used to have any of that, and I didn't want it. And now it looks like I have just a little bit more, don't I?"

Adam's eyes darkened, but he didn't say anything.

"The Talon Pack threw my mother out when she was pregnant with me. I don't know why." *Lie.* "But ever since then, we've been on our own. When she died, I became completely on my own." She ignored the pain that settled in her stomach and continued. "I don't know how to function in a Pack, and I'm quite fine being by myself. Usually. I never got a degree, and I never really did anything. I'm forty years old, and I have nothing. Is that what you wanted to hear?" Anger rose with each sentence, and she bit her tongue. She sounded like a loser who'd never had any ambition. But she'd been in hiding her whole life. She just couldn't tell Adam that.

Adam raised a brow but didn't say anything. She couldn't tell if he was judging her, but she didn't really want to think about that.

"I don't know how you lasted, Bay."

"What do you mean?" Did he know? Did he suspect?

"I've been in the Pack all my life. I've always felt them. I'm the Enforcer. Therefore, I have a closer connection to them than most. I don't know what I would have done with myself if I didn't have them. I've always known that, if I failed, I would have them to rely on and they would catch me if I fell. I've never been truly alone, even though sometimes I feel like I'm more alone than ever." He closed his mouth abruptly and widened his eyes, as if knowing he'd said too much.

She didn't say anything but lapped up the small details he let slip and relished them. Even though he didn't want to keep her, she was his mate. As long as they both lived, she'd always be his mate. She'd have to take what she could get.

"You can stay here in this house because that is what the Alpha requests." He growled that last bit, and she felt like crap. Of course, it hadn't been his decision. He would never have chosen her to begin with. But, it didn't matter now; it was all about the baby. "I will protect you because it's my duty. Nothing more."

She curled her lip and let out a small growl, even as pain radiated from her fingers down to her toes. The rejection ate at her, clawing its way through her body like her own wolf.

"Fine, your duty." She bit out the last word and inwardly cursed. Damn, she didn't want him to know what she felt. He had no right.

"It's nothing more. It *can* be nothing more."

She nodded and stood unsteadily, her ankles aching and swollen. She paced in the living room, resting her hands in the small of her back. Oh, what she wouldn't do to have someone rub her back for her.

Oh, God, even a bath would do. But she didn't have time for the luxury. She hadn't had a bath big enough back to her old apartment, and she hadn't felt comfortable using Adam's the night before.

"I don't know what it is you want me to say, Bay," Adam whispered, his voice low and filled with something she couldn't discern. "The night we spent together was supposed to end there. We'd had too much to drink and hadn't been thinking properly. Because if I had, I wouldn't have slept with a wolf and risked something like that."

She turned on him and growled, her wolf clawing to the surface. "Really, Adam? Because you think only wolves can mate to each other? You're an idiot if you think that. You know wolves can mate with anyone, that there are potentials out there for everyone, and if you look, you can often find one."

She took a deep breath.

"After that, the decision whether to mate with them is up to you. Sometimes the mating urges are harder than others, but it's your choice, Adam. You're the one who bit me first. You're the one who decided we didn't need to use a condom. You're the one who mated me. Don't put it all on alcohol. You're a fucking wolf. Your metabolism is high enough that, halfway through the night, your alcohol level would've been down and you would have known what you were doing. But, no, you decided to continue on. And, yes, it's just as much my fault as yours. But, I'm owning up to it. I know I'm about to be a mom, and I know that you want nothing to do with this. Fine. But, know this; I will not let you talk down to me just because you think you're all high and mighty.

"You're the one who couldn't keep his dick in his pants, and I'm the one who succumbed to it. Get over yourself and realize that this isn't going away. At least not for right now. As soon as everything is safe, I'll take the baby and go away. That way you won't have to deal with it. For right now, though, it's in your face, and I understand that hurts. You're going to have to get over it, just for the moment. Please."

She fisted her hands and turned away from them. She hadn't meant to say all that. She knew he was hurting from losing his mate and child. She *knew* that, and yet she pushed. Crap, this wasn't what she wanted. She didn't know what she wanted, frankly, but this wasn't it.

She heard Adam come up and stood behind her, and she braced for what he would say.

"You have spine. I like that."

She closed her eyes, letting the feel of his nearness envelope her.

"I don't know what we're going to do, Bay. But things will work themselves out. They have to." His voice sounded broken at the end, like he was giving up on something precious. She took a deep breath and tried not to let her emotions get to her. It was her fault he was feeling everything again. She didn't know how long his mate had been dead, but regardless, she knew she was bringing back the memories. And now that she was mated to him, she couldn't see him in pain. Her wolf whimpered for his wolf, and she lit a spark that sent a powerful flare, her wolf rolling over her and becoming more dominant. She didn't understand how she could do this while all the wolves had to change forms in order to be able to let their wolves become dominant, but she had been born different. She could let her wolf see through her eyes and act through her body, though she trusted her wolf enough not to do anything she wouldn't do.

Her wolf moaned inwardly, loving the feel of their mate close to them. Her wolf was allowed to feel the emotions that she couldn't. The longing, the need, everything.

"What the hell was that?" Adam shouted, and gripped her shoulders, turning her toward him. He looked as if he'd been shaken to the core.

She let her wolf fade back so Bay had control. "Nothing. It was just my wolf."

"I don't believe you. That was different. I've never felt that before. What the hell are you?"

"I'm a werewolf, just like you." *Sort of.*

"No, you're more. Tell me, now." He growled that last bit and let his power seep over her. He was the Enforcer, meaning he could sense threats and deal with them, as he needed. Damn, he thought she was a threat. She had to tell him something. Just not everything.

"I don't know why, but I have extra powers."

"Tell me."

"I've already told your father."

"I don't care, tell me now."

"Then let go of me please." She did her best to sound strong, to show that she wasn't scared. Her whole life she'd hidden, and yet now, the one person that could hurt her the most needed to know something she couldn't tell him.

He released her quickly then rubbed his hands up and down her arms, as if making sure he hadn't bruised her. She almost leaned into his touch then stopped, knowing that would be bad for both of them. He seemed to realize what he had been doing and pulled his hands back.

"Tell me, please."

"I have psychometry, meaning I can touch some things and see the past."

Adam's eyes widened, but that was his only reaction to what she'd said. Although she could still feel his wolf trying to lean into her wolf.

"It doesn't happen often, and I can't control it. But, with certain things I touch, I can see what others saw and feel what others feel."

"And is that what you did right there?" he asked, his voice strained.

"Something like that, but instead of someone else's feelings, I feel my wolf's. Meaning I can let her come to the surface more easily than a normal werewolf."

"What the hell, Bay? It felt as though you'd thrown power in the room and you looked like an Alpha for a moment."

She shook her head and fisted her hands, not knowing what else to do with them. "I don't know, Adam, I just don't know. I've always been able to do these things. Or, at least since I've been able to shift."

Werewolves were able to shift at the age of two or three, usually. She had been five by the time she been able to shift, scaring her mother to death. But she wouldn't tell him that.

"I've never heard of anything like that, Bay."

"I haven't either."

"What about your mother? Is that why they kicked her out?"

She could've lied and said it was the truth, but a wolf would've been able to smell that lie. She had to tread lightly. As it was, her lies were only leaving parts of the truth out, not lying head-on. "No, she was a normal wolf. I'm the freak." An understatement if there ever was one.

"I don't know what to do with you, Bay."

She gave a wry smile. "I don't know what to do with me either."

"Even though I've never heard of it, it doesn't mean it's not real. I mean, you're proof of that. There are many different powers in the Pack. Maybe yours is just special." He raised a brow as if asking her to contradict him.

"I'm just a wolf, Adam. Nothing more."

He looked at her like he didn't quite believe her, but she stood strong. She had to keep her secrets safe, not only for herself, but for her unborn child. Adam would help her find whoever was following her and take them out. That was his job and, as he said, his duty. He would protect them when she was unable to, and then she could leave, though it might kill her to do so. It wasn't just for herself; it was for the unborn child currently rolling in her womb, showing her how much it loved her. She bit back a sob, closed her eyes, and walked away from the man who was her mate. It was all too much. But this is what she'd asked for—a chance to live again, or maybe live for the first time.

# CHAPTER 7

T he leaves crunched under Adam's feet as he crouched down to the forest floor, the sickly sweet scent of the Centrals permeating and stinging his nose. He held back a curse and looked around, making sure he was alone. He'd been on patrol, searching around the outermost points of the wards to determine whether there'd been any intruders.

The wards possessed a natural ability to fend off humans. Meaning, that if a human came up to the Redwood den, they would have the sudden urge to leave or pass by without going any farther. Also, if for any reason they still continued on, which was highly unlikely, they couldn't pass through the wards, and they would turn around on their own. However, those with any supernatural ability could see the wards, feel the wards, and try to get through the wards.

Witches, other werewolves, and even demons could see their wards, but only those of the Redwood could pass through them easily. Others would need an invitation and have to be by the side of a Redwood Pack member.

However, what Adam smelled now was not the scent of a Pack member, but of their enemy, the Centrals. Rage simmered through him, boiling under his skin, threatening to burst. His wolf was still on alert, ready to attack. The fucking, piece-of-shit weasels of wolves thought it was okay to come to *his* land? He held back a growl and stood, his claws threatening to burst from his skin. Ever since that one fateful night eight months before, he'd had control issues. This time it wasn't about the redhead. No, it was about the fact that those bastards thought it was okay to encroach on their territory. They were at war, and this wasn't the time to pussyfoot around. He was the fucking Enforcer, and he needed to make a stand. Though the dark magic out there infecting the Centrals seemed to be overpowering, the Redwoods would not stand aside.

He inhaled their scents, the sweet sickness coating his tongue, and followed their trail. The two that had been sent to spy on the Redwoods were young, and inexperienced, they'd left markers and a clear trail. He would've laughed at the irony, but it wasn't the fact that they were wolves that made them bad. No, because they chose to summon a demon and let him into their hearts, their souls were black, and Adam had no use for them. He had no use for demons at all.

He came upon them, and they didn't notice him coming. He crept behind them, his wolf rising to the surface, loving the hunt. He was about two feet from them when they froze, fear and that sickly taint wafting from them. Adam gave a harsh smile and growled. They tried to run, but he was faster. He grabbed them by their collars and smashed their heads together, but not with too much force because he needed to hear them talk.

They groaned, whimpered, and cried out, and Adam shook his head. Really? This was the reason that the Redwoods were losing people? Weak wolves with a craving for power?

Adam growled again, letting his power flow out through him. The wolves paled and bared their throats. He would've bared his teeth and shown who was the more dominant wolf, but he wanted nothing to do with them, unsure of what would happen if he had a taste their blood. The scent of their disease slid into the air from their pores, and Adam almost felt sorry for the sick bastards.

"So, tell me, why are you here?" he growled.

"We were told to watch, nothing more," the smaller one whimpered.

Adam bared his teeth, and the other wolf, the one who hadn't spoken, growled and nipped at him. Adam growled and punched the bastard in the nose, almost enjoying the feel of its break beneath his fist. He was a wolf, not just a man. He didn't crave violence, but he didn't shy away from it. He did what he had to do to protect his Pack, and these infected wolves didn't deserve to live. Maybe if it had looked as if they had any remorse, or if their eyes had been completely black, tainted by the demon, he would've let them live. But he couldn't let them go back to Corbin and his pet demon and tell them anything they'd seen. It was too much of a risk.

This war was killing him death-by-death, blow-by-blow. But at least with this, he didn't have to feel what he had before and miss what wasn't there to miss.

"I could make you talk," Adam threatened.

"We promise; we don't know anything," the smaller one spoke again.

*"They are telling the truth, Adam,"* his wolf assured.

Because he was the Enforcer, he could immediately feel when there was a danger to the Pack or when something might cause a threat later. Though these two posed no threat to him other than being in the wrong place. If they left and went back to Corbin with what they'd seen, the danger to his Pack would increase, meaning he would have to take care of them. Permanently.

What would Anna have thought of who he had become?

In that moment of hesitation, the larger wolf reached out and clawed Adam in the face, its long nails piercing his skin, the pain radiating out like fire.

Adam roared and broke the bastard's neck in quick one movement. He didn't deserve a quick death, but Adam didn't want to deal with him anymore. The other wolf grew frightened and wriggled beneath his hold. With a remorseful sigh, he broke the other's neck.

He leaned back on his haunches and looked down at his hands. Though some might call it justice, others might call a murder. These days he didn't know what to call it. He hated who he was becoming but he didn't know how to stop it. Because if he didn't do things like this, his family wouldn't be protected, and he could lose everything, even if he didn't think he had much to lose.

He put a hand up to his face and winced. Damn, that wasn't going to heal quickly. He was pretty sure he could feel his cheekbone and cursed. He wouldn't be able to heal on his own. Even though wolves were fast at healing, they weren't as fast as portrayed in the movies. He would probably need North or Hannah to heal him. Frankly, he didn't want to see either of them right now. He'd rather sit up in his house and hide away. Oh yeah, look at the mighty Enforcer go.

He left the bodies where they lay, knowing they were too close to the Redwood wards to be noticed by humans. He'd leave the bodies there and let Corbin's next minions come and see the bodies. Though some part of him wanted to give the men proper burial, they'd wanted to harm his Pack, and he needed to make a statement.

He walked back through the wards, the magic feeling like honey sliding over his skin, and he made his way back to his home. He could've shifted to a wolf and made it to his home faster, but he didn't want to leave his clothes, and frankly, he didn't like shifting anymore. Even though, since Bay had come two days ago, his wolf had been happier, he still didn't trust it. He didn't know when he would be able to.

Yep, he had a pretty dysfunctional relationship with his wolf.

He made his way through the door and paused as Bay's scent hit him in the face. Fuck. He adjusted himself and groaned. Every second he spent in the house with her was sheer agony. Her body radiated health, wellness, and her pregnancy. He knew her breasts were bigger since the last time he'd seen her, and he hated himself for noticing. Even the sight of her swollen belly made him feel more like a man. No wonder Jasper and Kade walked around like cocks on the walk while their mates were pregnant.

That stopped in his tracks. Holy hell, he needed to stop thinking about her like she was his mate. Yes, they'd gone through the rituals of mating, but he didn't want her. He bit his tongue as his eyes burned. He couldn't want her. It was a betrayal of everything he had ever known.

Bay came from the back of the house, alarm on her face. "Oh my God, Adam. I knew I smelled blood. What happened?" She came up to him and lifted her hands as if she were going to touch him. He pulled back as if she'd burned him, and she winced.

"It's nothing, just part of the job."

"Shouldn't you see North or Hannah?"

"Probably, but I'm not in the mood right now."

She shook her head then let out a snort. "I swear all men are the same. Whether they are man or wolf, they don't like doctors."

He gave a big smile, showing teeth. "Are you calling all men babies?"

"If the rattle fits."

Adam threw his head back and laughed, surprising himself in the process.

"If you don't want to see North or Hannah, I can at least clean it for you. It looks pretty bad, but maybe if I just put some butterfly bandages on it, it'll be okay until you see them." She raised her brow, and Adam nodded his head.

"Fine, my first aid kit is in the bathroom."

He watched her go, and he sank down into the chair. What the hell was he doing? He was acting like this was the day-to-day thing and that it was okay she was taking care of him. No, it would only happen this once. He couldn't let her too close. His wolf begged and growled to claim her in more ways than one.

He hated this predestined mate shit. It was as if it were forcing him to have her. Because even as she kept saying that she'd leave and he'd never see her again, a little part of him didn't want her to go. That same little part wanted to know the baby inside her.

That little part needed to shut up.

She came out of the bathroom, her stomach leading her. She smiled at him, though her body

84

radiated tension. It had to be a bit uncomfortable for her to live in a house knowing she wasn't welcome. But no one else in the den would take her. It was as if there was a large conspiracy against them. The den didn't want to interfere, and they thought that Adam, being the Enforcer, could best protect her.

For some reason, he couldn't quite believe them.

"Okay, I'm going to do my best to clean it and then put on some bandages." Bay slowly sat on the table and cringed as it made a groan beneath her.

"It's an old table," he said as he tried to bite back a smile. Damn, this woman made him laugh more than he wanted to.

"Thanks for that. I really think North or Hannah should be looking at this though, Adam. It doesn't look good; I mean I think I see bone."

Adam ignored the dull throbbing in his cheek and shrugged. "I'll be fine; I've had worse."

"That doesn't make me feel any better."

"Just do your best."

She leaned forward and used a wet washcloth to wipe up the blood. As she worked, he watched the way her red curls framed her face and how her green eyes darkened when she concentrated. No matter how hard he tried, this little wolf was getting under his skin. He didn't know her, and he didn't know who had brought her here. He didn't know what the future would bring, and right now, the only thing he could think was if he could remember the taste of her lips.

Like sweet berries, the plumpest strawberries...

And that was enough of that.

"Okay, all patched up."

He blinked them focused on her. "Didn't hurt a bit, thanks." He focused on her lips and cursed inwardly at himself.

This was so not a good idea. Thoughts of Anna, his pack, and every other little reason on earth why he shouldn't bend down and kiss this woman flew through his head, but he ignored them.

"Adam?" she asked, breathless.

"I'm going to kiss you, Bay," he growled.

"Why?

"Because I have to."

"Because of the mating, right? Because you have no choice?"

He nodded, not knowing what else to say.

"Once we figure out what's going on and I leave, you'll just let me go?" she asked, her voice cold and no emotions showing on her face.

"Yes. That's all I have left to give."

"So you want to ride out the mating urge with me and not deal with the other crap?" Before he could apologize for his asinine comment, she nodded. "Okay. I can accept those rules. Because, frankly, you're not the only one dealing with a wolf that wants more."

His wolf growled, wanting to pounce on her, but the man held it back. He leaned forward and framed her face with his hands. He could feel the fluttering of her pulse, speeding up like a hummingbird. The scent of her arousal hit his nose, and he groaned.

"Shit, can we do this, you know, with the..." He gestured to her belly, not able to say the word.

Her eyes filled then she blinked the tears away, stronger than any wolf he'd seen. "Yes, we can do pretty much anything."

"You know this doesn't mean anything."

"I know," she whispered, her voice finally carrying a hint of emotion—fear.

"I will hurt you, Bay. I told you that."

"That's not the kind of hurt I'm afraid of."

He steeled himself and took a deep breath. "There's nothing I can do about that. I've nothing of that to give. I don't do love; I already did that. I don't want it again."

"Fine."

With that, he leaned down again and brushed his lips against hers. Shock rippled through him as he tasted her. She tasted of cool berries, feminine wolf, and Bay. She tasted just the same as she had that night, minus the tequila. But for some reason, that made her taste even more intoxicating.

He pulled back and rested his forehead against hers, his breath labored. "We're going to do this; it doesn't mean anything."

"Fine. I understand, stop saying it. Please." She ran a hand through his hair, and he growled, his cock straining against his zipper.

With that, he picked her up and cradled her to his body, ignoring the way she felt against him. Her soft curves were even more pronounced now than they had been before, and all he wanted to do was get inside her and relieve the aching tension. He placed her on the edge of the bed and knelt between her legs. Her belly was in his line of sight, but he ignored it. He stripped off her leggings and maternity dress and growled. Damn, she was fucking beautiful.

He stripped off her panties and took off her bra, leaving her bare before him, curvy and delicious. Her breasts were full and round, larger than they had been before. He cupped them in his hands, the heavy weight overfilling them.

"These are magnificent," he murmured, his voice low.

She laughed, low and husky. "They're getting freaking huge. I'm pretty sure they are their own shelf right now."

"What can I say? Apparently I'm a breast man."
He rolled both nipples between his thumbs and
forefingers, and she gasped, throwing her head back.

"I think I can deal with that."

"I'm going to be careful with you. I don't want to
hurt you." As his mate, he couldn't hurt her physically
without wanting to hurt himself. But that wasn't the
only reason, though he didn't want to think about
that.

She nodded, and he wasn't sure if she actually
heard him. He let his hands roam over her shoulders,
breasts, and lower. He made sure he stayed away from
her belly, not ready to feel what was beneath the
already stretched-out skin. Her thighs were creamy
and smooth beneath his palms, and he rubbed circles
onto them, loving the way Bay felt against his skin. He
spread her thighs wider and used his thumb to trace
her seam. She gasped again, and he grinned, liking the
control.

He slipped a thumb inside and groaned. "Holy
hell, you're already wet."

Bay's body blushed, and she looked down at him,
caution in her gaze. "I can't help it. You do that to me.
It's just a reaction."

Adam nodded, liking and needing the way she
reassured their agreement. "If you could feel my cock
right now, you'd understand it's the same way for me."

Her mouth formed the temptress's grin. "I'm sure
that could be arranged."

He didn't say anything, ignoring the warm pulse
that seeped into his icy chest. He crushed that,
remembering why they were there. They needed to
cool down the mating urge so they could move on and
get her the hell out of here.

Adam dipped his middle finger to the knuckle
inside her, and she clamped down, warm and needy.

He used his thumb to brush her clit, and she shuddered. He scraped the swollen nub with his fingernail, and she bucked off the bed. He gripped her hip to hold her steady and inserted two more fingers, curling them to reach that sensitive spot. Bay moaned his name, and he let it wash over him in a wave. Using a sensuous rhythm, he watched her body flush and her panting increased until, finally, she came against his fingers, her pussy tightening and a scream ripping from her throat.

He stood and removed his clothing quickly. She lay down on the bed and watched him with pleasure-darkened eyes. His cock slapped his belly as he walked toward her, intent seeping through every pore. Her breath hitched, and he groaned at the magnificent sight before him. His gaze traveled over her body and froze at her swollen belly. With great determination, he flipped her over on her knees, and she gasped.

"Can I take you from here?"

"I...I think so," she mumbled, a slight trace of fear edging her words.

Without thinking, he rubbed her back, trying to soothe her. His wolf growled in pleasure, and he pulled his hand back.

He swallowed hard. "Tell me if I hurt you; we'll stop if we have to."

"Of course, please, Adam, please."

He gripped his cock and centered the head at her entrance. He didn't put on a condom because it was way too late to be thinking about that. They'd already made that mistake. He gripped her hips and slid in inch by agonizing inch. When he was fully inside her, he stopped and tried to catch his breath. She fit him like a glove, a perfect fucking glove. She was hot, wet, and ready for him. They both moaned when he moved back slowly. He pulled out then thrust back in, loving the way her body arched with him, even with the awkwardness of her midsection. He set a rhythm, feeling her body close around him as she slowly climbed to her climax.

He increased the rhythm, their heartbeats syncing, their breaths doing the same. His balls tightened as she came around him, and he followed her, his seed filling her, warm and needy.

Before he caught his breath, he pulled out and set her on her side, careful not to jostle her. He watched as she closed her eyes and rubbed a hand over her belly. He swallowed hard and staggered away to the bathroom, locking the door behind him. Blindly, he turned the water on as hot as it could go and stepped under the steamy spray. The water scalded him, giving him a heavy dose of what he needed, pain, agony.

He crouched down, his legs giving out, his knees slamming into the floor. He didn't even notice the sharp pain as his body wracked in convulsions. Tears streamed from his eyes as he finally broke down, something he hadn't done in a very long while.

Yes, he'd slept with women after Anna. But that had only been to fill a need. But with Bay, this time, it had been different. He knew he could lie to himself all he wanted and say it meant nothing. But it did. And that was the worst betrayal all. He'd promised to love his Anna for the rest of his life, knowing at the time that, as a wolf, his life would be long. And yet, as he'd held Bay's hips in his palms, he'd broken his vow to his long-lost mate.

How was he ever going to forgive himself? And why should he?

# CHAPTER 8

B ay stepped out of the shower and placed her feet on the soft forest green bathmat. She wrapped herself in a fluffy green towel and sighed. She sat on the edge of the tub and rubbed lotion all over her. Even though she kind of enjoyed the fact that she was pregnant, in a scary sort of way, the stretch marks were going to kill her. She was pretty sure all women had to deal with them, but thankfully, she was a wolf and could most likely heal them later.

And yes, she was thinking about stretch marks and stupid trivial things. That way she didn't have to think about the fact that she'd slept with Adam, again. She closed her eyes and bit her tongue. Crap, she hadn't meant to do that. Yes, the mating urge had ridden her just as hard, if not harder, than Adam because of the hormones, but that didn't give her an excuse to make poor decisions. He kept promising he wouldn't hurt her, but she knew it was too late. Her heart was going to break it was going to hurt like hell.

And it was all her fault.

She pulled on a loose-fitting shirt and yoga pants, wincing as she stretched muscles that were a little too achy from earlier. She blushed as she remembered the way Adam had played her body like a fine-tuned instrument. She made her come twice before allowing himself to do the same. Her emotions ran her ragged, and she wanted to sob. But she was too strong for that. They had just had sex, not made love. That had not been love. That is been a joining of two bodies, and then he'd left her. Again.

She bit back another sob. She'd heard him break down in the shower, and it had taken every ounce of her energy and inner strength to not go in there and comfort him. He was not crying over her, but over the fact that he'd failed himself. What had she become? This was her. She was stronger than this. Yet, she cried at the drop of a hat over a man who'd used her. But really, they had both made the agreement that they would use each other. It was her own damn fault. Damn hormones.

The baby kicked, and she placed her palm over the little foot.

"I know it's not your fault," she whispered. Warmth spread over her at the thought of her unborn child. She already loved this little baby more than she loved anything else in her life. And although that wasn't saying much, considering her past, it didn't diminish the fact that this little guy or girl would be the center of her life.

The scent of pine and wolf entered her nose, and she froze. Adam stood at the door, a frown on his face. "Are you ready?"

She looked down at her dressed form then nodded. "I'm ready to go. Where exactly are we going?"

"We'll be inside the wards and in the part of the forest we usually use for hunts like this," Adam answered. "We haven't done a hunt outside the wards and in our outer territories since the initial attacks."

She nodded, sadness filling her. Though she was not part of the Pack yet, and hadn't even known these people, she still felt the pain of losing so many of their members at once. Corbin, the Alpha of the Centrals, along with his now deceased father, Hector, had come onto their land, burned as many buildings to the ground as they could, and killed as many people as they could. The demon, Caym, had even threatened to kill Willow and had kidnapped Reed. Thankfully, Reed had escaped, along with his two mates, Hannah and Josh.

"I'm ready to go; I need to shift."

"It's the full moon; I'm not surprised. When was the last time you shifted anyway?"

She shrugged. "I'm not sure, at least two weeks ago."

He shook his head then fisted his hands. "That's not smart when you're pregnant, Bay. You need to take care of yourself and your wolf so your body can take care of your baby."

She lifted her chin, anger filling her. She hadn't missed the fact that he always said 'you' or 'your' in reference to her child, as if taking own of their unborn even with words were too much for him. "I'm sorry I was a little busy trying not to die or whatever the hell was going to happen when that person found me. I tried to shift as often as possible, but I didn't have the den or safe place like this to hide."

"And whose fault is that?"

She let out a snort then stood up, her body sore and achy from their excursion. Her skin felt tight, like it was too small for her body. She needed to shift and

93

let her wolf run free. She could feel the setting of the sun and the moon coming toward her, pulling her.

She walked past him, careful not to let any part of her touch him. She didn't know if she could deal with that. She stood stone still and rested her gaze on him.

"I've never been in a full hunt like this before, Adam," she said in a small voice. "I don't know what to do."

Adam blinked at her, and she could almost feel him judging her from where she stood. Damn, she hated being a lone wolf sometimes, but it wasn't like she'd had any other choice.

"Shift when I shift, then follow me. We don't always hunt like a Pack; sometimes we go in smaller groups. Since we don't have as much space to roam because of the wards, everyone who will shift tonight is going to be one big group, at least to start. So stay by my side and you'll know what to do. You're a wolf, Bay. You'll know what to do instinctively."

She nodded, grateful he would show her what to do but also careful not to show him that. She couldn't let him have any more power over her than he already did.

"You have nothing to fear. I won't let anything happen to you. Whoever was following you and made you feel unsafe cannot get through our wards."

She nodded again, letting him think that that was why she was nervous. Better to think she was afraid of an outside force harming her rather than the man in front of her.

They walked out the back door and through the woods into the small clearing. The final rays of the sun sank below the horizon, and the moon brightened as night set in. A small wind blew through her hair, the red curls falling into disarray around her face. She hadn't had a chance to put any product in her hair or deal with the mass of curls that had been the bane of her existence after her shower. Plus, since she was going to be turning into a wolf, she didn't really feel the need. But as they came up upon the rest the pack, she felt wholly inadequate. Every single person looked beautiful, like freaking models. The most striking of all had the Jamenson green eyes set in the most model-like face she'd ever seen. This woman must be Cailin, Adam's baby sister, with her long black hair and green eyes. Bay wanted to hide her fat self and never look back. Why was it that whatever a woman saw another woman who was so beautiful she felt like the ugly spinster? Oh, she could hate a woman like that, except for the fact that she was the Redwood princess, and Bay couldn't really fault the woman for being beautiful.

Adam ignored her as he stopped, and Bay held her breath. She'd done her best to wash his scent off her just like she'd known he done the same with hers. She tried not to take it personally, but it still stung. She covered her belly with her hands and closed her eyes. Her skin rippled under the moonlight, and her wolf howled to be released.

She looked out over the crowd and saw Willow, who waved at her. Bay returned it with a small smile, grateful for a friendly face. Her mate, Jasper, wrapped an arm around her and gave Bay a slight nod. Relief filled her at the acceptance in his gaze. She looked out over the rest of the family, and they each, in turn, gave her a nod or wave of some kind. She didn't know what exactly all that meant, but at least she didn't feel so alone.

North came up to her side and gave her a hug. Surprised, Bay froze. Adam turned and growled, and North lifted his arm.

"It's good to see you again, Bay," North whispered. "How's the baby?"

She rested her hand on the swell of her stomach and looked up at the twin with no scar. "We're doing just fine. Thank you."

North nodded and looked her over with the cool gaze of the doctor, not that of a male. "Once you shift, yip or something if it hurts. Okay?"

Her eyes widened, and alarm spread through her. "What do you mean? I thought shifting was okay when I was pregnant. That's what I heard, and I've been shifting this whole time. Only, God, have I been doing it wrong? Have I been hurting my baby?"

Adam put a strong hand on her shoulder and gripped it. Though she was thankful for the comfort, she didn't want to read too much into it. North's eyes widened at the touch, but he didn't say anything.

"I'm sorry. I didn't mean to worry you. I just want to make sure you're okay. Shifting is natural. Therefore, your body will adjust while you're pregnant to shift that certain way. Your wolf needs it and wouldn't want to hurt your baby. I just want to make sure everything is okay. It's just the doctor in me."

She let out a breath, relieved. "Okay, I'll let you know. But you need to do better on that whole not-freaking-out-the-patient thing, okay?"

North gave a rueful smile and stepped back. That's when she noticed the other two wolves standing behind North. Maddox, North's twin, stood the farthest away, no expression on his face. The long scar that traced the right side of his face looked stark in contrast to his tan skin. The other person—a woman—had dark eyes, dark hair, and caramel-colored skin. She also looked like someone had broken her and she hadn't quite figured out how to put herself back together.

96

North looked over his shoulder and turned. "Bay, this is Ellie, our friend and member of the Pack." The other woman inclined her head, and they did the same. Tension radiated through the three newcomers, and Bay didn't really know what to think of that. She was missing a piece of the puzzle, but she didn't think it was really any of her business.

"It's time, Pack," Edward called out, his voice echoing throughout the trees surrounding them.

Bay lowered her head, showing proper respect to her Alpha. Though she had not grown up in a Pack, her body and wolf knew instinctively what to do.

Adam blocked her view of the others as they started to strip out of their clothes and shift. She felt grateful toward the man and quickly took off her oversized shirt and knelt on the ground. She wasn't quite sure what to think of Adam's gesture. Right now, all she could think about was changing. Her wolf howled, and warmth spread over her belly, cocooning it in a safe haven. Her limbs stretched, the bones breaking, the muscles tearing. Fur sprouted over her skin, and her back arched as her limbs reformed and reattached in new positions. She threw back her head and howled to the moon as she stood as a rusty-red wolf.

When she was finished, she looked over at Adam's wolf, awed at the beauty of it. He was large, bigger than her by at least twenty pounds, and was a beautiful chestnut brown. Half of his face was black, and he had black ears. He was magnificent.

North, Maddox, and Ellie surrounded them. The twins both had a mixture of gray and tan fur, while Ellie was a caramel brown. They bounded off together, Maddox taking the rear. Adam looked over his shoulder and took off after them. Not wanting to be left behind, she followed them, the ground soft below her paws. Through the link to the Pack and Adam, she could feel the others around her hunting in a unit for their prey. Even though they did not need to hunt for animals in this form, they enjoyed the rush of being able to let go and let their wolves take control. She let her wolf rise to the surface and followed that sweet pine scent she was falling for.

The feel of the Pack surrounded her, and she felt like she had come home. So this is what she had been missing being by herself for so long. She almost cried at the thought of what she had lost, but now she had gained so much, if only for the moment.

She heard the sudden sound of the pitter-pat of little feet on the ground and recognized it as the footsteps of a rabbit. The others moved on as she stopped. Her ears pointed forward, and she bent her nose to the ground. Her wolf kicked in, and she followed the trail and scent to the delicious rabbit. She crept behind it as it froze, aware that a predator had it in sight. It took one hop, and she pounced, taking its life out in a single movement so it would not suffer.

Though her belly was big in this form, as in her other form, she laid down on her side, eager to begin her meal. The sweet pine scent invaded her nose as Adam came to her side, another rabbit in his mouth. He laid it next to her and lay down beside it, not looking at her. They each ate their meal in silence, a peacefulness that came from being on four legs when the sound of more wolves came toward them. North, Maddox, and Ellie stopped about two feet away and stared. It was hard to communicate as wolves, but she had a feeling the men wanted to go off alone. Call it a wolf's intuition. She looked at Adam, who lowered his head and bounced off, North and Maddox following him.

Ellie came to her side, nudged the dead carcass away, and gave a wolfy grin. Bay barked a laugh then darted off, letting the other wolf know to follow her. They both ran through the woods, feeling safe under their wards and knowing that the other wolves were around them if there was any trouble. Finally, after another hour of playing, they made their way back to the center of the field where their clothes lay. They each shifted back, Bay wincing at the pain of shifting that never went away even as many times as she'd done it.

Ellie smiled at her, naked as a jaybird, and quickly got dressed. Bay did the same and tried not to notice the scars on the other woman's back. She didn't say anything, and she wasn't sure that Ellie had even noticed that she'd seen anything.

"It's nice to meet you by the way," Ellie said, and held out her hand.

They shook, and Bay felt a kindred spirit with the woman. "It's nice to meet you too. It was little hard to meet everyone with people staring and crowding."

"I know what you mean. And I'm new to the Pack as well, so it's nice to see another new face. I don't feel all alone."

"You're new, too?"

"They didn't tell you?" she said wryly. "I'm the daughter of our enemy. The Redwoods are amazing. If they can accept me—at least most of them—then they can do anything. They can win this. I know it."

Bay nodded but didn't say anything. As much she loved hearing that they'd accepted the daughter of their rival pack into their fold, Bay didn't feel very warm. Would they accept her if they knew the truth? No, she didn't think so. She hadn't even accepted it herself.

# CHAPTER 9

*Eight Months Before*
Adam let his head rest against the steering wheel as his body shook. Fuck. What was he doing here in a small rundown town in southern California? He'd needed to leave the Pack for just a little while to catch his breath. He'd never leave them for long; he couldn't do that. They were his family and had been by his side through everything heartbreaking his life, including the worst thing imaginable.

He clenched the steering will, his knuckles turning white. He'd left only a few weeks before, and now he could feel them calling him back. He was their Enforcer, and he needed to protect them. He couldn't do that this far away, but it wasn't time for him to leave yet. He didn't know what he was searching for, but he hadn't found it yet.

Maybe it was peace. He gave a harsh laugh and lifted his head from the steering wheel. Peace, sure, like that would ever happen. He'd lost his Anna and knew he'd never find peace. Maybe his wolf just needed to run...no, not yet. He didn't want to shift to his wolf and remember that feeling. He'd been doing okay for the past two decades, but one-by-one, as each brother mated, he felt a little part of himself die again. And when Reed had shown up with not one, but two mates, he'd needed to get the fuck out of there.

Maybe he just needed to get laid. A sharp pain radiated through him, and he cursed. Dammit, he hated urges and needs. Sometimes he wished he were a fucking eunuch.

On that thought, he got out of this truck, slammed the door, and prowled to the bar. He just needed a drink. He walked into the rundown bar that smelled of witches and magic and breathed a sigh of relief. Here he'd be able to get as drunk as he wanted and not have to deal with the humans staring at him.

When he walked up to the bar and the bartender raised an eyebrow, Adam grunted. The male witch seemed to know what Adam wanted and slid over an entire bottle and one glass. Adam grunted his thanks and found a table in the corner to sit. He leaned with his back to the wall. That way he could see if anyone came up to him. He was out of his territory, and he needed to be careful. He took a long swig straight from the bottle and relished the spicy taste as it poured down his throat. He poured some more in the glass because he didn't want to look so crass and took another drink.

People milled about; having conversations he didn't care about and played a game of darts, he didn't want to join. Four bottles of tequila later, he was just starting to get a buzz. The bartender looked up at him, and Adam put two hundreds down on the table to signify he wasn't quite done yet. The bartender nodded and looked around for something, what, Adam didn't care.

"I take it you want more?" a sweet voice asked, pulling out him out of his buzzed stupor.

"Yes, bring the bottle." And because his mom would kick his ass if he weren't polite, he tacked on a, "please." She didn't even glance in his direction as she walked away, but he caught a sweet berries scent that made his cock stand up and pulled a groan from him.

Holy hell, that had smelled like sweet heaven.

The tantalizing scent came back, and this time he took a good look. Oh, fuck. She was all curves, curves of sin that a man could pound into night after night. Or at least for one night. Red curls framed her face and bounced as she walked. And those damn green eyes of hers called to him even through the drunken haze.

"Okay, here you go, be careful," she said with a smile, and started to turn away.

He grabbed her wrist, and she started. He inhaled again and growled. "You're a wolf." A statement, not a question.

"So astute. I'm surprised you could even tell that with all the liquor running through your system."

He gave a laugh then took another swig of his drink, the sweet, spicy taste mingling with her scent and causing a dynamic that made him want to bend her over the table and fuck her right there to see how tight she was.

She turned and raised a brow. "Excuse me, why do you think it's okay to touch me?"

"Maybe because I don't want you to go."

She let out a sigh. "Really? That's the best you can do? That was just pathetic. Though at least you didn't ask me if it hurt when I fell from heaven or something. God, I swear, you'd think after all these years men would get better at pickup lines."

"Maybe they just needed you to teach them." He groaned inwardly at that, knowing that even though he was drunk, it had to be worse than what he had said before.

She threw her head back and laughed. "Oh, honey, that was just bad. But, I'll tell you what. I'm off my shift in ten minutes. Why don't I pick up another bottle or two and we can drink our worries away?"

"What type of worries do you have?"

She shook her head and grinned ruefully. "We don't know each other enough for that, but I will drink with you, and then we'll see what happens."

His cock twitched, and he smiled. "Sounds good to me."

He indulged himself and the rest of the bottle and waited for her to return. When she was done working, she came back with two bottles, one in each hand, and the seductive grin on her face. Hell yeah, this is just what he'd needed, a way to forget and indulge.

She sat down next to him in the booth, not across from him. He wrapped his arm around her shoulder, liking the way she felt against his drunk self.

"Do you know what bottle you're on now?" she asked, pouring a glass for herself.

"Does it matter?"

"I just don't want you to die on me."

"I think I'm a little far away from that, but thanks for worrying."

"Good." With that, she tossed back the shot and poured two more. He took a drink, letting it roll over his tongue as he inhaled her scent. She smelled of wolf, but also of something...more? Maybe it was the drink talking. He took her free hand in his and rubbed his fingers along her wrist. Her pulse raced, and he looked down at her eyes, liking the way she looked back at him, eager, wanting.

They finished the second bottle not really talking, just letting their arousal fill the room. The others filed out and the bartender called out, saying he was closing up and Bay knew what to do.

"I guess we should leave?" Adam asked, not wanting to let her go right then.

"My apartment's upstairs," she whispered, her words floating over him and making him growl.

"Sounds like a plan to me." He wanted to get in her quick and hard, and maybe slow and leisurely later. Maybe this quick fuck would drown away the pain more than the alcohol had.

****

Bay pulled Adam up the stairs after she'd turn off the lights to the bar. Her pulse beat in her ears, and she squeezed his hand for balance. She was a little too drunk to be doing this, but it didn't matter. She inhaled his sweet pine scent again and knew.

This man, this Adam, was her mate.

Oh, hell.

Could this be it? Had she really found someone to share the rest of her life with? Is that why she felt like she needed to writhe herself against him right now?

Could she trust him?

They made their way to her room, and as soon as she closed the door, he pressed her against the wall, his mouth crushing hers. She couldn't breathe, couldn't speak, couldn't think. She closed her eyes and moaned as his tongue worked its way into her mouth, mimicking that sensual motion she wanted to feel.

She felt his hands roam down her sides, and then he ripped the snap and zipper from her jeans. She gasped as he tore them from her body and threw them across the room. He lifted his mouth from hers, gave her wicked grin, and knelt between her legs.

Holy shit. Her wolf growled, and she did the same.

He pressed his face against her panties and inhaled, and the look of his dark hair against the white satin almost made her come at the spot. He looked up at her, the gold glowing around the iris of his eye and the green almost nonexistent around the dilated pupil. Her breath shuddered, and he dragged his teeth along her clit, sending shivers down her spine to end in her core. He caught the sides of her thong with his teeth and ripped, the strength of him causing her knees to buckle, and she almost fell. He caught her by the back of the thighs, and his strong hands lifted her so her legs lay draped over his shoulders.

"I want to taste you. Then I'm going to fuck you as hard as I can to see how much you can take. How does that sound?" His voice sent shivers along her body, and she shook.

"How about I just say do me now?"

"That can be arranged." Then he bent forward and licked her clit, her body shaking as she dug her nails into the drywall for leverage. He licked and sucked and feasted on her. Her body writhed against his face, digging in his shoulders, but he didn't drop her. She still wore her heels from working, and they dug into his back. He gently bit down on her clit, and she came, stars slashing behind her eyelids and his name on her lips.

She heard him growl but didn't have enough energy to move. She felt him take off her shoes, and he licked up her side, around her breasts, until he reached her mouth.

"I knew you'd taste like a feast. Like sweet berries and woman. And the way you look when you come...oh, fuck yeah, I'm going to enjoy pounding into you."

Her eyelids fluttered, and she smiled. "What are you waiting for?"

He growled and nipped her lip then licked the sting.

He laid her on the bed and stood back watching her. "Why are you just standing there? Aren't you going to touch me?" she teased.

"Greedy, are you? Oh, I like that."

He took off his clothes, and she lay mesmerized, staring at the long sexy lines of his body and the bulging muscles. Most wolves had a strong body, but he was sexier than most. And he was all hers.

Her eyes dropped down to his cock that stood out, thick and pulsating. She could already see the tip had a little drop of cum. And she was the one who'd done that to him. That made her want him even more. She writhed on the bedspread, her knees spread wantonly. He stared down at her, his eyes gold, and ran a hand up and down his shaft, twisting and squeezing. Holy hell, that had to be the hottest thing she'd ever seen. She'd never thought seeing the guy touch himself like that would be hot, but, apparently, she hadn't seen that before.

He lowered himself over her and kissed her, and she enjoyed the taste of herself on his tongue. She should have blushed at her brazen acts, but she only wanted more of Adam. He moved down her body, licking and sucking everywhere he went. He held her breasts in his hands and rolled the nipples in his fingers.

"These are delicious; I'm going to eat them right up."

She shivered and arched her breast into his mouth as he sucked on one nipple and played with the other with his fingers. He kept biting and sucking and twisting, and she almost came just by that. Her breasts were so large that she didn't usually have that much sensitivity and couldn't come from just that touch alone, but, apparently, all she needed was Adam.

He pulled up and looked down at her. "I don't think I can wait any longer. I need to be in you."

"Oh, thank God," she rasped.

She noticed that he didn't get a condom, and she didn't correct him. After all, this was a mating. She trusted him. Shouldn't she?

Before she could question that thought, he flipped her over so she knelt right above his cock, her breasts bouncing with the movement.

"You're going to ride me, baby," he growled, and gripped her hips with his hands.

She slowly lowered herself onto his cock and moaned at the feeling. He was so big that she felt so full. She hadn't even lowered herself fully, but she didn't think she could go any farther.

"You're really big."

He let out a rough chuckle. "You sure know how to make a guy feel good."

"Oh shut up. Give me a second to get used to it so I can go down all the way."

"Anything you want, baby."

She closed her eyes and rocked back and forth until, finally, her muscles loosened a bit so she could slide down the rest of the way. She stilled as they connected in the most intimate of ways.

He tightened his grip on her hips and pushed up. She closed her eyes and moaned.

"No," he bit out. "Don't close your eyes; keep them open so I can see them spark when you come."

She almost did just that with just his words, but she opened her eyes and looked down at him. She placed her hands on his chest and rolled her hips to match the movement of his. They rocked together in a furious rhythm, their bodies sweating and writhing.

They moved faster, and she came again, screaming his name. His dick twitched inside her, and he groaned and then flipped them. She could see in his eyes from their glazed look that the drink hadn't been exorcised out of his system yet. She lay beneath him, breathing heavily as he pounded into her with such a ferocity that, had she been human, he could have broken her. As it was, she would have delicious bruises from their lovemaking, and she didn't care.

He slammed into her, and she watched as his canines elongated. She tilted her head in their ancient custom, ready for him to mark her to start their mating. She needed—no, craved—this. He bit into the meaty flesh, and she came against him again, her body rolling in pleasure and sweet agony.

He pulled back, licked the wound, and then flipped them over again, his body still thrusting into her. Damn, the man had stamina. Poor guy hadn't gotten off yet and only cared about her pleasure. Oh, how she wanted to keep him.

Her wolf howled, and her teeth elongated. Adam tilted his neck, and she bit in, falling a little bit in love with him as she tasted him. He roared and came within her, his seed locking that final mating key. Their souls entwined, and she could feel him deep within her heart as well as her body.

He collapsed and let out a breath. His cock still hard inside her, he twisted so they both lay on their sides, their breaths in sync. She laid her head against his chest and felt him fall into a deep sleep as he held her.

She yawned, worn out in the best of ways. Contentment settled over her as she slowly fell asleep in the arms of her mate. Yes, this was the perfect moment. Nothing could crush this.

# CHAPTER 10

*P*resent Day
Three days had passed since the hunt, and Adam still didn't know what to do with himself. His stomach was in knots, and his skin felt ready to burst. He felt like a teenager again, trying to learn to control the shift with his raging hormones. He closed his eyes and tried to take a deep breath, though his body wouldn't let him.

He looked out the window of the bedroom and stared through the trees. The sun was just now setting, and pinks and grays shone through the gaps in the leaves like an odd array of twilight. This used to be Anna's favorite time of day.

He shook his head and almost beat his fists against his skull. Why the hell did he keep thinking about her?

He turned from the window, willing himself not to think about her anymore. Every time he did, he fell further and further into the spiral of depression. So, when he looked down, he muttered another curse. Bay napped on their bed, her cheek pressed against her hands, a calm expression on her face. Though it was only early evening, she said she had needed a nap since the baby had moved around the night before, keeping her up.

They'd taken to sleeping next to each other on his big bed, not quite touching. The couch wasn't big enough for either of them to lie comfortably, and frankly, it made his wolf would feel better to have her close. The better his wolf felt, the less stress he had himself. She moaned in her sleep, a curl falling on her face and he took a step back. Damn, he wanted to brush it away to feel the softness of her skin, her hair, her everything.

To top off his anger and other emotions, there hadn't been any developments in her case. It was almost as if the person who was searching for her had stopped completely. They'd looked into all avenues of her past but had come up empty. Adam's gut reaction was that it was the Centrals were following her. Either they had scented her new Pack status or they were following her for a much more devious purpose. Either way, it grated on him that they couldn't figure it out and that she still could be in danger once she left.

A part of him had almost wanted to put her up as bait to see who they would find. But as soon as that thought entered his mind, he felt like a shit. He would never endanger a woman like that, let alone a pregnant one.

The Pack could feel the magic pooling around the wards as the Centrals grew stronger, an inky black feeling like a sticky molasses that wouldn't go away. With each step that their rivals took toward the dark, the Redwoods were forced to make decisions. They couldn't cross that line and sell their souls to the devil, if only figuratively. But there had to be a way to find the gray. Because of Reed and his mates, they now held the trinity bond so they knew their wards would hold, at least against wolves. He knew they would not hold against the demon himself. And that thought scared him more than any other.

They needed to find another way to make themselves stronger that didn't include dark magic.

He cursed at their weakness.

He turned away from Bay, determined not to think of it for more than he already had. Meaning not every ten seconds. As he walked out to the hallway, he stopped in between the two closed doors that he knew his guest had entered. His fingers strummed against his thighs on their own accord, and he took a deep breath.

No, he couldn't, not without Anna.

He turned to his right and opened the door. He gulped, letting the wave of emotions wash over him. Since her death, he hadn't gone into this room, or the one across the hall, other than to clean them. He staggered back to the reality.

This had been their music room.

Their small piano stood on the corner, still tuned and dust free. Anna had used to accompany him while he played on the guitar. The old acoustic still stood on its setting, also in tune and ready for him to play. He took a shuddering breath as he glimpsed his old cowboy hat hanging on the peg on the wall. Anna had bought that for him, and he'd worn it every time they played. He used to fashion himself a werewolf cowboy. What an ass.

They used to play beautiful music together, though Anna couldn't sing to save her life. He chuckled at the memory and let the cold pain settle over him like an old friend.

*"Play, you know you need to. It's been too long. It's okay to mourn and grieve, but we can't let your life die along with hers."*

Adam closed his eyes at his wolf's words. The damn thing had been more talkative recently, and he blamed Bay for that. How could his wolf forget their first mate and want to move onto a new one?

*"That's not what I want to do, and you know it. I loved Anna and her wolf with every breath that I had, but Bay is our mate too. We need her. And she needs us."*

He closed his eyes and took a deep breath, his body shaking, coldness seeping into him like a blanket. He sat down on the chair and picked up the guitar. The cool wood felt like a distant memory under his fingers. Flashes of Anna's smile and the sound of her laugh caused bile to rise up in his throat. Could he do this?

He strummed his fingers along the strings, playing a few chords. The music drifted up and enveloped him. Gods, he'd missed this. Though he didn't hear her, he could feel Bay's presence in the doorway. With his back to her, she couldn't see his face, and he was grateful. He didn't know what he would do if he had to look into those eyes and see something that scared him to death.

Would he see pity? Or hope?

His fingers moved on their own accord and played a soft melody, the long years of practice flowing through them like a long-lost friend. He heard Bay sigh over his shoulder as he played. She held secrets from him; he knew it. He didn't quite understand the source of her powers. How could she sense a memory by just a touch? And how was it her wolf had more control over her than others had over their humans? She was hiding something, and he would do everything he could to find out. He could lie and say it was only because he was the Enforcer and he needed to protect the pack, but he dreaded the fact that there might be an underlying reason that had nothing to do with safety but existed because of their bond.

His thoughts drifted from her and her secrets, and he lost himself in the music. He didn't sing, only let the guitar do what it needed to do—play. With each note, he felt like he was losing Anna all over again. She wasn't here to play beside him or hear him play. How was he supposed to get over her?

He heard Bay shuffle behind him, her movements becoming more waddling with every passing day. Out of the corner of his eye, he saw her sit down on the piano bench, her gaze intent on him. He turned and scowled at her for invading his space, but she didn't move, merely lifted her chin. She turned to face the piano, her belly touching the wood, and placed her hands over the keys.

He almost screamed out, telling her not to touch what was not hers, but the words were stuck in his throat. Her fingers played a ghostly movement over the ivory, but she didn't utter a sound.

His finger stopped. He set the guitar down, the cold spreading over him. No, she couldn't play. She couldn't know how. Fate wouldn't be that cruel.

No, it was a bitch.

He slowly, methodically, made sure the guitar was on its stand, and walked away, leaving her there. He left the room, walked the too short steps to the other room across the hall, and laid his head against the door.

"What's in there, Adam?" Bay asked as she stood behind him.

He didn't answer, couldn't answer. Instead, he opened the door and stepped aside. Bay took two steps into the room and gasped. He looked over her shoulder and closed his eyes. He didn't need to look; he knew what was there. He'd seen it for twenty years. The pale pink walls of the nursery had faded over time, but he could still tell the colors. The crib and furniture were outdated but clean and dust free since he cleaned regularly.

He opened his eyes and tried to feel something, anything. No cold, no pain. Nothing. He was looking at what would've been his daughter's room and felt nothing.

Should he feel something?

He turned away from the room and felt Bay's pain through their mating bond. She cried softly, but he could still hear her. He couldn't be here right now.

"I'm going on patrol, and I'm going to take you to Jasper and Willow's," he said, his voice hoarse.

"Adam..."

He didn't wait to hear what she might have said, so he walked away. His past was coming back in full force, but the things he wanted most weren't coming with it.

\*\*\*\*

"Here's a muffin. You need to eat, honey." Willow handed Bay the fresh apple crumble muffin, and she reluctantly took it, not knowing how to say no to the warm woman.

"Thank you," she whispered, surprised she could even talk.

"What's wrong?" the other woman asked.

"Nothing," she lied.

Jasper grunted as he paced on the other side of the room with baby Brie in his arms. Brie babbled and shook her fists at him, a happy smile on her little face.

"Wolves can smell a lie, Bay," he warned.

"It's nothing, really," she stressed.

Again, she looked at Jasper holding his daughter, and a pang shot through her. She'd never have that. Not with Adam. He kept a tomb for his dead mate and child. There wasn't any room in his house or his heart for either of them. She placed her palm on her belly, and the baby rolled. She was truly alone.

Willow placed her hand on top of Bay's, and she turned to face the other woman. "Tell us."

As much she wanted to keep Adam's secrets, it wasn't doing him any good locking himself away. He may not want her, but the stupid part of her wanted him to be happy. So, she told them. Told them about the music room and the fact that she could practically feel in his ghost. When she told them about the nursery, Willow gasped, and tears flowed down her cheeks.

No one spoke for a while. Even baby Brie seemed to know something had changed. Uncontrollably, Bay joined in Willow's sorrow, tears sliding down her cheeks and sobs wracking her body.

Jasper cursed, breaking into the wordless crying. He murmured an apology to Brie and sat down on Willow's other side. Willow took her daughter and nuzzled her to her chest, seeming to need the comfort. Bay still held on to Willow's hand, needing it too.

"I never knew," Jasper rasped. "I should've known."

"I should have known too," Willow agreed.

"How could you have known?" Bay asked. "I don't think anyone knows. Well, maybe Maddox. He's the

Omega; he would have to have felt that pain, day in and day out."

Jasper frowned. "Yes, he would've felt that he needed to help, but Adam can't heal if he doesn't want to. Maddox wouldn't be much use if Adam wouldn't listen. By the sounds of it, he's worse off than we thought."

"I don't know how I can help him." And wasn't that just great? Because fate had given her a mate so deep into his own depression he couldn't even find a way out.

Jasper let out a sigh. "We need to talk about the elephant in the room."

Bay gave a watery laugh. "What are you talking about?"

"You two are mates. You're having his baby."

"No, I'm having my baby. And as soon as we figure out who was following me and put an end to it, I'm leaving."

"Could you really just leave him?"

Bay bit her lip and closed her eyes. "I have to; it's what he wants."

"But is it what he needs?" Jasper asked, his eyes filled with pain. "Adam lost everything a long time ago, and yes, it hurts. It hurts us all still. But it's time for him to move on."

"How can you say that? You don't really know. I don't know. I've no idea what he's feeling, but I know it hurts. I'm not going to sit around and be the reminder of the dead woman. It's not fair to me, and it's not fair to this baby." Inside, she wanted to curl up and die just a little, but she was stronger than that.

"No, I don't know, but Anna wouldn't have wanted him to live this way. He's going to be a father, Bay."

"No, he was sperm donor." She cringed inwardly at the icy tone of her voice. But if she didn't make this clear, it is going to hurt more in the end. And what if the Redwood Pack wouldn't let her keep her baby when she left? That scared her more than anything.

"You can't say that," Willow whispered. She leaned over and pulled Bay closer in a brief hug.

Bay pulled back and shook her head. "I don't want to think like that, Willow. Do you think when I was younger and dreaming about a mate that I thought I'd be in this situation? Adam made his decision, and I can't change that. I have to do what's best for me and my child. And that isn't living in that shrine to a dead woman." Her voice cracked, and she took a deep breath to hold her composure.

"You're going to have to work something out," Jasper warned. "You're Pack now. You're one of us." He leveled his gaze, and a mixture of warmth and fear spread to her. She could almost feel them being her center, the connection to being her home, but it wouldn't work out. It never worked out.

"I wish that were true. I wish I were Pack the way you want me to be, but some things are just not meant to be." And that was something she had experience with.

# CHAPTER 11

Adam hadn't gone home yet. The night had passed, and he still was on patrol. Though he could've gone home at any point during the night and let his other enforcers see their families, he couldn't. He'd left Bay on Jasper's doorstep and walked away. Talk about being a fucking coward.

They'd caught a scent late the night before and were still tracking. He and five of his men had combed the woods around their wards, searching for the potential intruder. The scent was coated with that putrid smell that now went with the Centrals' new persona. He fisted his hands and cursed.

They were using some type of dark magic to shield themselves. Adam could only find the leftover traces of their trail. It was as if something were cloaking them then fading over time, leaving breadcrumbs for him. He couldn't tell how many wolves there were, or what they were doing there. It wasn't a coincidence that their enemy was circling them like vultures waiting to pick off the weak.

He looked over his shoulder at his other men and gave a quick nod. They wouldn't stop until they found the bastards, even if it took all day. They couldn't let the others come near their territory again. Though the wards seemed to keep out the wolves, they knew even with the extra magic, they couldn't keep out the demon. But no matter what, Adam would do his best.

He crouched down low, inhaled that sickly sweet scent again, and prowled toward the east. He followed the trail to a grove of trees and froze. Once in the center of that, he knew he'd caught them. Or, had they caught him?

He looked around and muttered a curse. It was a trap; they'd walked right into it. Fuck, he needed to get out of his head and stop thinking about that fiery redhead. If any of his men got hurt because of him, he didn't know what he'd do.

He heard a growl, the sound creeping over him. He let his claws come out from his fingertips and bared his teeth. Eleven Central wolves crept out from the trees, their eyes a deep black, the power radiating from them unlike anything he'd seen before. These wolves were tainted, linked to the demon. There was nothing he could do; they would have to die.

Eleven against six. Doable. He risked a look at his men and nodded. They each stripped and shifted to wolves, their eyes focused on the enemy. Adam waited for them to be safe, as shifting took at least some concentration. He didn't want them to be vulnerable to attack. The other wolves seemed to be waiting; an aspect Adam didn't know what to think of. When his wolves were changed, he stripped and changed himself. He pulled on his wolf, the magic flowing over him, as his bones broke and his muscles tore and then rearranged themselves.

The others stood where they were, as if they had been waiting for him. He bared his teeth and let his power flow.

*Bring it.*

The other wolves charged, and he lowered his head and charged right back. A small gray wolf attacked his flank, and he turned, sinking his teeth into its pelts. It whimpered, and he shook his head, gouging the bastard. The injured wolf howled and tried to bite back, but Adam released his jaw and bit into the neck, severing the artery. The wolf let out a final gasp and stilled. Adam released him and turned as another wolf jumped on his back. Adam rolled and pinned him to the ground and sank his fangs into its flesh. He used claws to take out another hunk of fur, the blood pouring out of its side. He bit down harder, and the light in the wolf's gaze faded.

His men fought around him, winning against the uneven odds. The largest enemy wolf stood to the side, as if watching a play. Adam growled and ran toward him. How dare the bastard sit back and watch men die and do nothing? The wolf seemed almost to grin, then let out a growl, disappearing into the woods. Adam followed, determined not to let anyone leave alive, at least not without giving some answers.

The other wolf was lazy and left a trail easy to follow. He ran through the brush, twigs and leaves tearing at his fur, but Adam ignored it. He made it through an opening of trees and ended up at the edge of the cliff. Though they were situated in the mountains, Adam rarely came to the cliff side. The other wolf shot off to the side and growled, Adam doing the same. They leapt at each other, teeth, fangs, and growls meeting.

The other wolf was bigger than him, a rare feat. It used its immense weight to pin Adam to the ground. Adam twisted and turned, but not before the other wolf bit into his neck. He writhed with rage, the fiery pain shocking his system. Blood coated his neck and flowed down his side. Black spots floated over his vision, and his body grew heavy. The bastard must've struck an artery. Adam knew he had to move fast and get someone to plug it up, or he might not make it.

Fuck.

He pinned the other wolf to the ground and took a steadying breath as he grew weaker.

The other wolf shifted to human, and Adam did the same. Though they might both be two naked men, they were wolves first and didn't care about modesty.

"Tell me why you're here," Adam growled, surprised his voice was so steady, despite the blood loss.

"We just want the redhead," the other wolf spat.

Adam cursed. He knew it. The Centrals wanted Bay, but why?

"What do you want with her?" He shoved his forearm against the wolf's throat, forcing the other man's eyes to bulge.

"Caym wants her," he rasped.

"Why?" Why would a demon want her? What use was a lone wolf to him? Was it her special powers with no known origin? What about the baby?

"Like I would tell you." The other wolf sneered, twisted, and tore its claws into Adam's side then scurried away.

Adam screamed and lunged for him, but it was too late. The other wolf jumped off the cliff to its certain death.

Adam went to the side of the cliff and looked down. Even with keen eyesight, he couldn't see where the wolf had landed, but he knew there was no way he could have survived the jump.

Why would the wolf kill himself? What was so important about the demon wanting Bay that he'd rather killed himself than face torture and spill secrets?

Adam staggered and pressed a hand to his side. That wound didn't seem too deep, but the one on his neck was only barely starting to heal. He needed to get back home and get some help. His men came out from the trees dressed, with one of them holding a bundle of his clothes.

"Did you find out anything?" he asked, his body healing itself slowly as his strength started to return.

They shook their heads. "Nothing, they wouldn't talk," one wolf said as he handed Adam his clothes.

He got dressed, wincing as skin tried to heal, tugging at his wounds.

"Adam, we need to get you looked at. Let's get you to Hannah," Jason, one of his wolves, said.

He shook his head. "No, just get me home. I can heal on my own." He wasn't in the mood to deal with people.

"Are you sure that's wise?"

"Are you questioning me?" he growled.

Jason lowered his head in submission. "Sorry. Let's just get you to your home. Do you need help?"

Adam ignored the offer and didn't chastise the younger wolf for offering help. He hated showing weakness, but it wasn't their fault his wolves wanted to make sure he was okay.

They made their way to the den, Adam under his own strength, though it was waning. He needed to eat some protein and get some rest, so his body could heal. It would probably be smart to let North or Hannah look at it, but no one had ever accused Adam of being smart. He walked through his front door and scented Bay.

"What are you doing here?" he growled. "You're supposed to be at Jasper's."

Bay ran to him, as best she could being as big as she was, horror etched on her face. "What happened? Who attacked you?"

"Answer me."

She stopped and widened her eyes at his tone. "It's been over a day, Adam. I wanted to give Jasper and Willow break."

Something coiled within him. Fear? "So you took it upon yourself to come here, unprotected, and tempt your fate?"

The wolf in him wanted to hold her close, brush the curls from her face, and tell her everything would be all right. The man in him wanted to run and never look back.

She gave him an odd look and shook her head. "I'm not alone, Adam. Maddox is here to make sure I'm safe."

Unreasonable rage poured through him. He must have been really out of it if he couldn't even sense Maddox right away.

His brother walked up from behind Bay, his face expressionless. "Why aren't you at Hannah's?"

Adam clenched his fists, ignoring the pain in his side and neck. "Because I didn't feel like it."

"What's the point of them? This is the second time you've come back bloody and tried ignoring it," Bay said as she wrung her hands together.

"I'm not in the mood to be questioned like this. Maddox, get the hell out, I can handle this."

Maddox raised a brow and looked at Bay. "Are you going to be okay here with him?"

That had probably been the worst thing his little brother could've said right then. Without thinking, he shoved Maddox against the wall and tried to cut off his breathing.

"You need to watch your step, little brother."

Maddox merely tilted his head, and Adam sensed a wash of power flood over him. His knees buckled, and he fell to the floor. Bay rushed to his side, but he pulled away.

"What the hell was that?" Adam screamed.

Maddox flicked a piece of dirt from his shirt and rolled his shoulders. "That is what I've been holding back from you. Get your emotions in check, or next time I won't be so forgiving. If you, there will be nothing left for anyone. Get over yourself and take care of your mate."

"She's not my mate." He felt Bay flinch, but he ignored the urge to soothe her and take it back.

"Adam, Anna is dead, but Bay isn't. Figure it out." With that, his Omega walked out the door, leaving him and the person he was trying to ignore on the floor, blood pooling around him.

"Let me get you cleaned up. I don't want you to bleed all over your carpet," she said stiffly. She awkwardly stood up and walked toward the bathroom.

He twisted and leaned his head against the wall and closed his eyes. When Maddox had rushed him with that power, his emotions had broken free, suffocating him, pulling him down to a depth he hadn't realized could even exist. Is that what Maddox felt every day? Or was it just a personification of his own emotions? Adam didn't know, but he never wanted to feel that again.

"Can you come sit at the kitchen table? I'm too big to be bending on the floor like that, and I don't want you to ruin your couch." Bay set down the bandages and things to clean his wounds on the table and rested her hands on her belly. His eyes seemed to be on her stomach, something he tried to never do.

Her baby. Their baby?

He shook his head and winced as he tore open his neck wound again.

"Dammit, Adam. Don't do that. You're bleeding more." She rushed to him, and he held up his hand.

"I got it. I can stand. I don't want you to hurt yourself."

She stood back with a look on her face that said she couldn't quite understand why he was being somewhat thoughtful about her condition. He didn't quite know either.

He made his way to the chair and sat down, cursing as his side flared with pain.

"What happened?

"A few of the Centrals' wolves didn't take too kindly to us for keeping them off our territory."

"Are they dead?" she asked, no emotion in her tone as she cleaned his neck. He winced at the sting but held back a curse.

"Yes."

"Good."

His wolf liked this feisty wolf of his.

No, he couldn't think of her as his.

"Did they say anything?" With somewhat shaky hands, she took off his shirt then cleaned his wounds.

"Not much."

She finished bandaging up his side and neck and tilted her head. "What did they say? Or is it too classified or whatever for me?"

Adam barked a laugh. "Classified? You're making the Pack sound like some secret ops military project."

She shrugged and then cleaned up the mess, leaving Adam to sit in pain at the table. "I don't know how these things work. Are you supposed to let everyone else know what you're doing? Or is that all secret to protect the Pack from itself? Just seems really odd."

"I can tell my trusted circle what I need to. So pretty much my family and my enforcers. Others can ask, and I can tell them some things, but you're right. Some information is best kept close to the heart and the situations."

"So you can't tell me. I understand," she said, though her tone betrayed the slight.

Though he didn't want to man up to it, he had to be honest. Even if nothing would come of it, the woman in front of him was his mate. At least by mark, if not by heart.

"It concerns you, so I'm going to tell you."

She dropped the box of bandages in her hand and paled. "Me? They were after me?"

"Yes, though I don't know why. Do you have something you want to tell me?" He still didn't trust her and these special powers of hers.

"I'm not sure why they would be following me or wanting me."

He couldn't taste a lie, but he couldn't quite tell what she was hiding either.

"They were after you, but now they're dead. I don't know why, but the demon wants you. You need to tell me why, Bay. If you don't, you may endanger in my family. And if you do that, no amount of mate marks could protect you." He narrowed his eyes as he said the last part, and she thrust up her chin.

"I'm telling you, I'm nothing special. Maybe they're just after me because they want to get you. After all, they can scent I'm your mate."

That thought hadn't occurred to him. Was it his fault?

"Whatever it is, we'll deal with it. Just remember, I don't know you, and I'll protect what I have to."

"Fine. Oh, and by the way, you're all bandaged up. Thank you for killing those bastards, but the next time you decide to play hero, try to protect yourself too. I'm getting tired of playing Beauty to your Beast."

He gave a soft growl and watched her walk away to their bedroom. Dammit, the longer she stayed, the more complicated it got. She was hiding something; he knew it. He just needed to figure out what.

# CHAPTER 12

"So, how are you liking the Redwoods so far?" Josh asked as he tugged the wiggling toddler toward him.

Adam's brother-in-law, Josh, was babysitting Kade and Mel's son, Finn, for the day and had stopped by the house to pick her up so she could enjoy the fresh air. She relished the chance to get out of that small, enclosed space with the man she wanted to strangle one minute and make out with the next. Josh was also relatively new to the Pack and had only just recently married and mated with Adam's brother Reed and their other mate, Hannah. He'd once been a Navy SEAL and then a security officer before he'd rescued and fallen in love with the both of them. During that time, he'd also been bitten by a demon and turned into a partial one, meaning he was stronger than most humans and carried some of the demon characteristics. Though he wasn't a full demon, he still most likely could live a long life. She thought about how they'd welcome him into the fold, even though the one who'd bit him and made him who he was also their enemy.

Finn stared at her and waved his chubby little hands then smiled, deepening his dimples as he giggled. She waved back, and he walked toward her and put his little hands on her stomach.

"Baby?"

Oh, what was she supposed to say? Did toddlers know where babies come from? Oh, God, she was going to be a horrible mom.

Josh threw his head back and laughed. "Talk about throwing you into the deep one. Finn, yes, that will be a baby soon. Stop making your Aunt Bay uncomfortable." He blew raspberries on Finn's neck as the little boy kicked his feet in the air to try to get away.

She smiled at them on the outside, but on the inside, she froze. Aunt? Well, she had mated into the family. Guess that did make her an aunt. Jesus. Why had she come here? Even though she needed help, she was ruining the lives of everyone in this family.

"So? How do you like it so far?" Josh asked again, and she blinked.

"What? Oh, sorry. I need to stop thinking so much in my head."

"This is not where you normally think?"

"Oh, you're a funny one, are you?"

Josh shook his head but grinned. "Not usually." He scratched his arm and she looked down at the spiral tattoos that covered them. She knew they were the mark of the demon, and not just a decorative piece.

"But to answer your question, I don't really know. Everyone's been so nice and helpful, but I don't really know anyone. I'm afraid to do that. Because, you know, I'm leaving." She needed to say it over and over again until people believe her. They all thought she was going to stay with them. But she couldn't, not with Adam being the way he was.

The red rims around Josh's irises flared a bit before he blinked. "You do realize you're pregnant with the Alpha's grandchild, don't you?"

"Actually, I'm pregnant with my child."

"You know, it did take two?"

Finn stared between the two of them, his face growing cloudier as the conversation took a turn she didn't want to go.

She took a deep breath and traced a finger along Finn's jaw so he would smile. He obliged, and she looked directly into Josh's gaze. "I'm not going to stay here, Josh. I can't. Adam doesn't want me to, and I'm not weak enough, or strong enough, to stay with a man who doesn't want me. I will not raise a child in a situation like that."

Josh nodded, obviously thinking on how to tread lightly. "We'll just have to see, won't we?"

She didn't say anything, as there really wasn't anything to say. She wasn't going to say anything that could change his thinking.

Finn giggled and took off toward the center of the park. Bay kept an eye on him but let him run and roll across the grass by himself. He was only about thirty feet away when the hairs on her arm stood on end, and she froze. The den seemed to stand still, the magic surrounding them turned oily, slick.

Oh, God, no, not now.

"Do you feel that?" Josh asked, his voice low, his eyes red.

She stood, cradling her belly.

"Get Finn, now." She tried to speak calmly, but the fear bubbled up within her, and she wanted to scream.

Josh took off without another word. No one else was around them, so it was up to only him and her. He'd almost made it when something appeared before them. No, not something. Someone.

Caym. The demon.

The man her mother had warned her about. She'd never met him...but she knew him.

He stood like a fallen angel, his dark hair flowing in the wind, his chiseled cheekbones like ice. He grinned, one so evil that it sent chills down her spine.

"Josh! No!" She tried to call out to stop him, but it was too late. There hadn't been enough space for him to stop. He growled and tried to punch the demon, but Caym was stronger. In one quick movement, he lashed out with a knife and slit Josh's throat, blood pooling. Her new friend gurgled, blinked, then slid to the ground, motionless.

She screamed in agony and ran toward him. Though she was pregnant and wanted to protect her baby, she couldn't just stand by and watch a man die, but what would happen to Finn?

She could hear other people running toward them, their shouts and screams as they tried to reach their fallen brother. But she had eyes only for the demon. Finn stood frozen, as if he had no idea what he should do. But he was a baby. How was he supposed to know? Finn blinked as if he knew he was supposed to move, but it was too late. Caym reached down and picked up the little boy. Finn was an Alpha through and through and kicked and screamed and bit to try to get free. She ran as fast as she could to them, but as soon as she made it close, Caym threw the boy across the field. She choked on a sob as the little boy landed with the deafening crunch.

"Ah, just the person I wanted to see," Caym crooned.

She tried to bend down the help Josh, but Caym grabbed her by the neck and shook her. She choked, trying to take in air and protect her belly at the same time.

"At last, we meet."

She could feel the other wolves around them, but Bay couldn't reach them. It was as if Caym had put a special ward around just them. She could hear Hannah's and Reed's broken sobs as they watched Josh bleed out near her feet. She fought for breath and from the corner of her eye she could see Kade and Mel trying to break through the barrier to get to their son. But it was hopeless. Caym came from the fiery depths of hell and was stronger any one of them and all of them put together.

She clawed at him, her wolf rising to the surface as she tried to break away, but he wouldn't let go.

"Don't you see, Bay? I need you."

He released her throat just long enough for her to rasp out a word. "Never."

"Oh, little girl. You say that as if you have a choice. I'm going to gut that baby out of you and see if I can use it and then torture him to use you to get what I want. The wolves around you will die, and it will be your fault."

She struggled against his hold and kicked. He squeezed harder, and black dots danced behind her eyes. She was a wolf, darn it. She was stronger than this. She reached again with that special power she'd wanted to ignore all her life and let it flow through her. She focused it and pushed as hard as she could. Caym screamed and let her go, the wards around them dissolving.

"Don't think that means anything, little girl. I'll come back for you and that little mutant you carry. " He dissolved away, and Bay fell to the ground.

People scrambled around her, screaming, crying, their movements hurried and frantic. She lay on the ground and watched as Hannah leaned over her mate, her hands holding his neck together as Healing power flowed through her. Bay didn't know if it would be enough.

"Josh, please, don't die. You can't die," Hannah sobbed. Reed held the both of them, their bond flaring. Bay couldn't see it, but she knew that the trinity bond would be doing overtime to heal Josh. If he could be healed.

She took a steadying breath, her throat raw and scratchy and looked over her shoulder at the form she didn't want to see. North kneeled at Finn's side, a grim look on his face.

Mel and Kade hovered around, careful not to touch the little boy, afraid they'd break him even more by the merest of touches.

"He's breathing," North said, fear lacing his tone. "But I'm going to need Hannah. I can't heal this. Not without a miracle."

Mel broke down in sobs, her body shaking. Kade held his mate closer and howled a howl that shook every Pack member to the core.

Hannah looked over her shoulder, past Bay, and took a shuddering breath, tears flowing down her cheeks. Blood stained her clothes, her hands, and her face. "Trade with me, North. I'll do what I can. Just heal him however you can; he needs stitches." She sobbed each word but was stronger than any woman she'd ever known. "I can Heal Finn." She stood on shaky legs, and Reed held her. North ran to Reed's side with his medical bag and began working on Josh. The rest of the family stood around each broken family member, watching as their doctor and Healer

134

put every ounce of their strength into saving their patients.

Bay lay between them both, her hands cradling her stomach. No one had spoken to her or had even looked at her. She could feel the bruises swelling on her neck, but she didn't say anything. As soon as they healed their family, they'd ask questions she didn't want to answer. And she'd lose them. If she'd even had them to begin with.

\*\*\*\*

Adam looked as Bay sitting on the floor, the stark mottled bruises forming a ring around her neck. He warred within himself. On one hand, he wanted to make sure she was okay; on the other, the utter betrayal of her actions shocked him to the core. Though he had never trusted her, he'd never once thought she'd been in line with Caym.

His body shook as he held Josh's hand because Reed and Hannah could not. Hannah needed Reed to aid her powers so she could heal his nephew. She had done all she could for her mate and had to leave him in the hands of North and his western medicine. With a deft precision, even in the outdoors, North cleaned and irrigated the wound then stitched it up.

"It's the best I can do right now," North said, a stern promise of retribution on his face. "We need to get him back to my clinic, give him some blood, and figure out what to do. I don't know what he is, Adam. I don't know how to do this."

"I think I know who might," Adam growled.

Over his shoulder, he nodded toward his father. The Alpha nodded back and helped North carry Josh away as Adam released his hand. He stalked toward Bay and tried to rein in his temper, though he knew would be a futile battle.

"Come with me," he ordered Bay. Under any other circumstances, he would've just left her there to rot, but he held out his hand to help her up. The two sides of him warred, and he wanted to scream.

She looked up at him, her green eyes wide and tears streaming down her cheeks. "I...I'm sorry," she stuttered.

"Sorry isn't good enough," he spat. "Do you see what you and your lies have done?" He picked her up and forced her to look at Finn. "Every bone in his body is broken, Bay. Every bone. Only because of his Alpha blood is he still breathing. Hannah and North will heal him because they are powerful." He twisted her toward where his father and North had carried Josh away. "Josh had his fucking throat slit because of you. He may die, and I need to know how to help him. He's a partial demon. What do we do to give him blood? I think you know. Tell me."

Some part of him wanted her not to know, hoping that she would be innocent. But he knew that wasn't the case.

"He can use any blood as long as it's his blood type. At least, that's the case with me."

He looked over his shoulder and nodded at an enforcer, who would run to North's side and tell his brother what he'd heard.

Adam growled and turned her so she faced him. "What do you mean by that?"

She gulped and steadied herself, the bruises purple and blue around her throat. "I'm a half-demon."

He let go of her like she'd burned him. Fuck. A half demon. His enemy. An abomination. Josh had been bitten, not born. His brother-in-law was a human who had a curse. Bay was a part of evil. It was inherent in her blood.

Tears slid down her cheeks, but she held her head high. "A demon came to the Talon Pack and raped my mom. She got pregnant, and the Pack kicked her out. I was born, and she took care of me. I had never met my father...until today. As soon as I saw him, I knew. I can't explain it."

Adam rushed toward her and gripped her again. "You're telling me that fucker Caym is your father?" he roared.

She paled and nodded.

He let her go, and she staggered back. "You're lucky you're pregnant."

"I didn't call him here."

"Why don't I believe you? Did you know who was following you? Or were you lying about that too? Were you here to be his mole? Are you working for Daddy?"

"No! I'm here because I needed to get away from him."

"So you knew it was him."

"Yes. I'm sorry I lied about that, but I didn't know how to tell you. I'm a werewolf-demon hybrid. I don't know anyone else like me. I'm not evil. I promise. I just needed to feel safe." She let out a breath and rested her fingers on her stomach.

Her stomach.

The baby.

He turned to the side and vomited. It would be a hybrid, a mutant. Just like her.

"Adam, there's nothing evil about me. I'm just a bit more powerful than Josh."

"You mean you're more demonic than the man who almost died by your father's hands?"

She closed her eyes then took a breath. "I'm a half-demon, meaning, when I'm not pregnant. I'm stronger than a normal werewolf and have those powers I already told you about. But that's it. I can't control fire, flash, or call other demons."

He glared at her, betrayal settling it.

"And I can feel Caym. I know him because he is of my blood. At least I think that's why I can."

He roared and turned, unable to look at her.

"Adam, I know we're mates—"

"No, you're a whore who I took to bed. We're not mates."

She looked as if he'd struck her, and he cursed.

"Bay, I'm sorry, I didn't mean that." He would never call a woman that.

"No, you did. But you don't understand. I'm alone, Adam. I know this. I know I'm a half-demon and people want me dead because of my blood, but that doesn't mean I'm going to let anyone walk all over me."

"You're a demon."

"Half."

"Semantics. You lied, and now we have to deal with it. I don't know what you are, but any trust you thought you had is gone."

"Trust? You never trusted me. You just used me as a good lay and then tossed me aside. Twice. We're mates, and as much as you want to, you can't run from it. I can help, Adam."

He closed his eyes and took a deep breath. "Go back to the house and stay there. I can't look at you right now. I need to be with my family."

"Adam—"

"Go."

He watched her waddle off, and he cursed. Fuck, he'd have to have North go and look at her once he was done with Finn...or maybe Hannah. Bay was hurt, and the wolf inside him clawed at him to get her healed. He was fucked up.

The mate he didn't want was a half-demon and the daughter of their enemy. Fate really wanted to screw him over. And this time, he didn't know how he'd move on.

# CHAPTER 13

Adam sat on Jasper and Willow's porch, letting the sun hit his face. He hadn't wanted to be at home yet, not with so many emotions running through him. Bay was his mate, there was no turning back, but he didn't know what he wanted with it. With her.

"Adam?" Willow came out to the porch and sat next to him. "What's wrong?"

"Bay's a half demon."

She nodded then gripped his hand and squeezed. "I know. How do you feel about that?"

He shrugged and his wolf snorted.

*"Why don't you just tell her, Adam? Like the fact that you actually like and care for her? Or the fact that would want to be her mate?"*

Adam scowled and ignored his wolf. "I don't know," he finally said.

Willow turned to him so she was sitting sideways on the bench. She frowned and tucked a piece of her light brown hair behind her ear. "I don't know what you want me to say, Adam. It wasn't her fault that she was born from a demon. She didn't choose her father.

140

And if the way he acts now is any symbol of how he did then, her own mother might not have even had a choice."

He nodded. "I have a feeling you're right about that. We don't know much about her mother, other than the fact that the Talons banished her."

"And that they didn't care about Bay."

"So, now the Redwoods aren't going to do the same?" he asked, knowing the answer.

"We can't turn her away, Adam. She's your mate."

He winced as his chest ached.

"Adam, you need to face it. Wallowing and ignoring her isn't helping things. You're making it worse by treating her so badly. We all see it. Don't you."

He turned from Willow, not wanting to see the censure in her eyes.

"Adam."

"What do you want me to say? She's not Anna."

"No, she's not. She's alive."

Adam growled and faced Willow. "What the hell?"

"Don't you growl at me, Adam Jamenson. Anna died twenty years ago and yet you're hurting your mate because you don't want to let go. I can't tell you to do that. I can't tell you anything but Bay is here now. You mated her. You need to deal with it."

"I know that."

"Then what are you going to do?"

He sighed then leaned into her open arms, letting the Pack envelop him, something he rarely, if ever did.

"I like her, Willow."

Willow ran a hand through his hair and sighed. "I know, Adam. You need to try to make it work. You'll only hurt each other if you walk away now without trying."

"I don't know if I can."

"Just try."

"How?"

"Be the man you want to be, not the man you've become. Be the man I watch movies with. Be the man that makes Jasper laugh. Be the man that beat my mate down in the forest when he was acting like an ass."

He smiled, remembering his fight with Jasper.

"I can try."

"Do it, you like her, Adam."

He let out a breath. "I do."

"Then fight for her."

Could he do that? Could he let go of his Anna and be with Bay? He had to try, he wasn't doing anyone any good not to. But how could he?

****

Bay looked at herself in the mirror and hardly recognized the reflection. The bruises around her neck had begun to fade since yesterday. She'd been put under house arrest for the others to decide her fate. Though she didn't blame them for that. They'd almost lost two of their own because the man who claimed to be her father wanted her to join him.

It was like a bad case of *Star Wars*. No, she didn't want to join the dark side. Frankly, she just wanted to find a home. But that wasn't going to happen here. She sat on the edge of the bed and rubbed her hands along her aching back. She was due any week now. She just wanted it to be over with. Maybe once she had the baby, she would be able to leave and be strong enough to protect herself.

She groaned and closed her eyes. It was a stupid plan. It always had been. No matter what, she'd set her fate in stone when she'd come to the Redwood den. She didn't think there was any way that they could defeat the demon, meaning she'd have to hide here forever. There was no leaving Adam, or his family. The same family who she was pretty sure hated her at this moment.

Due to the blood that ran in her veins, she was outcast. She'd known from the moment Caym, the man who claimed to be her father, stepped onto this plane that she was being followed. Though she had never met him, a demon knew a demon. She just didn't want to claim him in return. She could feel the slight pulse from his existence, but she'd known, due to the fact that she wasn't a pure demon, he couldn't feel her quite as well. Most demons would be able to feel another of their kind and locate them in a heartbeat. Because of her diluted heritage, neither of them could find each other with any ease, she knew he was near, not where. They could only sense that the other was alive. Whenever she thought of Caym and their connection, she could feel like a cloying pressure on her heart that threatened to break her ribs and suffocate her. What would she feel if she was a real demon? She shuddered to think.

She'd come to the Redwoods as a last-ditch effort, and now she was stuck. It was because of her that Josh had been severely injured. Josh was currently in recovery at North's clinic but would eventually be okay. Caym had sliced Josh's neck open deeply. The cut had gone through tendons, muscle, and his trachea, leaving Josh permanently scarred. Only the demon blood running through his veins due to the bites from Caym had allowed him to survive at all. If he had been a werewolf, witch, or human, he'd have died. Not to mention the fact that his mate Hannah had used her power to Heal him, and North been right there to administer everything he could. As it was, he'd have a scar running along the length of his neck, and his voice would be more gravelly. But he was lucky to be alive.

Finn, on the other hand, was in worse shape. Because he was so small, the impact had broken every bone in his body. It was only because he was the son of the future Alpha that he hadn't died instantly. He was also too young to shift and heal. Werewolves did not shift for the first time until they were two or three. Finn still had at least a year to go. Hannah had used every ounce of her strength to Heal him. His bones were fixed, but he still hadn't woken up. That was a lot of pain for a little boy to go through. Kade and Mel were beside themselves, and she knew they blamed her. She blamed herself.

After Adam had exploded after finding out the truth behind why she was there and what she was, they came back to the house. He hadn't said a word to her other than to tell her what had happened to Josh and Finn. She figured the only reason he had even said that was to make sure she knew the consequences of her lies. If she had just gone to Caym in the beginning and sacrificed herself, none of this would've happened.

She still had time to have her baby, leave it with the Jamensons, and make sure she would never be used again. But she couldn't quite do that because whatever blood ran through her veins would also run through her child's.

Bay didn't know what she had to do, but whatever it was, she did need to talk to Adam. They couldn't go on living like this. The mate bond was so strong between the two of them it seemed to almost override the fact that they were supposed to hate each other. Though he never looked at her with longing, other than for a quick lay, just the fact that she was still alive and living with him told her that the main bond meant more to him than he would admit.

She walked into the living room and watched as Adam sat on the couch and looked at his computer. She knew he was looking at the different satellite images of their den, making sure it was safe. Though they were werewolves, they liked their technology like the rest of the world.

"Adam?" She was surprised at how steady her voice was.

He looked up at her and gave a small smile. Her heart raced at that small gesture, but she didn't let it show that she liked it.

"What is it?"

"I just wanted to know if there is anything I can do." She walked over and sat on the couch next to him, her ankles too swollen to stand long.

Adam closed his computer and sat so he was facing her on the couch. "Not really. Our defenses are strong against werewolves and witches. But there's no way we can control it against the demon. Unless you have any ideas."

She searched his face for any disdain or horror but didn't see any. "I don't know. All I know is I can sense that he exists. I don't know where he is really. Or how to stop him."

"I figured. You would've told us if you could."

She looked at him sharply, her heartbeat racing. "Does that mean you trust me?"

He took a deep breath before answering. "I think so. At least with that. There's so much you could have done if you had been working for him. Plus, my wolf is telling me that you care more about your child than your own life, like any wolf mother. You can't help who your father was, but that doesn't mean I like the fact that you lied to me."

She let out a breath, and the tension eased out of her shoulders. Never had such words made her feel so...wanted...happy. He trusted her, at least partially. "If there's any way I can help, I will."

"I know; it's your Pack."

"What? You mean I can stay?"

He looked torn, like he was trying to relive the past and still stay in the future. "I've been an ass, I know this. You didn't ask for any of this, yet here you are. You're Pack, no matter what happens between the two of us. I'm trying to get through this, Bay. I'm just not handling it well."

She'd watched the way he handled everything in his life, from his family, to his Pack, and had fallen just a little bit in love with him. That scared her more than the demon. What would it be like to have a man love her the same way that he had loved Anna? She was too scared to hope it would be the same with her and Adam. In fact, she didn't even have an inkling of hope that he would love her back.

"I don't think there is a way to handle this well, Adam. I'll do what I can to not mess anything up." *And to not fall in love with you anymore than I am. Because that would be stupid.*

"Finn and Josh will be okay. It was the demon that did that to them. Not you. I tell myself that."

She bit her lip and shook her head. "No, it's my fault. He was looking for me."

"And he would've killed whoever he could to get what he wanted. But that doesn't mean it's your fault. He's eventually going to come back. We have to find a way to fight him."

146

He brushed a curl behind her ear, and she froze. The action was so sudden and uncharacteristic of him that she didn't know what to think. The heat from his hand warmed her face, and she wanted to lean into it. But she didn't. He looked down and seemed to realize what he had done and pulled back sharply. He mumbled an apology, and another part of her died.

No matter how much she wanted their mate bond to work, he couldn't overcome that. She was competing with the ghost and losing. She knew because of the demon blood she wouldn't be good enough for any wolf, but she hadn't thought she'd feel lower than dirt.

He cleared his throat and stood up abruptly. "I'm going to drop you off at my mom and dad's. They want to get to know you, and frankly, I think my mom needs someone to talk to about that scenario. She was still a little shaken over what happened to her grandson."

"I think I'm still a little shaken too."

"We all are. But I need to go do another run, to see what I can do to help. Plus, with Reed and Hannah out of commission because they're staying at Josh's side, someone needs to go do some research."

"Research?"

"The elders have always written down everything in our history, but it's not yet in the digital age. So we're all taking turns looking through the old stacks and trying to figure out anything we can about demons."

"I can help with that. I can't really do any physical labor right now, but I feel like I'm going to explode. I can do reading. That is, if you trust me enough for that."

He gave her a long look, and she waited for the blow. "I think they'd like that. My mom has a few volumes at the house that she hasn't had a chance to look at yet. I'm sure the two of you could look over them while you're trying to keep her mind off of Finn."

She smiled at him and tried to stand. When she wobbled back and almost fell into the couch, he caught her and pulled her against him. For a moment, she leaned against his heat and relished the fact that the father of her child cared. But then she got a cold dose of reality when she remembered exactly what terms they were on and pulled back. "Thank you. I seem to be having balance issues."

"No problem, it's a pregnancy thing I hear." He still wouldn't look down at her stomach, but least he was saying the pregnancy word. That had to be better than nothing.

"Okay, then. Let's head out." With that, he walked her out of the house and into the car. The drive was short because the Jamensons all lived in the corner of the den relatively close to one another, but far enough away that they had their privacy. After all, werewolves could hear sounds, smell things, and see things stronger. Meaning they needed a little bit more space if they want their privacy.

Pat walked out of the house as soon as they pulled into the driveway. She was smaller, a little more round than most wolf females, and usually looked as fierce as any werewolf mama. She gave them a weak smile and held the door open as they walked through. Once inside, she gave the each warm hugs, and Bay settled into hers. It was times like these she missed her mom most of all. Though her mom had never been very strong, due to the fact that she had felt broken inside, she had still been stronger than most, based on the fact that she had survived as long as she had.

"I'm glad you're okay, Bay," Pat said as soon as they walked into the living room.

Bay gave a small smile and nodded. "I'm so sorry, Pat."

Pat gave Bay another hug, letting this one linger. "It's not your fault."

She didn't quite believe that, but she let it pass.

"Okay, Mom, I'm going to leave now, but I'll be back soon as I can. Bay said she could help you with the texts if you wanted to keep your mind off things." He leaned down and brushed a kiss on his mom's forehead then did the same to hers. She blinked but didn't say anything. The spot tingled where his lips had touched.

As he walked out the door without another word, she watched him and tried not to let the tug on their mate bond mean anything. Every touch and familiar feeling of their bond reminded her that she wanted him and he didn't want her. His off-and-on-again thing wasn't working for her. Somewhere deep inside she'd always held the belief that, because of their mating, he could maybe love her, but he couldn't. He still loved Anna, and Bay didn't think anything would change that.

"Bay? Is everything okay? You look like you're lost in your thoughts." Pat had opened an ancient-looking text, its paper cream and worn.

She shook her head and tried to temper the energy that wouldn't go away. "I'm fine, just pregnant."

Pat looked at her stomach and gave a watery smile. "I'm really happy you're here. Really."

Bay gave her a smile, telling her she didn't quite believe her.

Pat hiccupped up the chuckle. "I guess I can't fool you, huh? I'm so sorry, Bay. We are blessed that you are going to give us another grandchild, never mistake our cautiousness with hatred. We just weren't expecting you."

Bay gave a nod but kept quiet, knowing the other woman needed to speak her mind. After all, this was the Alpha female of the Pack.

Pat gripped her hands, the strength radiating from the other woman. "Don't mistake me. I want you to be my daughter-in-law. You are Adam's mate, no matter what he says. I know you have a long way to go in finding out who you are and what you are to each other, but no matter what, we're here for you. I want you to be our daughter-in-law. I do."

Pat took a deep breath, and fear clenched Bay's stomach at what the other woman was about to say.

"Anna was such a part of our lives. She was the first marriage in our family. And she was going to give us our first grandchild. When we lost her, it was as if the Pack lost the thing that made us whole and we became blurred. It'd taken a long time, but we were finally moving on. My sons were getting married, and I was getting grandchildren. And Adam broke again. And I didn't know why."

Bay refused to cry or show any emotion. She had known she wasn't worthy. She had known it would hurt this much.

"We want you with our family, Bay. Adam does too. He just needs to let go of his past."

"You know he can't do that. Anna is with us every moment of every day."

The other woman nodded. "I know. And that may be my fault. I let him stew and mourn for so many years. I don't think he knows how to pull himself out of that."

"He's a grown man. It was not your fault then, and it's not your fault now. He lost his mate. Throwing in another mate on top of that isn't going to help matters. I know he doesn't want me. You don't have to try to make me feel better."

Pat shook her head then dabbed her eyes with a tissue. "You're pack. You need to remember that. We're not just going to let you go. You're holding one of our members within you. Remember that."

"Is that a warning?"

Pat leveled her gaze at her, and Bay lowered her own. "I know you are the daughter of Caym, and that his blood runs through your and Adam's child. But I also know that you came for protection, not to hurt us. I am, at least, that much a judge of character."

Relief spread through her as Pat confirmed Adam's thoughts.

"You didn't hurt Finn and Josh. The demon did. You did your best; we all have. But it isn't good enough. We need to figure out a way to protect our family."

Pat continued to speak and then moved on to discuss the books, but Bay wasn't listening. She was an idiot for endangering the family. What the hell could she have been thinking? There was nothing she could do for them, and by just staying here, she was offering a beacon for her father. The Redwoods were in danger no matter what, but maybe if she weren't here, Caym would focus his attention elsewhere.

Abruptly, she stood and schooled her emotions. "I need to use the bathroom; I'll be right back."

Pat nodded absentmindedly, taking notes from the books she read to try to find a way to protect her family. Bay would do one better and protect them, even from her. Quickly, and silently, she crept out the house and ran. She didn't have time to get her stuff or her car, but she could run as fast as she could, even pregnant, and make it to the wards. The others would be able to find her, but maybe if she ran fast enough, they wouldn't care enough to follow.

The trees tugged at her clothes, and branches scratched at her, but she ignored everything, only cradling her stomach to protect her child, the only thing that mattered. She'd find a way to protect him or her, no matter what.

Her heart hurt at what she'd have to do. She didn't have a mate who loved her, only one who offered to protect her, and in this stage, she wasn't strong enough to protect herself. She'd do what she could to keep the demon's eyes off the Pack, have her child, make sure it was safe, and say goodbye.

She bit her lip and jumped over a rock awkwardly. She felt the warm pulse of magic as she slipped through the wards, and she was free. She ran faster, knowing she would only make it so far in her state. There had been only two choices when she had felt the demon coming for her—find Adam and be safe within the Pack walls or sacrifice herself for her child.

Adam's disdain for her had chosen her course.

She tripped over some roots and braced her hands on a tree to break her fall. The bark gouged at her hands, and she cursed. She looked around her and sighed with relief when she spotted a cave in the deep rock face. She'd be able to rest for a few moments, get her bearings, and find a way to get farther away. She'd been stupid to run when she did; she should've made a plan. But sitting in Pat's house and hearing all about Anna had caused her to act without thinking. Crap, she had once been a strong independent woman, and now look at her.

Her wolf snorted inwardly, and she rolled her eyes. Apparently, her wolf didn't even want to speak to her. No wonder. Bay had made stupid decisions in the past, but this one had to take the cake.

She slipped inside the crevice, and her breath caught. It had to be the most beautiful cave she'd ever seen her life. The cave opening at the other end led to beautiful mountain range with lush greens. Inside was a pool of what had to be ice-cold water that glittered over crystals and shiny rocks. Stalactites, or maybe those were stalagmites, came down from the cave ceiling and made beautiful shadows. The whole scene made this an oasis.

This couldn't have been a secret from the Redwoods. It was too close and too beautiful. She couldn't stay here long. She's stay only long enough to find her bearings and her breath.

"What the hell do you think you're doing?"

Bay turned quickly and slipped on a rock. She waved her arms around and tried to catch herself, but it was no use. She was falling. Adam's arms wrapped around her waist and caught her. He clutched to his chest and held her tightly.

"Why did you leave like that? You could have been killed. What the hell were you thinking?" he growled as he rubbed his arms down her back and sides as if checking for injuries.

She closed her eyes and inhaled his masculine scent, letting herself sink into his hold for just a moment. Dammit, he wasn't supposed to find her so quickly.

"I can hurt your family, Adam. I needed to leave." She didn't open her eyes nor did she step away from him. Call her weak, but she wanted his touch for just a moment.

"You're an idiot, you know that? Caym will come after my family no matter what. You leaving doesn't change that. All it does is make you another target."

"That was the point." She pulled away and hid her hands so he wouldn't see the shaking. "If I would have stayed there, it would have made it worse."

He growled, and the sound sent shivers down her spine. "No, don't you see? No matter what, you're in danger. But you are Pack, meaning we work as a team and find out how to protect and help ourselves. A Pack is better as a whole, not broken off into parts. You can't just leave and expect everything to be okay. You can't run from your problems."

"Seriously? You have the nerve to say that me? You been running the entire time I've been here. I'm trying to protect you and your family. Don't you understand that?"

"So you're just going to go off and hide and hope that you can protect the child you're carrying?" He shook his head and spat, "What was your plan?"

She lowered her head, ashamed.

"Really? You didn't have a plan. Just run and hope for the best. What were you going to do if I hadn't found you, and you would've had the baby, huh?" He walked a few feet away, the tension in his shoulders evident.

"Found a way to get him or her back to you or your family," she whispered.

A dark look passed over his face, and he stomped toward her. She froze but met his gaze head-on. She had to be strong, had to.

He stopped right in front of her, the warmth of his body seeping through her pores and heating her chilled bones.

"I'm not going to let you sacrifice yourself for an ill-conceived plan or idea."

He tipped up her chin with his finger, and her breath caught. Damn, she hated this mating bond. She did care about him.

"We need to work out who we are. What we are. We can't keep going on like this... I can't keep going on like this." He took a deep breath, and she bit her tongue from saying anything. What was he talking about? "You're making me feel things that I shouldn't want to, Bay."

"What?" she whispered.

"Fate has decided we're supposed to be together, but we haven't. I don't have anything left to love, don't you understand that? I've done that, and I have nothing left to give. But when you stand there and look at me, all I want to do is hold you and make sure you're okay. I don't want to be that man. I want to have everything like it was, but it's not ever going to be like that."

Her heart raced yet froze at the same time. What was he saying?

"Much as I want it to happen, you're not going away."

"Thanks," she said wryly.

He let out a breath and rubbed his hand over his face. "We're it, Bay. We have a bond, and like it or not, I have to accept that. You have been amazing, and I've been an ass. A bastard. Do you think I want to treat you the way I do? But every time I see you, all I think about is the fact that Anna's not here and I don't want to do this."

He punched the cliff wall, winced, watching the blood rush over his hand.

"You're going to break something," she admonished.

"I don't like the wolf I've become. I don't. I don't know what the future holds for us, but I can't run away from it. You ran away and could have died, mostly because you were stupid and didn't have a plan, but because you didn't feel safe with me. What kind of Enforcer am I if I can make you feel that way and do that?"

"I don't want to think about us as just a member of the Pack and the Enforcer. We're mates. Reckon we have to deal with that."

"I know; I'm trying."

"Not good enough." She knew she was laying it all out on the line, but if she didn't say everything, she wouldn't be able to live with herself.

He brushed his non-bloody hand against her cheek, and she leaned into it. "I don't know what we're going to do. You can't run away again. I already lost a pregnant mate because I wasn't there. I can't lose you too."

Oddly touched by those words, she let that small kernel of hope settle into her heart.

"Come back with me, please."

"I can't be your sense of duty. An obligation."

He looked at her for a long time, as if searching for the right words to say. But she wouldn't give him any help. He had to come up with this on his own.

"Okay. We'll try it."

"And the baby?" She hadn't failed to notice that he had refused to look at her stomach and hadn't acknowledged the fact that they were having a child together. She couldn't raise a child in that environment.

He gulped and closed his eyes. "One thing at a time."

"Not good enough. This baby comes before me, always."

"Give me time, please." He lowered his lips to hers, and she let him kiss her. She closed her eyes and fell into the kiss, his lips soft, demanding, but not rough. When he pulled back, she was out of breath, and she wanted to kick herself for letting him get away with that.

"I'll go back with you, but only for the baby. I'm sorry I left without thinking."

"It was a stupid thing to do."

"Stop calling me stupid."

He grinned at her, and for a second, she caught a glimpse of the man that he had been before everything had been taken away and gone to hell.

"Sorry, Bay. But you got admit it wasn't the smartest thing you could have done."

"Well, I didn't really have any choice. But I won't do it again; at least not without a set of wheels."

He coughed a laugh and shook his head. "At least if you plan to get somewhere."

Where, she had no idea. At least this was a step in the right direction, right?

# CHAPTER 14

A stick snapped under Adam's foot, and he cursed. He had to start paying more attention. He'd left her back at the house with Maddox watching her. For some reason, it grated on him that his little brother kept being the one to watch over her. Though, the way the man kept hiding from his twin and Ellie, Adam wasn't so surprised that Maddux kept volunteering for the job.

At least he hoped that was the reason.

For most of his life, Adam had always put his job first, leaving his family second. He had to do that because his job was to protect his family. Anna had understood and had been amazing at staying at home and making sure everything was right there. She'd had her own hobbies, a job, and friends, but she'd separated her life from his work life, as he wanted it. That helped him focus solely on his job during his work hours.

It wasn't the case with Bay. She occupied his thoughts day in and day out. Plus, he couldn't keep thinking of Anna like that; it was getting tedious. And it wasn't fair to Bay. The more he thought about Anna, the more depressed he got that she wasn't there and the fact that he kept thinking about her in the first place.

He checked the wards one more time, nodded to his second-in-command, and went back home. He couldn't stay out any longer. Though he and Bay had talked about what they would do in the future in general terms, they still had to iron out the details.

Like whether they were going to act like a real couple for the rest of their lives.

Could he love her?

His body shook at the thought. His wolf howled and stretched at the surface to say yes. But he couldn't. Not now.

He walked through the front door and inhaled Bay's berry and ice scent. He'd grown accustomed to it. He wanted it to sink into his pores and never wash off. And that made him feel guilty. This never-ending cycle was going to turn him into an old man.

Bay waddled out toward him, and he gave her a hesitant smile, which she returned. He laughed inwardly at the fact that she waddled now, and yet when she needed to run for her life, nothing had seemed to slow her down. He'd followed her trail from his mother's house the moment he'd felt something wrong in the bond. He'd grown shaky, his wolf ready to attack at any moment until they could be sure their Bay was safe. He hadn't even waited for his mother to apologize for saying something she shouldn't have. He'd just known Bay was in trouble and she needed him. And that fact had scared him. It made him think that maybe this could work out.

"You're home early," she stated, and looked a little bit uncomfortable.

"Why are you standing?" It came out sharper than he'd intended, and Bay frowned.

Fuck, this was going to be harder than he'd thought. No wait, this was going to be exactly as hard as he'd thought.

"Because I wanted to greet you at the door." She lowered her head and looked really small. "I guess it was a little foolish. I'm not really good at this whole mate thing."

He walked up to her and brushed a red curl behind her ear. "I'm not really good at it either, but I don't want you to be in pain or uncomfortable. Okay?"

She looked up at him and blinked those big green eyes. "Okay."

"I'm going to head out if you two are settled then," Maddox said as he strolled past them, a knowing look on his face.

"Thank you, Maddox, for babysitting."

A weird look passed over his face at the mention of the word babysitting, but Adam shrugged it off. He just wanted his little brother outside of the house so he could get on with this mating business. Maddox walked out without another word, and Adam turned toward Bay again.

"So what do you want to do tonight?"

Her eyes darkened, and he held back a groan. Hell yeah, but he didn't think she'd be up to it.

"How about we play some music?"

He swallowed hard and nodded. This was one step closer toward getting over Anna. He could do this.

She tugged on his hand and led them to the music room. On his way, he looked over her shoulder at the closed door to the nursery. The night he'd brought Bay back, he'd gutted it, leaving it empty and ready for something new. He didn't want to think about the fact that it might be, no, *would* be, another nursery. But at least it wasn't a stark reminder.

Bay sat down at the piano and played a soft melody. It seemed to ease the tension out of her shoulders, his as well. He sat down on the bench across the room and picked up his guitar. Slowly he strummed the strings and joined her. She hummed a soft harmony, and he did the same. When her stomach bumped the edge of the piano and she missed a note, she threw her head back and laughed, and he watched the long lines of her neck.

He continued to play absentmindedly but let his gaze lower to the swell of her belly. There were having a baby, a real living being that he had so far refused to acknowledge. With everything going on around him, he'd done his best to ignore the fact that, yet again, things were going to change.

Anna would have wanted him to move on and treat Bay right.

He *knew* that, and yet he couldn't.

They continued to play, their music blending. As much as he tried to deny it, Bay had inserted herself into his life, and he was growing to like it.

But could he love her?

\*\*\*\*

*Twenty years before*

Anna smiled up at him, her small body, with her rapidly growing stomach, looking like it could teeter over at any moment. Adam leaned down and kissed her softly, relishing how she sank into him. God, he loved this woman.

"You'll be safe, right?" she asked as she rubbed the large swell of her stomach.

"Of course, we'll be fine. I just need to take out the adolescent pups for their first full moon without their parents. I'd rather stay home with you, but they need this too."

She beamed, giving him a huge smile. "I just like to be selfish with you. I love you."

"I love you too." With that, he walked out the door and made his way to the open meadow where he would watch the adolescents change to make sure they were letting the wolf come without forcing it, and then they would hunt.

"Are you ready for this?" Maddox asked as he jogged to Adam's side.

Adam let out a breath and rubbed a hand over his face. "Not really. Anna has been up all night for the past week because she just can't get comfortable."

Maddox patted him on the back and laughed. "She'll be okay soon. She's really excited about the baby. I think that's why."

"You can feel all her excitement, can you?"

"Yep. I actually kind of like it. Usually I can't stand it when one of our Pack mates is pregnant. All that joy and stress just gets a little bit under my skin, you know? But since it's my sister-in-law, I think I like it."

"I don't know how it is you can live all those emotions running through you."

Maddox shrugged but didn't say anything.

"Okay, let's get this over with."

"Don't let the adolescents hear you say that. They are freaking out over the fact that they get to go on a full-moon hunt. You don't want them to know you don't want be here."

"True."

They made their way to the cluster of adolescents, and he growled at them. They each lowered their head in submission, and Adam was inwardly pleased. Most of the wolves here would be submissive, but a few would have alpha tendencies. However, no matter what their attitude and characterizations, they needed to learn the hierarchy. Without that, they wouldn't be able to function as a Pack in dangerous situations.

He watched them all change, noting to himself who he would have to talk to later. Then he and Maddox changed as well, and they were off. He watched the younger wolves use their senses and try to figure out where the deer would be. They didn't normally hunt for wild game, as they ate in human form and enjoyed it that way. But, it was good for the adolescents to learn how to hunt as a pack. Later they would learn how to hunt other wolves by acting and playing.

He'd just jumped over a large fallen tree when pain hit his heart so sharply he felt as if someone had stabbed him. He grunted and rolled to the ground, breathing heavily. Bile rose in his throat, and his body started convulsing, shaking. He tried to stand, but his heart felt like someone had crushed it.

Maddox howled behind him, screeching an unearthly tone that caused Adam to look sharply at him. He froze. Something was very, very wrong.

He barked a strangled sound, and the younger wolves ran to him. They nipped and looked at him, as if trying to soothe him but nothing would help.

Maddox howled again, his wolf body writhing on the ground until he passed out. Adam groaned and shifted back to human, ignoring the intense pain radiating from the quick shift. He staggered to his feet, naked and sweaty. The younger wolves looked at him, some with frightened eyes, others determined. They went over to Maddox's body and nudged at him, but his brother wouldn't move.

He picked him up and groaned. "Get back to your homes. Get me the Alpha," he ordered in rough tones, and the younger wolves darted off. He carried Maddox to the Grove and dropped to his knees. Pain radiated through him sharply again as he tried to breathe.

"Anna," Maddox whispered, and rose to shaky legs to get dressed.

Adam threw on his jeans and ran to his house. His brothers were all at the house, their tension radiating toward him. Jasper stood in the doorway, his long black hair in a mess around his face as rage poured through him.

"The bastards took her," Jasper growled. Reed and Kade growled with him, their bodies taut with energy.

Adam threw back his head and howled, agony whipping through him. "Who?" He growled.

"The Centrals," Kade said as he came up to Jasper's side. "The smell is all over your house."

"We'll get her," Reed promised, a dangerous look in his eyes.

Maddox stumbled toward them and dropped to his knees. "Get her quick. She's scared." Maddox stared up at him with watery eyes than howled before passing out again.

North ran to his twin's side and checked him over. "Fuck, he's in a coma, I think. I won't know more unless I check him out at the clinic. You need to get to Anna fast." Desperation filled his gaze, and Adam shook.

No, not like this.

Adam could feel only their bond, and the sharp hits it was taking. Each time something happened to Anna, he could feel her tug on the bond as if screaming his name. His heart ached, his body pulsed as his wolf clawed beneath the surface, begging to get near their mate. With each strike or burn Anna took, Adam could feel it. They weren't a newly mated couple; their bond was old, settled, more connected. They could feel each other better than most mated pairs. But Maddox could feel every emotion and most of the pain his mate was feeling. Since Maddox could only feel a small fraction of the physical pain, it meant Anna was feeling more. Too much more.

They jumped into Jasper's truck and drove toward the Centrals' den. It'd been years since they'd fought with this Pack. Why was something going on now? The pain intensified in his heart and his mate bond shook, the tendrils between them straining.

Then nothing.

No snap, no spark, no twinge.

Nothing.

His breath caught in his throat, and his body shook. He threw his head back and howled in the cab of the truck, the metal encasing them vibrating with his pain.

"Anna...I can't feel her," he whispered, his voice hoarse.

His brothers didn't say anything; they knew.

If there was no mate bond, there was no mate.

They'd driven maybe another two hundred feet when Jasper stopped abruptly and cursed. Adam was afraid to look up, but he had to. In the middle of the road lay a lump—a naked woman. The moonlight bounced off the light-colored flesh. And Adam staggered out of the car.

Anna.

Like a blind man, he made it to her side, tears running down his face. He fell to his knees, the gravel digging in and cutting him through his jeans. But he didn't feel it. Couldn't feel it. She lay on her side, cradling her stomach. She was naked, bruised, and bloody. The bruises covered her side, her face, and her legs. He noticed the bruising around her inner thighs, and he turned to the side and threw up.

His brothers came up beside him, quiet and cautious.

He brushed a lock of hair from her forehead and kissed a bruise. He cradled her to his body and howled. She was gone. Their baby was gone. His future. The Centrals would pay with their blood.

He would never forgive them. Never forget.

# CHAPTER 15

*resent day*
Adam cracked open his eyes as the sunlight shone through the blinds, and he exhaled a breath. He hadn't had a dream like that in a while, thankfully. He didn't like to relive the most painful moment in his life.

Bay moved in his arms, her naked bottom rubbing against his erection. He held back a groan and shifted so he wouldn't wake her. She snuggled closer, and he let her. Her very presence seemed to heal a part of him he didn't know could be healed. It was as if she'd filled in that place in his heart that he'd lost yet wanted nothing to do with. She wouldn't and couldn't replace Anna, but she was a healing presence all on her own.

But was that fair to her? Didn't she deserve more than just being someone who tried to heal him? He was getting used to her being in his life, and he enjoyed it, though reluctantly. Could he love her?

Bay turned so she was facing him, and he smiled. He had been doing that a lot recently, smiling. It was weird. When she'd first shown up, he hadn't wanted anything to do with her, didn't even want to *want* anything to do with her. And yet slowly, over time, he'd begun to like having her in his arms, even though he still used the excuse of the mating urge to get her into bed. But that was all it was, an excuse. He really did like her next to him. Scary.

"Good morning," she said, her voice a husky whisper.

"Good morning. I'm going to take you on a date today." His eyes widened as he heard what he'd just said. He hadn't meant to say that.

She stiffened and gulped. "Why?"

"Because we're mates," he said simply.

"No, that's not a good excuse. Just yesterday, you wanted nothing to do with me. You can't just change your mind like that."

"Yes, I can. And I did."

"No, that's not fair to either of us."

"Maybe I've accepted the inevitable and made a new decision."

She shook her head and tried to pull away from him, but he held her closer, his hands gripping her ass so she was flush against him. "I have no idea what you're feeling, Adam. What happened to make you change your mind? What did you do?"

"You left."

"I left and suddenly you felt that you couldn't live without me? No, that doesn't make any sense."

"I don't know, Bay. I just want you by my side."

"For now."

"I don't know."

She let out a sigh. "I can't just play house with you."

"That's what we're doing now, isn't it?"

She groaned and rested her head on his bicep. "I told you it wasn't going to leave again. You don't have to say you love me to keep me."

"I like you here."

"You like me for sex."

"True, but I want to figure out how to do this, okay? I don't know what I'm doing or what we're doing. But I don't want to be that person anymore that sits around and mopes and has children flee from them. I want to move on, Bay. Please."

He hadn't realized that had been the reason. But it was true. He needed to move on and grow up. Two decades of mourning might not be enough, but that had to be. He had a woman he was mated to and he needed to show her that he was worth it. He might not love her yet, but he didn't want her to hate him.

His wolf rumbled its content. A first in too many years.

She blinked up at him, and he kissed her nose. "Please," he repeated.

"I don't want you to go." Her voice broke at the end, and she blinked away her tears.

That had been the most emotion she'd ever put into anything he'd heard from her. He couldn't hurt her, couldn't.

"I won't go, Bay. I'll stay."

"But you don't love me."

"I can't, Bay. I can't. I want to, Bay. I do. But I can't love you. I don't have it in me."

"I don't love you either," she said quickly, and he wasn't sure if he believed her. But it wouldn't be fair to push her for the truth.

"Okay. But we can like each other."

"That will have to do."

He leaned down and kissed her, sealing their agreement. She moaned, and he licked the seam of

169

her lips, asking for an invitation. She opened them, and his tongue delved in, tangling with hers, the sweet berry taste dancing on his taste buds. He groaned when she arched against him, awkwardly with the swell of her stomach. But he didn't care and ran his hands up and down her back, cupping her ass, thrusting his erection between her thighs. They couldn't get closer in this position so he turned her so she faced away from him.

He played with her nipples, and she moaned. He grinned and lifted her legs, and he slid right inside her. They both let out a whimper as her hot core encased his cock. He thrust slowly and rhythmically while playing with her nipples with one hand and rubbing small circles over her clit with the other. He licked and kissed her neck, slowly filling her over and over again until he felt her tense and shatter in his arms, her pussy clenching around his cock. His fangs lengthened, and he bit into her neck, marking her again, as his seed spilled within her.

They both lay silently, their chests heaving with the exertion.

"You marked me again."

"It seemed like a good idea at the time." In all honesty, he hadn't meant to do that. But he had promised her he wouldn't go, and that had been the best way to seal it.

A bump pressed against his palm, and he tensed. Without thinking, he had rested his hand on her stomach, and the baby had kicked. It was this first time he'd let himself do that. The first time feeling her, *their* child.

Bay froze, and he felt the kick again. He turned her so she was on her back, and he looked down into her eyes.

"We'll find a way to make this work." It might have been an empty promise, but at that moment, he wanted nothing better than to stay in bed with her and never get out.

They kissed a few more times and took a shower together. He washed her, paying extra special attention to the parts of her he liked best.

They had just sat down to eat breakfast when his phone rang. He walked toward it and he heard a scream from the outside. He went on alert and answered the phone quickly.

"We're under attack. The Centrals have broken our wards, Adam," Kade yelled through the phone. "Get Bay safe and come here. We need you." With that, his Heir and brother hung up, and Adam shook.

"I heard. What you do you want me to do?" Bay stood straight, fear in her eyes, but not her stance.

"The wards are gone like you heard." She was a wolf so he knew she could have heard all of Kade's side of the conversation. "I need you to stay here and use the gun I showed you how to use. It's in the closet. There's nowhere else for you to go."

She nodded, a look of determination brightening her eyes. Unable to help himself, despite the turmoil outside, he leaned down and took her lips, hard. She kissed back, pulling at his hair.

He bit her bottom lip, marking her. "Stay here and be safe." He tried not to think of how he had also said that to Anna all those years ago. This time it was different; it had to be.

Adam left the house, prepared to fight for his life to protect his Pack and Bay. Jasper came up to his side and nodded.

"Is Bay safe?"

"For now. Willow and Brie?"

"Yes, at the house. Let's get these bastards off our land." His brother's eyes glowed gold, and Adam growled in agreement.

Thankfully, they'd attacked on the south said, away from most of the house. This was happening too often. He needed a way to strengthen their wards and find out how to kill the demon. Maybe Bay could help with that. After all, the demon's blood ran through her veins. But that was something to think on later, after he killed the bastards who'd dared to encroach on their territory.

As soon as they crossed one of the streets on their southern end of the den, the putrid smell of their enemy invaded his nose, and he grunted. These bastards would die. A wolf came out of the brush and pounced on Adam. He let one arm shift to a claw, and he gripped the wolf around the neck. He squeezed, and the wolf squirmed. Adam growled and twisted his wrist so he broke its neck in one movement. He threw the wolf against the ground and prepared to take on the other two wolves that were coming at him. Jasper stood by his side and guarded his flank as he took care of the wolves that came at him. Though the Centrals could do more now that they had black magic, they were still not as strong physically as the Redwoods.

He killed the other two swiftly then ran toward the large group of wolves attacking his enforcers. They worked as a group, killing them all. The metallic smell of blood lay heavily in the air, but none of his men was down. The largest enemy wolf grinned at Adam before darting off into the woods toward Adam's house. Adam howled and followed the bastard, determined not to let him get far. He jumped over a fallen log and tacked the gray wolf. He gripped the enemy around the neck and let his claws pierce its flesh.

"Shift," he growled, his voice hoarse from holding back the change.

The other wolf shifted to human, revealing a bulky man with dark eyes and nothing in his soul.

"Why are you here?" Adam asked. "You know you can't win without your demon. What is your purpose?"

"I'm here for the master's daughter. Our pride."

Rage poured through him, and he slid his other claw into the other wolf's side, cutting him deep. The bastard screamed in agony, but Adam didn't move.

"What is your name?"

"Samuel."

"How could you find where she was?"

"Caym gave me his blood so I could sense her."

"Did he do that to anyone else?"

"No, I'm the master's favorite. Please don't kill me. I'll go away; I swear."

Adam lifted a lip to show his fangs. "You shouldn't have come to my home and attacked my people and endangered my mate."

"But—"

Adam broke Samuel's neck and lifted off the dead wolf. His body shook as he thought of her alone with a demon after her. He would do all in his power to protect her and his Pack. She was the reason he could move forward. She couldn't die.

\*\*\*\*

Bay gripped the gun in her hand and listened to the sounds of fighting wolves fade. With each growl and howl, she'd tense and pray that Adam would be okay. She knew he was a strong wolf, if not one of the strongest ever, but that still didn't alleviate her fears.

Plus he wanted her. She shouldn't feel so giddy about that, considering what was going on at that very moment, but she couldn't help it. He wanted her. He said he didn't love her, couldn't love her. But she could live with that. She could live with the fact that he wanted her and wanted to be her mate. She didn't know what had changed, but she'd take it. She felt a little twinge of loss at the thought that she might love him and he would never love her, but she would get over that. She had to.

She heard footsteps on the porch then relaxed as the scent of pine invaded her nose.

Adam.

Thank God.

She unloaded the gun and put it back in the closet then waddled out to him. He was in the kitchen, washing off his hands, the scent of blood rising in the air.

"Are you hurt?"

He didn't turn to her but shook his head.

"Adam?" she asked when he wouldn't say anything.

"We took care of the last wolf; you're safe." He turned off the water, wiped his hands on a dishtowel, and turned to her.

His eyes were still wolf, and she shivered at the rage she saw in them.

"Is everyone okay?"

"Yes, none of our own were hurt, and we got the wards back up. They don't do us any good from Caym and those with his blood, but they help against others at least."

"Maybe I could help."

Adam nodded and stood in front of her, his presence so large she just wanted to crawl into him and make sure everything was okay.

"I think there's something in your blood that we can use. I'm not sure, but I know the elders are looking into it. But I don't want to do anything until the baby is born, okay?"

She nodded, a sense of peace washing over her at the thought of being part of something bigger than herself. Not to mention the fact that he'd thought about or mentioned the baby twice in one day. They were progressing faster and better than she had ever hoped.

He brushed his thumb along her cheekbone, and she closed her eyes, leaning into his touch.

"There was a wolf after you."

She tensed, opening her eyes, searching for what he had meant.

"His name was Samuel. He said your father wanted you, and he had given Samuel his blood so he could go through the wards and find you. That's how I know your blood will help us. But don't worry; I'll protect you. I killed the wolf. He won't be a problem."

She exhaled, finding a strange sense of peace at his brutality. The wolf in her was thrilled by the fact that her mate could be strong and ruthless when he needed to be. Something a human would never understand.

"Good."

His eyes widened as though he were surprised she agreed with him. They had a lot to learn about her. She wasn't just some fluff who would stand aside. But she had this baby. She would stand by his side and help him be the Enforcer. That was her job as his mate. And she would do it. No matter what.

She tugged on his hand and led him to the bedroom. She stroked him and stripped herself. The both got into the bed, and she turned so she snuggled his front to her back. They spooned, quiet, content.

This could be it. They could finally be moving on. She smiled and closed her eyes, pressing her hand on top of his, which lay on her stomach.

His breath evened out, and she knew he was falling asleep.

"Anna."

Just one whispered word and everything crashed. She knew he didn't mean it. She couldn't replace the woman he'd lost. But that didn't mean it didn't hurt. She wanted to cry, but she didn't. She had to be stronger than that.

Dammit, she needed to stop acting like she was the center of his universe. If she didn't, she might just lose herself. How could she be a mom when she couldn't even take care of herself?

# CHAPTER 16

Adam took a sip of his coffee and winced as it burned his tongue. He blew on it and took another sip, closing his eyes at the sweet taste. Bay was standing at the stove, cooking bacon because she had a craving. He'd offered to help her, but she had just given him a sad look and shook her head.

Adam held back in a sigh because he knew what had upset her. He'd whispered Anna when he had been falling asleep. His fallen mate had come to him in the dream and faded away, and he had merely been saying goodbye. Something he hadn't ever said to her. Yet to Bay, it had looked like the worst. He didn't know how to say he was sorry for something that would, or had, broken her heart. He should tell her what Anna had said and that it was a goodbye, but he didn't know if Bay would believe him.

So instead of speaking, he stood by her, showing her that he wouldn't leave. Though he didn't love her, couldn't love her, he'd made the decision to stay by her side. He'd been the one to bite her first. She deserved more than what he could give her, but he was selfish enough to not her to go. And that made him one sick bastard.

Just as Bay turned to put more bacon on the plate, she grabbed her stomach and shouted.

He quickly put his coffee cup down along her side. "What's wrong? Is it the baby?" Fear crawled up his spine, even though he had no idea what to do.

She closed her eyes and scrunched her face in pain. "I don't know; it just hurts."

"Are you having contractions?"

She narrowed her gaze at him and grunted. "How would I know? I've never had a baby before."

"Okay, let's get you to Hannah and North. They'll be able to help."

She nodded, panic rising in her face, and he did his best to remain calm. If he freaked out, so would she. Well, more than she already was.

He gripped her elbow and had started to walk her toward the door when she froze. A puddle appeared at their feet, and she groaned in pain.

"I think my water broke."

Adam gulped and looked down at the puddle of fluid on the floor and tried not to pass out. He could do this. He was the Enforcer. A little bodily fluid wouldn't hurt him. He hoped.

"Okay, you're definitely in labor. Let's get you to Hannah."

Bay nodded, her gaze fixed on the floor as well. "That sounds like a good idea."

Adam took a deep breath and slowly walked her to the door. But as soon as he got there, she curled over and winced in pain.

"Damn! I'm a freaking wolf. Why can't I handle this?"

"Because apparently childbirth is hard?"

"So not helping."

He nodded then lifted her into his arms, cradling her to his chest.

"Adam! What do you think you're doing?"

"I'm taking care of you. Stop fidgeting."

"Oh." She looked genuinely confused but leaned into him as she groaned again.

"I should call Hannah shouldn't I?"

"Probably, but we'll just surprise them, right?"

"I'm not doing a very good job with this."

"Well, it's your first time."

He nodded and walked her over to North's clinic, which thankfully wasn't that far. As soon as he reached the porch, Hannah came running to them.

"I felt her pain all the way from home. Let's get her set up and maybe we'll have a baby soon." She led them to the back where North was already setting up the equipment so they would get comfortable.

He sat Bay down on the table, making sure he didn't hurt her, then backed away. Tension squeezed his shoulders, and he didn't know what was going on. For all he had thought about getting over his issues and being with her, he hadn't thought about the fact, really thought, that there would be a new life.

A baby.

Oh, Jesus.

Bay screamed as another contraction hit, and she threw out her arm. Instinctively, he gripped her hand and moved closer so he could be near her. She looked up at him, fear in her eyes, and gave a weak smile.

"Thanks for being here."

"Nowhere else I'd be." The words surprised him, but when he thought about it, he knew they were true.

North and Hannah set her up and got her dressed to be ready for the birth. He held back a growl as North touched her, but his wolf relented. After all, North would help make sure everything was okay.

Plus, he didn't love her, so he shouldn't feel so territorial.

Right.

Hannah rubbed small circles on Bay's stomach, using her Healing powers to bring down the pain. Bay immediately calmed but didn't let go of his hand. Frankly, he wasn't sure who needed the strength more, him or her. Josh walked to the door and stood by his mate. Adam watched as Josh rubbed his hand up and down Hannah's back and kissed her temple. He still had a large scar on his neck that looked brutal, and he would probably have it for the rest of his life.

"Everything's going to be okay," Josh said, his voice lower and more gravelly than it had been before.

Jesus, the Centrals were taking too much from their family. It had to end.

Hours passed. Adams didn't move as Hannah worked her magic, though she seemed more sad than usual, but Adam didn't know why. Finally, Bay pushed and pushed until she screamed, and then a baby's cry filled the room.

The cry seemed to pierce something in Adam, and he let go of Bay's hand. He took a step back and watched how North and Hannah cleaned up the small little bundle and brought it over to Bay.

Hannah put the blanket-clad baby on Bay's chest and smiled. "You have a little boy. Congrats, Mama. What did you decide to name him?"

Adams's tongue grew heavy, his mouth dry. He blinked, trying to make the back spots go away.

"Micah. Baby Micah," Bay whispered as she traced a finger down his little chubby cheek.

The room seemed to go out of focus, and it started to buzz in his head. He took another two steps back and shook his head.

It was all too real. He couldn't do this. Couldn't be the man she needed him to be, couldn't be whoever the little blanket-clad being needed, couldn't be anything but the shell of a man he'd existed as for so long. He needed to leave. He needed to just breathe and get out of there.

With that, he turned on his heel and stomped out of the room, ignoring the disappointed faces of his family as he passed.

He couldn't do this. He couldn't.

**\*\*\*\***

It felt as if someone had taken the most perfect moment and stabbed her in the chest. Bay took a deep breath, and she watched Adam walk out the door, leaving her and her child alone. Just what she'd always thought they would be.

Alone.

She shouldn't have trusted he would've stayed. It made no sense that he would want her. She should have known.

The crevice opened up in her, threatening to swallow her whole. The cold slapped at her, breaking through her skin, seeping into her bones. He was gone. He hadn't even looked at Micah.

Their child.

No, her child.

She looked down at his chubby little cheek as he nursed. She felt so connected to him, like he'd settled into her heart when he'd been in her womb. In all that had happened, she hadn't thought about a new life as much as she should have. This little person was dependent on her for everything. She needed to hold it together for him.

Especially since he still had the demon's blood running through him.

She traced his little face with her finger again, loving how soft the skin was below her fingertip. Pat came to her side and squeezed her hand. Bay held on for dear life but didn't cry. She couldn't, didn't, have anything left.

"He looks so handsome," Pat whispered.

"Your grandson is precious." Though Adam would never claim him, she knew he would always be part of the Jamensons through Pat and the others. At least he had that.

"You did a wonderful job."

Bay nodded but wasn't really listening. How had everything gone so wrong so quickly?

She cleared her throat and looked up. "Do you think I could just have some time with Micah?" She was surprised at how strong and steady her voice was. Inside she felt like she was dying, but she knew she couldn't hide it from the alpha wolf. At least Pat didn't outwardly show her pity. Bay didn't think she'd be able to take that.

"Of course, dear." She touched Micah's face and then Bay's before leaving. As she walked out the door, Maddox walked in and then closed the door in North's and Ellie's faces. She heard growling from the other side, but then they left.

Without saying anything, Maddox got onto bed with her and held her and Micah close to him.

"Mating sucks." She looked pointedly at the door when she said it, and he coughed a laugh. He held her closer, and she cried into his shoulder, letting everything she'd held in come out.

When she pulled away, she patted his damp shirt and rocked a sleeping Micah.

"Thank you, I needed that," she whispered.

"I'm the Omega. That's what I'm for."

She looked up at him and saw the sadness she felt reflected in his gaze. It seemed like nothing would be fixed, or could be fixed. She would just have to move on and be strong, for her baby and for her.


The next day Maddox came to Bay's house. Or rather, Adam's house, even though he still had not come home from wherever the hell he had run off to. She'd ignored the hurt and pain and coldness from his departure and now was just pissed off.

Maddox sat on the couch holding Micah, but he didn't quite know what to do.

"I thought you said you babysat Finn before."

"Yeah, and I was scared to death to do it then too. These things are just so little. You could break them at any moment."

"Don't call my son a *thing*," she growled lightly.

He just shook his head and waved his fingers in Micah's face. Her little guy scrunched up and gave a small smile.

"Hey, he's smiling at me!" Maddox looked so cute in his response to the gesture that Bay almost didn't have the heart to tell him the truth.

"It's gas, hon. You're going to need to check his diaper."

A look of horror crossed over his face, and she held back in a grin. "Uh, I think I will let you take care of that. After all, you need the practice."

"Thanks," she said dryly.

Bay took Micah from Maddox. She changed her little baby's diaper then went to sit back on the couch and watch her little one take on a whole new world. But even as she tried to focus on the good things, Adam's blatant absence ate at her more and more.

"We just have to give him time."

"Stop intruding on my emotions, Omega."

"I can't help it if you're blaring them out at me. But really, Adam will come back. You know he wants you. He's just being an as—butthead."

"I already gave him time. I know I'm not what he wanted. I guessed that. But he left without even looking at his son. How am I supposed to forget that?"

"Don't forget it. But forgive him when he comes back. And kick him in the ass."

They visited for another hour or so, and Bay put Micah in her room to sleep. She hadn't felt comfortable enough to put him in the nursery yet. Then she had noticed that Adam had cleaned it out for the baby. Why had he reacted so cruelly?

Maddox left, needing to deal with his normal Pack duties. As soon as he left, the door opened again, and she tensed. Adam walked into the living room and fell to his knees before her. She'd been standing near the couch and was unable to move. His body shook, though he didn't reek of alcohol. At least he hadn't gotten drunk this time. He laid his head on her stomach, but she couldn't move, couldn't breathe.

"I'm so, so sorry. I'm so, so sorry." He just kept repeating it over and over again, but Bay didn't move. "Please forgive me for leaving. I know I said I wouldn't, and I did. I'm a coward. Please."

He rubbed his arms on her sides and wrapped them around her. Still, she didn't move.

"I would've forgiven you if it had only been me when you walked out. I even understand it completely. You're not ready. I know that. But it's not just me anymore. You *left* your child. You never even looked at him. You *left* him. How am I supposed to trust you when you do that? You don't know what he looks like; I didn't know if you even cared.

"You can't get over the fact that you never got to hold your child. The other one. The one who died. Well, guess what, Adam? This one didn't die. And it's not fair to either of us, Micah and me, to let you keep doing this. I'm not strong enough to say no every time. You need to learn to grow a spine and take responsibility for your actions. You are a grown man and a grown wolf. Act like it. For the rest of my life, I'll always remember my son's birth with the sight of you walking out on him.

"How am I supposed to get over that, Adam? What am I going to do next time you decide to leave and I don't know if you're coming back? What's going to happen if you do it when Micah is actually old enough to remember? How are you going to explain to him you don't love him? I know that you don't love me, and I'm strong enough, at least I hope I am, to get over that. I'm not strong enough to watch you break my child. *My* child. Not yours. You lost that right."

Tears streamed down her cheeks, and she shook with each word. She could feel Adam's tears against her stomach as he hugged her tighter, as if the harder he hugged, the more he proved he wouldn't let her go. But she didn't trust him.

She heard Micah's cry from the bedroom, and Adam looked over his shoulder. He didn't look like he was going to run away. But how could she know?

"My son deserves his father. And because of that, I'll give you one more chance. But if you walk out on him or treat him like anything less than the best thing in your life, I will leave, and you will never see him again. Do you understand me?"

Adam stood and kissed her softly. She didn't kiss him back, not wanting to give him the wrong idea.

"I can't, Adam. I don't trust you."

He traced a finger down her brow line and nodded. "I'll earn it. It was just too much right then, and I hadn't thought about what it meant to have a new baby in my life. It was selfish, cruel, and unthinking. I know you don't trust me, but I won't do anything that will make him think I don't want him. And it's the same with you. I'm so sorry, Bay."

She nodded, upset with herself for wanting to believe him. But Micah deserved more than her bitter attitude so she nodded and walked toward the bedroom. She stood by the bassinet and looked down on a whimpering Micah. She knew he was just fussy for attention because he had a full belly and a clean diaper. It was amazing how quickly she could learn this mom stuff.

Adam stood by the side and gulped. His eyes widened as he looked at her. "He looks just like me."

She gave a soft smile. "I know." And that would have killed her to know that every day she'd be looking at the image of the man that left her. She prayed that wouldn't be the case.

"I'm going to go wash my hands." He went into the bathroom, and she heard him wash up. She held back a smile at his nervous tendencies.

He walked back in and looked scared to death.

"You've held a baby before, right?"

"Not since Cailin."

She nodded at that tidbit of knowledge. Apparently, this baby thing was more than just Micah, considering there were two relatively new babies in the family.

"Go sit on the bed now and I'll bring him to you, okay? We'll take the slow."

186

He did so quickly, and she picked up Micah and held him to her chest. He looked up at her, and she knew he looked so much wiser than a one-day-old should. She carried him over to Adam, and he held out his arms, as if he knew instinctively what to do. She held back a smile and gently placed Micah into his father's arms. Adam cradled his son's head and bottom and looked down at him as if he'd never seen something quite like him. Bay had done a similar thing when she'd first seen him.

"We made him," Adam whispered in awe.

"I know. We didn't do too badly."

"We did perfect. He's perfect."

Unconsciously, she leaned into him, resting her head on his shoulder. He twisted so he could kiss her forehead, and she closed her eyes. This was how it should've been. Not storming out and lost glances. This.

She watched her mate hold their son, praying she hadn't made a mistake by letting him come back. Their enemies were out to get them, people were dying, and yet in this small room, her greatest fear was she wouldn't be strong enough.

# CHAPTER 17

It still wasn't working. No matter how much Bay wanted it to, it wasn't. Adam tried to be warm, but he couldn't do it. She didn't know what he was thinking. Did he love her? No, that couldn't be it. He'd told her that he couldn't love again, and she was starting to believe it. The stupid woman inside her had clung to hope of something more. But, even though he was warming up to her, doing all the right things, and saying all the right things, she couldn't quite believe it.

He didn't love her. She knew that. But she didn't think he loved Micah either. And that was something she couldn't handle. She'd come to the den for protection and even some comfort, not to be shut out and watch the man she loved try too hard for something that wouldn't come.

Micah turned in her arms and nuzzled her breast. She gave a tired smile and unbuttoned her blouse so he could have his breakfast. Her little boy was a machine when it came to eating. Every two hours, on the dot, he had to eat. Apparently, it was a Jamenson trait. Pat had told her that all of her boys had been the

188

same way. They had to eat all the time so they could grow as big as they were. Bay was not a small woman by any means, but she had a feeling her little boy would be bigger than her in no time.

She rocked back and forth in the rocking chair Jasper had made for her. She looked around the freshly painted nursery and tried not to let her heart beat too fast. Her new family had decorated it and made it look like new, essentially cleaning out the tomb of Adam's lost child. He hadn't said anything about it, and that worried her. Even though they slept together, made love, if she could call it that, and they were trying to raise a baby together, she didn't know much about him. They didn't talk. She didn't know about his past. Most of the time they sat in silence across from each other, and she would fret away on the inside and had no idea what he was thinking. When they did talk, it was as if they could only fight. She hated it. The only time she felt at peace was when they played music together. And even then, she didn't really know if he felt as if he was in the same room with her. For all she knew, he was reliving his past with Anna through her.

They needed to talk. But she didn't know how to broach the subject. If they were going to make it, and, oh, how she really wanted that to happen, they would have to talk. They would have to cross that line and talk about Anna, the baby, his past. Even she hadn't opened up completely to him. Yes, she'd talked about her nomadic lifestyle, her mom, and her job. But she hadn't disclosed her hopes and fears. Because if she did that, she would feel as if she were opened up and raw, while he was steady as stone.

Micah whined again, and she lifted him up to her shoulder to pat his back. He let out a belch so loud she was afraid her eardrums had popped.

"Dear Lord, Micah," she said with a laugh.

"That sounds like a Jamenson, all right," Adam commented from the doorway.

She froze then quickly buttoned up her blouse. She hadn't felt or heard him come in. Damn, she was so messed up and deep into her thoughts, she couldn't think of anything else. What if Caym had come in while she was deep in thought? She had to stop. She had to talk to Adam and figure out how to move on. If she didn't, it would be dangerous for all of them.

She juggled Micah so he lay cradled in her arms. Bay got out of the chair and walked over to the crib. He closed his little eyes sleepily, and she smiled. He was so precious. A perfect blend of Adam's and her features. If only everything else would blend just as well.

She didn't fail to notice that Adam hadn't walked into the nursery. Nor did he offer to help her hold their child. No, he stood off to the side as always and watched with a torn expression on his face. Every time she saw him, a little piece of her fell apart. She didn't want to be this emotional, weeping woman. She had to be stronger than that.

"Is it his nap time?" Adam asked as he backed away from the door.

She nodded and walked out of the nursery, the baby monitor attached to her hip. She closed the door partially and walked out to the living room.

Steeling herself, she took a deep breath. "We need to talk."

Adam gave that annoyingly charming smile then said, "Why is it that whenever someone says that, there is always something bad to say?"

"Because there is."

190

"I thought we were doing okay. I mean... we're trying." He stuck his hands in his pockets and looked genuinely confused.

"When is my birthday, Adam?"

He scrunched his brows and shook his head. "I don't know. Did you ever tell me that? What's that have to do with anything?"

She let out a sigh and paced the room. "It has to do with everything. We don't know each other. Yeah, we have sex, but what does that mean?"

Adam narrowed his gaze and clenched his fists. "We're still learning. Give it time."

"But we're not doing anything to learn. Do you understand that? We know nothing about each other, and yet we're not trying to move on." She took a deep breath, closed her eyes then opened them. "I want to talk about Anna."

"No." His voice was low, cold.

And with that, her heart broke again. She hadn't thought she even had any left to break.

"Why not? She's as much a part of this relationship as I am. You know what? I think she had an even bigger part."

"She has nothing to do with us, and I don't want to talk about it."

"You don't want to talk about a lot of things. But that doesn't really fucking matter right now. I'm losing you when I never really had you to begin with. Anna is as much a part of our lives as you want her to be. Do you understand that? Unless we talk about her, she's always going to be the ghost in our relationship. She's always going to be the one taking you away from me."

"Anna was my mate. You have no right to say anything about her."

"I am your mate now," she growled. "I'm not asking you to forget her. Quite the opposite. I want to know more about her. That way I can know more about you. She is such a part of your life that until I know who she was, I can't know who you are. How are we supposed to act like mates and be together if I don't know you?"

"I'm trying, Bay."

"That's not good enough. Not anymore. That little boy in there is our son. Yeah, you came home and held him that one time. That's it. You barely even look at him."

"I'm trying."

"Stop saying that when you aren't. You're as much of a ghost as she is. I need to know you're here. I deserve to know, Adam."

He rubbed his hands over his face and shifted from foot to foot, anger radiating off him.

"I'm here, aren't I? You came waltzing into this place, my home, pregnant. I opened my door for you to stay here. I like you, Bay. You know I do. You also know that I can't love again, and you said that was okay. You said that we could be mates and live on like we were. I can't talk about Anna."

"You won't."

"Fine, I won't. She's gone, and no good will come from talking about it."

She looked up at him sadly and shook her head. "Even if you don't talk about her, she's still here. I know she's more important to you than I am. But I don't know if I can live with that."

With that, she walked back into the nursery and closed the door behind her. She leaned against it as she sank down to the floor, tears pooling in her eyes. She deserved more than what she had, but she knew she wouldn't get it. Not when Adam was so firmly lost in the past that he couldn't even see his present.

\*\*\*\*

Adam walked out of the house, slamming the door behind him. He stormed to the backyard, through the forest to the area behind it, and ended up at his hidden meadow. Jesus, Bay was asking for everything. She wanted to be part of his life, to know every little piece of him and his past.

Though she deserved it. He knew, even though he tried not to, he was falling in love with her. Day by day, it felt a little bit less like a betrayal to do so. Anna had been gone for two decades. He needed to move on, and he had thought he was doing that with Bay.

He could see Bay in his future, standing by his side as they watched their pups grow. He could see her act as an Enforcer's mate and hold her own. He could see her with him...and he liked it. He loved it.

He loved her.

God, he loved her, didn't he? How the hell had that happened? Yes, his wolf had wanted her from the start, and fate had brought them together. He hadn't thought he'd fall. What scared him most was the fact that he wasn't scared about loving her. He was just scared about letting go of the past.

But it was time.

Despite what he had said to Bay, he had been thinking about saying goodbye to Anna. It'd been on a loop in his mind since he had met Bay in that bar that fateful night. He'd fought tooth and nail, claw and fang, in order to hold onto what he thought he needed. But he'd been wrong.

He stepped onto the soft grass and knelt before the stone grave marker. The cool breeze drifted over his shoulders and into his hair. It felt as if someone had slightly brushed their fingers across his face.

Anna.

He'd buried his mate himself in this hidden meadow, marked with a sole gravestone amongst the wildflowers on a grassy knoll. He traced his fingers over the letters and closed his eyes.

*Anna Jamenson*
*Mate, Mother, Heart*
*Jessica Jamenson*
*Too early for this world*

His wife and daughter were buried beneath him, long gone from this world. He came out here weekly, to tidy up the grass and flowers, to clean the stone. Bay had been right. He'd created a tomb in his home, not a site of remembrance.

Tears leaked out from his eyes as he traced his finger along the edge of the stone.

"I don't have anything for you today, Anna. I came here in a moment of decision; though it's been a long time coming."

He swallowed hard and clenched his fists. "I'm so sorry for letting you die. I shouldn't have left you alone and unprepared. You were most at peace taking care of others, not fighting for them. And yet I didn't do my duty as your mate to make sure you could protect yourself and our child. I'm so sorry. Please forgive me."

The tears flowed freely now, washing away the sins.

"I'm never going to forget you. You have to realize that."

A twig snapped behind him, and he turned quickly. He didn't smell anything out of place since it was downwind, but it must've been a dear or other animal.

He turned back to the grave and dried his tears. "I know you probably already know, but I've met someone. Her name is Bay. She's amazing, Anna. I think you would've liked her. She's strong, capable, and has a fiery temper just like her red hair. I made a mistake at first because I didn't think about the consequences. Now that she's living with me, I love her, Anna. I couldn't, no, I *wouldn't* let myself think about it because I love you. But just because I fell in love with her doesn't mean I love you any less. You're part of my past, part of me, and I'm never going to forget you. But I'm going to try to move on and try to be happy."

He could swear he felt that wind hug him and caress him, and he leaned into it. "I have a son, Micah. He's so tiny that I don't know what to do. I'm almost six-and-a-half feet tall, but you know that. He's so little in my hands that I feel like I could crush him. That's why I'm nervous to be around him. But I think Bay thinks it's because I don't love him. But as soon as I saw the little green eyes, I couldn't hold back. They're my family, Anna. You were my family and you'll always be part of me, but I'm ready to move on."

The wind hugged him again, and he closed his eyes. His wolf rumbled in pleasure, and he said goodbye to his lost mate for the first time—no, the last time. He stood and started walking back toward his home. To his and Bay's home. He was ready to start a new life. He just needed to tell Bay that.

****

Bay clutched Micah closer to her, and she rushed back into the house. She'd been an idiot to follow Adam. Just watching him kneel at Anna's grave saying he would never forget her made her want to weep. It was a lost cause. She'd lost him. No, she'd never really had him.

Micah squirmed and squeaked a cry. She held him closer as tears streamed down her face. She'd have to leave. She'd find a way to protect her son, but she couldn't stay here. Not anymore.

The door opened and closed, and Bay quickly sniffed and wiped away her tears. She couldn't let him see her crying. That would only hurt her more.

"Bay?" Adam called out as he walked closer to her. "Hey? Were you crying? I'm so sorry, baby, for leaving like that. I shouldn't have left without saying anything."

She gave a stiff nod and put Micah back in his crib. "It's just hormones. Don't worry about it."

He brushed his thumb along her cheek, wiping away trail of tears. "I'm sorry. We can talk about anything you want. Okay?"

She bit her lip and shook her head. "It's not important now."

"But it is. I want to know everything about you."
*It's too late.*

"I'm just all hormonal because of the baby. Just give me some time and I'll be okay."

He looked as though he didn't believe her and pulled her into his arms. She stiffened then melted into him, furious at herself for doing it. Their mate bond pulsed between them, calming her wolf and making her feel loved. Dammit, he didn't love her. Why was fate so fucked up?

He rubbed his hand up and down her back, little tendrils of sensation flooding her with each fingertip and caress. He rubbed his cheek on the top of her head and held her tighter.

"I'm sorry again."

"Don't be," she whispered. It wasn't his fault that he was the love with another woman. It was her fault for believing he could change.

He shifted and led her toward their bedroom. He cradled her face in his hands and looked down at her. She gazed into his jade-green eyes and hated herself for loving this man. He slowly lowered his head and brushed his lips against hers. His tongue tentatively traced her lips, and she opened for him. He tasted of man, coffee, and Adam. He groaned into her mouth, and she sighed. Why did this feel different? Why did it feel like he wanted this more than anything, and yet she felt as though it were a goodbye?

She was weak and wanted him if only for a moment.

He wrapped her hair around his fist and tugged. Pleasure shot down her spine at the slight pain, and she rubbed herself on him. Wanton and needy, she ignored their problems and deepened the kiss.

He pulled back, his eyes dilated and glowing with arousal, his chest moving with deep frantic breaths. "I'm going to make love to you, Bay, and then I'm going to fuck you hard. I've missed being with you."

She raised a brow. "It hasn't been that long."

"It's felt like it." He nibbled up her jaw and her ear lobe, and she shuddered. Because she was a wolf, she didn't have to wait the normal amount of time after having a baby to have sex. Thank God. She needed to have this at least for a reminder of what they could have had before she left.

He pulled on her hair again, forcing her head to the side. He nibbled over the mate mark, and her pussy clenched. She'd always heard it was an erogenous zone, but, dear God, she could come with just his licking. His hand cupped her breast, and she started.

"I'm nursing, so you're going to have to be careful."

He kissed her, and then quickly and efficiently unbuttoned her blouse, removing it from her body. "I love your breasts, Bay. I loved them before, when they were plump and overfilled my hands. Now they're so full and swollen, I slowly can eat them all up. Do they hurt?"

She shook her head. "My nipples are supersensitive, but other than that, they're just like before. Well, except for the fact that they may shoot milk at you." She blushed and tried to hide her face against his chest. His very naked chest. When had he stripped down to his boxer briefs?

He grinned at her, and she shivered. She loved that grin, the mixture of sexiness with a little wicked thrown in. He quickly divested her of her pants and panties, and then Adam unclasped the front hook of her bra. Her breasts fell heavy and aching. She tried to cover up her stomach, but he pulled her hands back.

"Why are you trying to cover yourself up? You're beautiful."

"I still haven't recovered from the baby. I may be a wolf, but it does take a little bit. Plus I have stretch marks."

"Aren't those called tiger stripes or something like that? You know, badges of courage and bravery?"

She let out a laugh and threw her head back. "How much *Oprah* have you been watching?"

"*Oprah* isn't on anymore." He blushed and shut his mouth.

"Oh, my God, you used to watch *Oprah*? How modern aged of you." She grinned, and he pinched her hip. "Hey! Don't pinch me."

"Then don't make fun of me and my love for *Oprah*."

"Oh, my God, you love her? I was just kidding."

"I didn't say anything. I have no idea which you mean."

"Does your family know of this obsession?"

He growled then kissed her hard. "Shut up. I was just saying that you're fucking beautiful. Take the compliment and let me lick you all over."

She swallowed hard. "Okay."

He backed her to the bed, so she sat down. He grinned, knelt before her, and spread her legs. She blushed as she lay open to him, feeling vulnerable.

"Uh, you know I just had Micah. Things may not be... you know...the same." She blushed again and closed her eyes.

He traced a finger down her folds, and she sucked in her breath. "You're beautiful," he said with a raspy voice.

He brushed his thumb over her clit, and her hips rocked toward him. He groaned and leaned closer. She could feel his warm breath against her, and she moaned. He rubbed small circles on her clit, each movement causing a cascade of pleasure through her. She rose higher and higher, almost reaching that peak, and then he pulled back, and she cursed.

"Adam, don't tease," she grumbled.

He didn't say anything but lowered his head farther so his lips touched her core. She bucked off the bed as he sucked and licked, causing her to scream as she climaxed. Her body blushed, and her nipples ached as she came against his face. He kept licking, sucking up all her juices then slowly licked up her mound to her belly button.

"Not my stomach, please." She was still too self-conscious for him to see her like this.

"I love every part of you."

She tensed at the word love but knew he only meant it in terms of sex, not emotion. Dammit, her body grew cold at the damning thoughts of what the relationship truly was.

He tilted his head and looked at her, completely confused. She gave him a stiff smile and tried to look like she was happy. No use ruining what would be their last time. With his tongue, he traced every stretch mark and bump on her stomach. Tears fell from her eyes as emotion welled within her. He continued his path and licked around the globes of her breasts. Warmth spread through her as he softly caressed each nipple and licked and kissed them.

"I don't want you to feel uncomfortable, so I'm going to be very careful, okay?" he rasped out, his breath uneven.

"Okay," she breathed.

Her body felt light and heavy at the same time, her pussy hole wanting him inside her. Even though she'd just come, she wanted him. Now.

"Adam, please."

"I like the sound of you begging."

"Don't be an ass. Get in me."

He threw his head back and laughed. "I think that's the sexiest thing you've ever said, my sexy redhead."

She tried not to glow under the *my* part of his statement. It was just sex after all. He pulled back, and she groaned.

"What are you doing?"

He grinned and stripped off his boxer briefs. She almost swallowed her tongue as she watched his cock bounce back up and hit his stomach. A tiny droplet of cum dripped out of the seam at the top, and she licked her lips.

"Fuck, every time you look at me like that, I almost come. I need to get a condom first, okay?"

He rummaged through his nightstand and shouted as he found one. "I'm so glad North makes us keep these in here."

Protection. Damn. She hadn't even thought of it. Now that they were fully mated, and she wasn't pregnant anymore, she could get pregnant with just one time. As werewolves, they couldn't get pregnant without mating first; it was just the way they were wired. Thank God he'd thought of it, or she could've been walking away from him pregnant. Again. If she had been staying, she would have talked to Hannah about some herbs to make sure she was on birth control.

He ripped open the foil packet and rolled the condom down this thick length. She followed his hands with her gaze as he squeezed the base of his dick. She licked her lips, and he grinned.

"I like you there, watching me hold my dick as you arch against the bed, wanting me. I can't wait to stuff you full with my cock and have your pussy clench around me. And you know what, baby? Today, I'm gonna play with that little ass of yours to get it ready for me. Because coming up soon, I'm gonna stuff that little ass full and watch you scream my name."

Damn, she loved to talk dirty like this. She'd never had anal sex before, and though she knew she never would with him because she was leaving, just the idea sent shivers down her spine. She wanted him there. She wanted him everywhere. That was the problem.

"Scoot your butt up and grip the headboard," he ordered, his voice low and growly.

She obeyed instantly, letting herself get into the moment. She wrapped her hands wrapped around the firm oak of the headboard, and she spread her legs. He grinned then got on the bed to kneel between them. In one quick movement, he grabbed below both her knees and pushed them closer to her head, then slammed into her.

She shouted as she came around him, but he didn't let her rest. He pulled back out, her pussy clenching onto him like it didn't want to let go. He groaned and slammed back in, over and over again. She held onto the headboard as it slammed against the wall with the force of his thrusts.

He pulled her back and set her on her knees. "I don't want that slamming to wake up Micah," he whispered, and she cooled. Fuck, she hadn't even though of the baby. Talk about a way to take her out of the moment.

He gripped her hair and pulled back her head back so her lips met his. He thrust his tongue inside her mouth, and their teeth clashed together with the force of this kiss. "I'm sorry. Let me get you back in the mood."

She grinned as he licked and kissed his way down her spine, ending at her bottom. He spread her cheeks, and she blushed.

"Damn, I think I love every part of you."

Just as she was about to say something, she felt his tongue at her back entrance. Holy shit. He gently probed the area and licked and sucked. It should've felt weird and invasive, but for some reason, it turned her on as all hell. He kept licking and probing and, at the same time, massaging her cheeks. She blushed as she moaned and wiggled against his face. He slowly lowered his tongue and licked her pussy. She could feel him groaning against her, and then she felt a finger slowly replace his tongue. She froze as he slowly rimmed the entrance then pushed his finger in. She clenched around him, and he groaned.

"You're so tight baby but don't worry. I'm just going to get you ready. It's gonna take a few times. I won't hurt you."

She nodded but ignored that. He was already hurting her more than he knew. Just not physically.

He continued to play and tease her until she thrashed against him, needing release. He moved so his other fingernail could gently scrape against her clit, and she came. She breathed his name as he slid into her. He was so deep that she could barely breathe, barely think. He gripped her hips and pistoned into her. Her body was boneless, her energy waning, but she could feel herself about to come again. She didn't think she could take anymore. But Adam didn't think the same apparently, so he pushed in one final time, and they came together. She felt his hot seed within the condom and let out a whimper at the loss. She and her wolf both had wanted to feel him in her fully. But it was for the best.

They collapsed in each other's arms, and she closed her eyes. She felt him pull out and get off the bed to take care of the condom. When he got back into bed, he wrapped them both in the blankets, reached over to make sure the baby monitor was as loud as it could go, then fell asleep with her in his arms. As he drifted off, she swore she could've heard him mumble something about love. But she ignored it, too afraid she would hear Anna's name at the end.

Her body grew cold, even with the furnace of a mate surrounding her. She needed to find a way to protect herself and her baby. She knew she'd be broken far more than she was now once she left.

# CHAPTER 18

G lass shattered, and the room grew still. An oily black feeling crept over her arms and threatened to suffocate her. She floated weightless along the current, the air a misty hue of what it once was. Dark eyes loomed in the distance, a red iris striking against the Black. Whatever haunted her cackled, the sound like knives leaving cuts and blood in its wake.

Bay sat straight up in bed, her heart in her throat. Just a dream. It had to be just a dream. A fucking weird dream. She immediately put her hand on Adam—no, on Adam's cold side of the bed.

The irrational part of her felt like someone had hit her in the stomach. He couldn't be gone. He's said he'd stay. But no, just because he wasn't there for the moment didn't mean he was gone forever. She needed to get over her low self-esteem issues.

Bile rose in her throat as she thought of the dream. She didn't know exactly what it meant, but she knew who it was.

Caym.

Her father.

Well, sperm donor. She didn't count the bastard as much more than that. A chill hit the air, and goose bumps rose on her arm.

Micah.

Unease filling her, she tossed back the covers and ran to the nursery. She couldn't sense Adam in the house, but something else was there.

Something dark.

Her wolf clawed to the surface, and she let her claws slice through her fingertips, ready to protect her child. She slammed open the door and froze.

Caym stood over Micah's crib, a spine-chilling smile on his face. He turned his head to the side in a way that reminded her of that silent episode of *Buffy the Vampire Slayer*. The episode that had given her nightmares and made her want to cry like a baby. Caym straightened and licked his lips but didn't utter a word.

She couldn't move, couldn't think past the fact that the demon who'd haunted her life, who'd slit Josh's throat and broken every little bone in Finn's body, stood over her son's crib. The demon wore a crisp black suit with a shockingly white silk shirt and black tie. The sharp angles of his face looked like they could cut glass.

Thankfully, she'd taken after her mom with her curves and Micah already looked so much like Adam. At least that part of her tainted genetic code hadn't contaminated her son. Caym smiled again, and she tried to take a step forward, the need to save her son stronger than her fear. He flicked his wrist, and she flew back into the music room door across the hall, her head slamming into the wood and stars bursting behind her eyes.

She tried to get up, and he laughed.

Laughed.

"Oh child, why do you fight it?"

His voice was like a smooth cognac. It slid over her and made her want to vomit. She ignored the pain in her head and the blood running down her fingers and tried to stand.

Wait. Blood?

She'd sliced her hand against the lock on the doorframe as she'd flown threw the air and hadn't even noticed it. The copper scent stung her nose, and she blinked. God, she needed to get up. Needed to save her son. She stood and growled.

The demon laughed again.

"Do you know why I wanted you, blood of my own?"

"I don't give a fuck. Get away from my son," she growled.

Where was Adam? Why wasn't here protecting their child? Blood roared through her ears at his rejection, but she ignored it. Micah was far more important.

"Yes, my grandson. Quite a feat for you. You fucked a Jamenson, and the fates smiled upon me. Now I'll raise your son in my image. The blood of the Jamensons runs through his veins, yet he'll rule by my side. I love the irony. You did me well, child."

She narrowed her eyes and tried to calculate the odds of her making it out of this alive. On one hand, he would want her to live in her misery. On the other, she would do her best to injure him, most likely getting herself killed in the process, but maybe, just maybe, Micah would live.

That was all that mattered.

Where was Adam?

Oh, God, what if he were already dead? She tugged on her bond to him, and she felt him move.

Good, he was alive. But not here.

Damn.

"You can't have him. He is my son."

"Oh, Bay, you have your mother's spirit." He grinned, and a darkness settled over him. "I loved that I fucked that spirit out of her. She fought like the bitch she was, but don't worry, fate wanted you here. After all, she was my mate. How else could you have been born?"

Her stomach clenched, and she wanted to vomit at his cruel words. Rage pooled through her, and she lunged. He moved slightly, drawing Micah into his arms. She scraped her claws down Caym's side, and he kicked out, throwing her against the dresser. She got up quickly, ignoring the pain, but it was too late. Caym blinked away, her son in his arms.

"No!"

She screamed until her throat was raw. She screamed Micah's and Adam's names, but neither of them were there. Shakily, she got to her feet and staggered to the empty crib. She clutched Micah's blanket to her nose and inhaled his baby scent laced with pine. Tears streamed down her face, and agony ripped through her.

"Bay!" Adam roared from the front door as she heard the wood splinter from its frame.

She heard his footsteps as he ran closer and wrapped his body around hers, his pine scent enveloping her. She didn't melt against him like she would have before this. She didn't close her eyes and inhale his musk and think "mate."

He hadn't been there when she needed him.

"Where is he? I can smell that demon. Where is he?"

His words lashed out at her, and she pushed him away with such force that he staggered back.

"Caym's gone. He took our son and left. He said he was going to raise him as his own and make us watch. But where were you? Where were you?" With each statement and question, her voice rose to a screech. She could hear the others in the room as they gathered in their home. She felt the tension along her skin as the others felt the shock of hearing one of their own was missing.

But they'd felt his before after all. With Adam's first mate and child. This was just a repeat performance.

Not on her watch. She strode away from him and stormed into the living room.

"What do you plan to do?" she screamed. "You're the fucking Redwood Pack. Don't just sit back and let my baby be lost."

Everyone in the room froze, and Edward lowered his head. That this man, this wolf, would do that floored her.

He raised his head, his eyes glowing gold. "We will find your son. The Centrals will not have your child. He is ours. He is our blood. We will fight for him."

Jasper, the Beta of the Pack, came to her and bared his throat. Her wolf whimpered, not liking the submission and apology in their eyes. "We will fight, but we may lose. Know this. We are strong, but the demon is stronger."

"Josh and I have his blood. We are strong too," she promised.

Josh nodded, the scar on his throat stark against his tan skin.

"I know; that's what we're hoping," Kade added. "We won't let anything happen to Micah."

"Don't make any promises you can't keep," she growled, aware that all might be lost but not wanting to voice it.

"Bay," Adam whispered from beside her.

She'd known he was there. She'd felt his presence like a second skin. Her wolf had cuddled close to the surface to feel his, but Bay had ignored it.

She was broken. Damaged. She was losing everything, sinking in quicksand, yet could do thing about it. Nothing yet.

"Bay," Adam repeated.

She turned on him, her wolf in her eyes. "What?"

"I'm sorry."

Out of the corner of her eye, she saw the others leaving the house, most likely regrouping to plan their attack. She would follow later as she would not be left out of this. But, first, she had to deal with an Enforcer.

"You weren't here."

Pain shattered the expression on his face as he went to his knees. "An adolescent snuck out of his house tonight to see a girl, and I had to deal with him."

"So you left your family to deal with a kid who couldn't listen? Caym walked into our home because you weren't here. He might not have come if you were."

He growled but didn't contradict her.

"Where were your enforcers? Where were your men?"

"They were dealing with other things."

"Bullshit. You put your job before your family."

"They are my Pack, and they needed me. I was coming right back."

"And yet the demon came."

"And what would I have done if I were here, Bay? Caym is stronger than me."

"You would have been here!"

He kissed her bloody knuckles, and she closed her eyes. "I would have died for you and Micah. I *will* die

210

for you two. I will not let that piece of filth raise our son. With every last breath I have, I will find a way to defeat him and get our son back."

She fell to her knees and held him close. "I was so scared." She hadn't been mad at him, not really. It wasn't his fault. He had been doing his job. Caym had come into their home, and Adam's presence wouldn't have changed that.

He wrapped his arms around her, and she cried onto his chest.

"I'm so sorry, baby. I'll find him. I will."

"I'll be by your side."

He kissed her softly and growled. "I don't want you there."

Hurt laced through her. "What?"

"I want you safe."

"I'm stronger than all of you. I can do this. Besides, everyone else knows I need to be there. I'm part of this, Adam. You can't keep me away. I'm not a submissive mate. You know this."

He kissed her again and ran his hands through her hair. "I know. I just don't want you to get hurt."

"I want Micah."

"I know."

He held her close for a few more minutes before they both stood up and got changed. They needed to go to the Alpha's home and make their plans. They needed to save their son.

****

Adam stormed back into the house after the Alpha's meeting and roared. No matter what they did, they might lose. But he'd die before he'd just *let* Caym have his son. In two hours, Jasper, Adam, Josh, Bay, Maddox, and Cailin, along with a handful of his enforcers, would invade the Centrals den.

The rest would prepare for a second wave and protect their own den. He wasn't happy that both his mate and sister would be in the first wave, but he had no choice. With the blood of the demon running through her veins, Bay would be strong. Not to mention she was a momma wolf on a warpath. He'd protect her to the death, but she could handle herself. And despite the fact that Cailin was the baby and princess, she was a fierce warrior and top sharpshooter. They needed her as well.

Bay paced behind him, and it took everything in him not to grab her and hold her in his arms and never let go. If he did that, they might not leave. They needed to focus. As he walked toward the bedroom a fresh, tangy scent made him pause.

Fuck.

The demon had returned, though he wasn't there now. Adam ran to the bedroom, checked his surroundings, found them empty, then picked up the note on the bed.

Bay wrapped an arm around his waist, and he did the same as they read the scrawl of the handwritten note.

*I will kill your child, your Micah, if you, Adam Jamenson, and your bitch mate, Bay Jamenson, do not come to me personally. Do not tell others of this note, or I will kill your child myself. Slowly.*

Adam roared, and Bay took the note from his shaking hands. She leaned against him and gasped as rage poured through him.

"Bay?"

"I see him."

212

He put his hands on her shoulders and turned her to face him. "What?"

"My powers. You know how I can use them to see pasts and memories with objects? I can see Corbin; at least that's who I think it is. He at least looks like the man you described. Oh, Adam, he and Caym aren't at the den. They're in the cave. The same cave I ran to before where you found me. Oh, God, they have Micah."

He kissed her temple and held her tightly. "We have to go. We can't let our families go to the Centrals."

She nodded, her gaze off in the distance.

"We can't tell my father where we're going, but we can tell them not to go to the Centrals."

She nodded but didn't say anything. Worry crept through him as he gripped her chin.

"Bay?"

She kissed him, hard, then pulled back. "I'm sorry, Adam. I love you."

Confused, he pulled back as she gripped his shoulder. Pain ricocheted through him through a pressure point, and he fell on the bed, darkness falling over him.

"I'm sorry," she whispered as he passed out, his mind on the fact that she couldn't betray him. No, she was saving him. Or at least that's what she thought.

Darkness.

****

Caym strolled through the cave and took a deep breath. It would be over soon. It had been easy to snatch the brat, but he wasn't strong enough on his own to kill all the Redwoods. Damn.

Bay and Adam would be there soon.

His daughter.

What a novel idea.

He hadn't loved her mother. No, she had been just a wolf who'd had the ill fate to mate with him. He'd taken what he'd wanted and apparently left his baby in her belly.

This Bay was too wild, too independent. He didn't think he'd be able to use her for what he wanted. He would most likely give her to Corbin then use her child. His grandchild.

He would raise it in his image and kill everyone in his path. Oh, he liked that idea.

His body went on alert as he felt Bay walk toward the cave.

Ah, she'd come alone. This would be good.

"Corbin. Take care of her."

Corbin grinned and walked toward the entrance. Caym stood back and watched as Bay walked in with her chin held high.

Corbin would enjoy beating that confidence out of her.

Caym ignored what they were saying; it wasn't important to him. He just wanted this to be over with so he could move on and take over. It was taking too long as it was. He smiled when Corbin backhanded Bay and she flew into the air, crashing into the wall.

Progress.

# CHAPTER 19

A droplet of water hit a rock near her face, and Bay jerked. She tried to move, but her arms were at an odd angle, and she discovered she was chained to the cave wall. She forced herself into a sitting position, ignoring the fiery pain in her shoulders. Her lip ached where Corbin had slapped her. She looked out into the cave and sighed. Before where it had looked like in an oasis inside of a forest, now it looked like a death trap. No, the pools and trees hadn't changed, but what it represented had. Before she had ran into this cave as a place to hide, not from the people who loved her, but for them. She hadn't wanted them to get hurt, so she had run, not thinking. And now, she had run directly to the enemy for the same purpose. To protect those she loved. She couldn't let the family that had taken her in get hurt by attacking the Centrals. It was a war they could not win. Maybe if she'd had more time she would have been able to figure out a way to strengthen the wards. But as it was, it was too late.

She rested her hand on her flat stomach and held back a sob. Her Micah was out there somewhere, in the hands of her enemy. She could feel that he was close, that bond between the wolf and her child wouldn't fade for a few years. But it scared her that not even the Alpha could feel her child. That meant he was near the demon. It was only because of the blood in her veins she could even feel Micah.

"Ah, I see you've woken up," Caym drawled from the edge of the cave opening. Bay stiffened but didn't lower her head. She wouldn't, not for this piece of trash. She would go down fighting to the end. "It's about time. I had been afraid that my Corbin had hit you too hard. But really, it would have been a shame for you to have died...so soon."

The way his eyes gleamed when he had said "my Corbin" made her want to vomit. There was no love in that gaze, only a desire for power.

She could almost feel sorry for the wolf, almost.

Caym took short, measured steps toward her, as if knowing each time he moved closer she had to bite her tongue that much harder not to flinch. He squatted in front of her, resting his forearms on his thighs. He still wore his suit pants and pressed shirt, but he'd lost the jacket and tie he'd worn the other time she'd seen him. His hair was smoothed back so his cheekbones were even more pronounced, and his eyes were their usual black orbs of darkness, but now the red flashed with each breath.

She didn't want to be like him, nor did she want her child to be raised like him. She'd die first.

And she probably would.

"I'm not surprised you came, darling," he said softly as he traced his finger down her cheek. Against her will, she flinched away from his touch as it left a trail of cool numbness in its wake.

She lifted a lip and showed some fang. Her wolf wanted to pounce and tear out his throat, the woman not too far behind. But she couldn't do anything rash. Not when she knew she wasn't yet strong enough to do it and when she didn't know where Micah was. Her baby had to come first. Then Adam. Then her. That's the way it had to be.

"Uh uh uh. Watch your attitude, little girl." He twisted his finger so his nail ran across her cheek instead. She flinched at the sharp sting then held back a growl as blood seeped from the wound.

"Good girl. I know you want to growl and make a fuss, but that won't do you any good, will it?" He smiled a wide smile, full of sharp teeth, and she wanted to crawl into a ball.

So much for being a strong wolf. One look at this demon and she knew she'd met her match.

"I know you came for your baby, and not me. That much I understand. You're a selfish child for not wanting to be near your daddy, but it's okay. I'll beat a new attitude into you." He smiled again then stood, leaving her chained to the wall. "You really are an idiot, aren't you? Like I'd let Micah live with you after this. No, I'll raise him in my image. I really do think Corbin and I will make great parents." He gave a malicious grin, and her heart stuttered.

No, dammit. No. He couldn't have her little boy.

"As for you, well, you're so wild and independent, and that won't do. I'll let Corbin have you to play with for a bit to see if we can make you a little more manageable. Yes, he'll rape and beat you, but really, it's your own fault. You should have come when Daddy called you."

Chills ran up her spine as bile rose up into her mouth. This creature was truly evil. That he'd say that to his own daughter made her want to throw up, but the fact that Corbin was just as sadistic and of her own kind wanted to make her scream.

But, wait, she was also a demon.

Thank God she was more wolf than demon.

"I'm a gracious sort, so I won't kill your Adam right away. No, I'll wait a bit, just so he knows how lucky he is. Then I'll kill him and the rest of his bastard Pack. Those Redwoods piss me off more than you can ever imagine. If they'd just get over it and surrender already. They don't have a chance, not against me. And, their trinity bond pissed me the fuck off even more. Now I can't call the other demons. But no worries, I still have you and your little boy. And I'm going to make more babies with the Centrals' wolves. What do you think of that? Those women spread their legs for anyone. Well, it might be due to the fact that their Pack bonds are tainted, but whatever. Then I'll have Corbin sire some whelps with you. I like that idea."

"We can't have children if we're not mated."

"Corbin already has a child with a mate of his, I'm sure we can find a way to make it happen with you. Though the bitch left him before he could raise the bastard. Don't worry, we'll find them. Pity your whore of a mom mated me."

"Don't talk about her. You don't deserve that right."

"I can do whatever I damn well please. And I know we can't sire babies without mating. But with a little bit of dark magic, I can try and make demons."

Revulsion slid through her. "What?" she breathed.

"I'm going to fuck those little bitches until they breed. Along with some dark magic, I'll be able to procreate at least *something*. It won't be pure wolf, or demon, or even what you are. But according to my old texts, *something* will come."

"You're a sadistic monster."

"Yes, yes I am. But I'm winning."

"They'll fight you. The Redwoods won't let you win."

"Oh, I can't wait. I want to see the blood of their fucking Alpha on my table. I want to see your precious Adam plead for his life. Then I'll kill him in front of you. Just because I can."

"I hate you."

"Good."

With that, he walked away, leaving her chained to the wall, her hopes crashing down to the floor. She'd known it had been a long shot to come here and plead. But maybe if she went along with Caym's plans, at least for a little while, she'd protect the Redwoods. At least long enough for Adam to save Micah. Then she'd let Corbin kill her, anything to protect Micah.

Bay rested her head against the cold wall and tried to break free. The metal dug into her wrists. She looked a bit closer and cursed. It was spelled metal, meaning no matter what she did; she wouldn't be able to break through. And even if she shifted to her wolf, the clamps would expand or shrink to fit. There was no way she would be able to break free so she'd have to wait until one of them unlocked her. But then what? She couldn't run, not with Caym's ability to flash. And she would never leave Micah here.

She could only hope that Adam would come for their baby. It was really the only way. She couldn't have let Adam come with her at first because he too would have been caught or killed. And she hadn't let him in on her plan because, if she had, he wouldn't have let her come.

God, she hated that fucking demon.

The sound of feet against stone forced Bay to turn to the side. Though she was incapable to protecting herself, her wolf still rose to the surface, on alert.

Corbin grinned as he walked closer, and Bay's heart stopped. He held Micah in his arms in a surprisingly nurturing gesture. She didn't want to set him off and have him drop Micah or crush him. He was a wolf and could break those little bones so easily.

Her wolf growled, and she had to bite her tongue to keep from doing the same. She couldn't provoke the man, not when he held her everything.

"Your Micah is quite a little bundle of wolf, isn't he?" Corbin sneered. "I like him. He'll do well by my side."

She couldn't help the growl this time.

"Tut-tut. Watch your temper. You never know what could happen." He held out Micah with one arm, and she held back a gasp. "I wouldn't want to drop him. He's so tiny."

"I'll do whatever you want. Just don't hurt him."

Corbin frowned and held her baby closer to his chest. "See, now that's not fun at all. You weren't supposed to cave so easily. Well, it's not as if I believe you. I mean I'm still going to have fun cutting you up to see you bleed. I need to be sure of your loyalties. Because, right now, you're still that Redwood bitch. But, don't worry; I'll take care of you." He smiled, showing way too many teeth, and set Micah on a pad of blankets near the edge of a pool. She worried her lip thinking that if her son moved just two inches he'd fall in the water. Corbin followed her gaze then threw his head back and laughed. "If he's a fucking idiot and falls in the water, then it's all on him. I gave him a blanket and everything. He can deal."

Corbin stalked toward her and grinned. Nausea rolled through her, but she kept her chin up. She might not be able to beat the demon, but she was of higher rank and power than this sadistic wolf—she wouldn't cower from him.

"Oh, you think you're a badass?" He sneered. "Well, fuck you." His hand shot out, and he stuck a needle in her neck. A sensation like warm oozing honey flowed through her, and her body went lax. "It's just a mild sedative. Okay, not too mild, but whatever. You'll stay awake—I like it when they stay awake for this—but you won't be able to fight back. At least for now. Once I get you strapped onto my table, you'll be able to thrash a bit, but that just makes it more fun. Isn't my Caym amazing? He brought my table all the way from our den." Corbin sighed, and Bay wanted to throw up.

"You should know that this table has a special place in the Redwoods' hearts. I've played with Hannah and Willow on it." His eyes grew stormy, and he snarled. "Oh, and that bitch Ellie, since apparently she's a fucking Redwood now. I can't wait to see her again because I'm going to gut that bitch. Slowly."

Bay struggled not to panic. If he were talking about his own sister like that, she didn't want to think about what was coming. She just hoped Adam got there quickly to save their son and maybe they'd kill her quickly.

God, what a fucking weakling.

Her body lolled and grew limp as he released the shackles and threw her over his shoulder. He palmed her ass, and she retched, throwing up along his back.

"You fucking bitch!"

He threw her against the wall, her face taking most of the impact. She felt her cheekbone shatter, and tears streamed down her face, but she couldn't move. She looked out of the corner of her eye and watch Corbin strip and jump in the pool. He quickly got back out and stormed toward her, his body wet and his eyes gleaming.

"You'll pay for that." Naked, he dragged her by her leg toward a table that stood in the center of the cave opening. He lifted her in one movement and clawed off her clothes. Inwardly, she fought back, her wolf howling with rage. Outwardly, she lay limp as the medication took hold.

Corbin sneered and grabbed a sharp looking knife from a nearby table. Without speaking, he sliced five long ribbons on her stomach. Pain laced through her, and she tried to move again.

"I'm going to enjoy this."

"Get your fucking hands off her," Adam growled from the edge of the cave. The scent of pine washed over her, and she growled.

*"No, he can't be here; he needs to save Micah,"* her wolf pleaded.

Bay tried to talk, but her tongue wouldn't work.

Corbin laughed and lunged at Adam. Adam moved to the side and twisted so Corbin would trip. The other wolf fell to the ground, growling.

"Touch my mate again, and you'll wish I'd have killed you sooner."

Bay used all of her strength and moved a finger. Thank God, the meds were winding down. Apparently, Caym didn't know her strength. Good. She couldn't let her mate fight on his own. Not now, not ever.

\*\*\*\*

Adam picked Corbin up by the throat and shook the bastard. Rage poured through him at the sight of Bay lying naked on the table, fear in her eyes, and her body seemingly paralyzed. When he'd awoken from

Bay's attempt at leaving him, he'd growled and wanted to kill something. But he'd held back, knowing Bay had done it for a reason.

They couldn't risk his family. He'd known that. And although he'd have preferred she not run off, he knew he wouldn't have let her go by herself. Once they got out of here, they'd have to have a long talk about not running away, but before then, he needed to make sure his family was safe.

He'd followed her trail to the cave. She hadn't done anything to hide her tracks, and that's how he'd known she'd been expecting him to follow her. Whether to save her or their son, he didn't know. But it didn't matter; he'd save them both regardless.

When he'd entered the cave, he'd crept along the wall, away from where Caym and the others were. He'd seen Micah right away and hidden him outside, knowing his family would follow his trail and find him. He hadn't come with them because he too was afraid of what Corbin had put in the note. He needed to take all precautions.

Corbin growled and turned on him. Adam ducked to the side and gripped the bastard's arm, twisting at the same time until he heard a break. The other wolf howled in rage and clutched his arm. Adam took the knife from the bastard's hand and stabbed him the belly, twisting the knife as he did. Corbin screamed, and Adam stabbed him again. Corbin lay in a heap on the floor, breathing with a shallow rasp.

Adam didn't waste any time. He ran to Bay's side and started to undo the clamps.

"Bay, baby. Talk to me."

"Tr...trying." She winced and closed her eyes.

"Baby, I know it hurts." Her cheekbone looked broken, and there were long cuts on her stomach. Other than the external damage, he didn't think any of them were life threatening. She was a wolf, she could handle it. Thank God.

"Drugs."

"Fuck, he drugged you?"

She tried to nod and whimpered.

"Okay, baby. We'll get out of here."

"Mic..."

"He's safe. Let's get out of here. I love you so much, Bay. I should have told you before. I love you so much." He kissed the bruise on her cheek and felt the soft spray of tears against his lips.

"I love you, too," she whispered, and his wolf howled.

"Oh, you stupid wolf. Why would you think that?" the demon drawled.

Adam whirled around at the sound of Caym's voice and growled. "I'm going to kill you, you fucker."

Caym threw his head back and laughed. "You really think you can take me? You're a puny little wolf who can't even protect his mate by keeping her at home. You're going to die, and I'm going to make sure your Pack knows how weak you truly are."

He could feel Bay trying to move behind him, but he kept his focus on Caym. The demon was stronger by far, but Adam could hope that he could keep him off Bay and Micah long enough to get her out.

"You won't get her." Adam settled his weight on the balls of his feet, letting his claws slowly come out of his hands so he could attack.

Caym shook his head. "Oh, how little you know, you arrogant wolf. I already have her. She told Corbin she'd do whatever he wanted."

"Under duress," Adam growled.

"He hadn't even strung her up yet. She caved too easily if you ask me. Must be that wolf blood in her."

224

Adam felt the slow rumble in his chest as his wolf clawed at the surface, ready to claw the fucker's face off.

"Why are you doing this? Did the other demons throw you out?"

*"Oh, that's good, just antagonize the demon," his wolf said as he rolled his eyes.*

Adam ignored his wolf, though he did agree with him. Being a sarcastic ass probably wasn't the best thing to do, but he needed to get Bay to safety, and the best way he could see to do that would be to distract him. Even if it meant dying.

Caym's eyes flashed red, and he charged. Adam rolled to the side, landing in a crouched position, and swiped at the demon's legs. Caym moved away before he could touch him and rolled a ball of demon fire between his palms.

Fuck.

Adam ducked to the side as the fire flew past him, singeing hair on the side of his head. Pain shot through his scalp, and he patted down the flames. Ah hell. Caym came at him again, but this time Adam stood his ground but lowered his head. He socked the bastard in the stomach, enjoying the gasp the other man released, then moved away.

They went at each other, fists flying, attacking with fire and claws. His chest heaved as he caught his breath, but Caym didn't give him any time. The demon took him by the neck and threw him against the cave wall, clearly tired of playing with his toy. Adam cursed as his head smacked against the sharp rock, pain blinding him. His leg slid down and wedged between two boulders, and he froze.

Fuck. Fuck. Fuck.

He tried to get out, but he couldn't move. Spots danced in front of his eyes as he felt blood seep down his back from where he'd hit the cave wall. He couldn't see Bay, but she had to have moved by then. Hopefully, she wouldn't do anything stupid, and she'd leave him to go get Micah.

He gripped the walls of the cavern and tried to lift himself up to no avail. The demon laughed and moved closer. Adam growled and used all his strength to try to break free.

"The little doggie is stuck in a trap I see," Caym sneered.

"Fuck you."

"Oh, I just might, little wolf. If there's anything left when I'm done." His eyes flashed red, and he gripped Adam's side. Fiery pain seared through his leg as Caym ripped Adam from the rocks. His body convulsed as an odd, hollow sensation swept through him. He looked down at the blood pouring out of him and blinked.

Oh, shit.

His head lolled back, and he tried to gather the strength to fight back but couldn't. His vision dimmed, and he cursed.

He'd lost.

Just as he passed out, a blur of red crossed his vision.

*Oh, Bay, no love, you should have left. You can't be here.*

Not now.

\*\*\*\*

Bay screamed and sliced the knife through Caym's wrist, forcing him to drop Adam to the cavern floor.

226

She watched as her mate slid to the ground, blood pooling around him where his right leg had been.

*Oh my God.*

Caym turned to her and howled. "That hurt, you little bitch."

"Get off my mate."

"Oh, I love it when wolves get all territorial. It's all 'mate this' and 'mate that.' Well, fuck you and your mate. I'm tired of all this wolf bullshit. Do you know how hard it is to get the wet fur smell out of my clothes? Fuck this. I'm just going to kill you and your precious little mate now. Though it seems like your little Enforcer may be dying now as it is. What-the-fuck-ever."

Rage poured through her, and tattoos spiraled up her arms. She looked down and froze.

"I see you've come into your power. All it took was killing your mate. Nice." Caym nodded and looked over her naked body. *Gross.* "You might just be useful after all."

"Fuck you." Power stretched and ebbed through her. He body pulsed, thrummed. She stood straighter, ready to fight. She was part demon, she could take him. She felt stronger, ready. She didn't know exactly what had happened, other than she had broken looking down at Adam.

"People keep saying that, yet here I am, fuckless."

She roared and lunged. Caym didn't move, underestimating her. She slashed out with her knife, stabbing him above the heart. His eyes widened for a moment, then he looked down at the gaping wound. He staggered back, breathless. Bay kept her eyes on him but lowered herself to Adam's side. She tore off his shirt and tied it around the wound as tight as she could. As it was, he'd lost too much blood.

*Oh my God.*

Bay looked up as Caym came at her again. She reached for the second knife she'd taken from Corbin's passed-out-but-not-dead body and threw it at him. The blade ripped through the air as fast as lightning and slid through the demon's eye. He roared in pain as blood gushed from the wound.

"Bitch!" He flashed away, and Bay let out the breath she'd been holding.

"Adam? Adam?"

He didn't move, and tears slid down her cheeks.

"Oh, God. I'm so, so sorry, baby. I love you so much. We need to get you to North. We can fix this."

She looked over to where his leg was jammed between the rocks and let out a sob. There was no way she would be able to get it out, carry him, and find Micah at the same time. Reeling from the decision she had to make, she stood, naked as she was, and gripped under his shoulders. She took a deep breath and dragged him to the edge of the cave. Though he wasn't heavy to her, he was way too big and at an awkward angle for her to carry him any other way.

When she'd made it out of the cave, a small whimper caught her attention, and she let a breath out on a sob.

Micah.

She carried Adam to a grove of bushes and lowered him to the ground. Micah lay in a grouping of blankets, his face red and angry from hunger, his little fists bunched up as he cried. She lifted him to her and sobbed as he nuzzled her neck. Her baby was okay.

It had only been two minutes or so, but it had been too long. She moved Micah away, cradled his crying form in her arms, and lifted Adam again. Her body groaned, and her cheek was in pain, but she started moving through the forest. She needed to save her family.

228

A wolf broke through the trees, and she screamed.

Kade.

Thank God.

He quickly shifted to man and froze. "Oh shit." He ran to her side and lifted Adam from her hold. "Oh damn, Bay. Oh damn."

"He's alive, but he needs North now."

"Where's his leg?" his voice cracked as he said it, but as the Heir, he was still strong.

"I had to leave it. I couldn't hold it and Micah.

"We should go back for it," Kade said, his voice cracking.

"No!" Bay screamed. "No, I can still feel Caym close by. We need to go. I know Adam will hate me for making this decision for him, but I can't risk him and Micah. We need to go. Please."

Kade nodded, sorrow in his gaze. Jasper and Reed broke through the trees and shifted.

"Holy fuck," Jasper breathed, and took Adam's other side so he and Kade could carry him easier.

"Oh, God, Bay." Reed looked pointedly at the new tattoos on her arms and blinked. "I'm so sorry." Without saying anything else, Reed lifted her into his arms. Though she wanted to be strong and walk on her own, she didn't have anything left to do so she cradled Micah closer, and her new family carried them out of the forest, away from the demons and evil.

As the memories of what she'd seen and done came to her, she closed her eyes and wept.

# CHAPTER 20

Adam groaned and reached for his leg as it flared in pain. When he hit air, he froze. What the hell? What happened?

He thrashed against the bed, his fists clenching, his body writhing in pain. He could feel the cool, clammy beads of sweat form on his brow but couldn't bother to wipe them off. He tried to open his eyes, but his eyelids were too heavy.

"Adam?" A voice... but not the one he wanted, needed. "Adam, open your eyes. I need to know you're okay."

Adam mumbled something but couldn't form the words he needed.

"Adam, it's me, North. You need to wake up. I can't give you drugs, and Hannah can only heal you so much. I need to know where you're at."

Adam relaxed somewhat at knowing his brother was by his side. North was always there when he needed him. Adam knew he would be okay.

But what about Bay and Micah? Oh, God, he'd left them.

Flashes of how he'd got to where he was flooded him. The fight with Corbin, seeing Bay lying on the table in pain, Caym.

Caym.

He remembered the blinding pain of being ripped from the rock.

His leg.

Fuck.

He gritted his teeth, fought back the overwhelming urge to vomit from the pain, and cracked open his eyes. He could feel North's relief emanating from him when he did so.

Adam opened his mouth, his lips cracked and dry, and tried to speak.

North shook his head. "Don't try, Adam. It's enough that you're alive. We'll take care of you."

Adam closed his eyes, forced himself to gain the energy to do what he needed to do, and opened them again. He swallowed and winced in pain then opened his mouth.

"Bay. Micah."

It was all he could say, all he needed to say.

North gave a small smile then gave him some water. "They're fine. Your mate is freaking amazing."

Adam tried to smile, but he just wanted to go back to sleep at the relief of them being okay.

"Bay got you and Micah to where we could find you all and is okay. She's a little banged up." He patted Adam's shoulder as Adam growled at that. Bay couldn't be hurt; he wouldn't allow it. "She's fine. Micah is fine, just hungry, but Bay took care of that. You're the one we're worried about."

Adam nodded and sank back into the pillow. "She's an Alpha," he whispered, his voice rough and sore.

North nodded then shifted from foot to foot. "Do you remember what happened?"

Adam closed his eyes, unable to speak. Someone put a cool glass to his lips, and he started, opening his eyes in surprise.

Ellie's eyes widened, that frightened deer look of hers becoming more pronounced. "Sorry, I thought you might want some water."

Adam tried to smile to make her feel better. Now knowing firsthand the acts of brutality the Centrals could wield, he had a newfound respect for one of their newest Pack members.

He let the cool water flow down his throat; it was almost healing. He swallowed down almost half the glass before she took it away.

"I don't want you to drink too much too fast and get sick," she whispered.

Adam nodded then looked behind her at Maddox, who seemed to be frozen in place. He met his brother's eyes and felt all the resentment and guilt slide off him. He'd known he'd always felt off near his Omega brother because of the connection he'd had with Anna in those final moments. But now he could feel only such an agonizing pity that Maddox had to go through that.

"Hey, man," Maddox grumbled. "You didn't answer North's question. But I think I already know the answer. Don't I?"

Adam nodded. "I remember everything about my lack of limbs."

North sighed and sat on the other side of him. Adam turned his head and faced his brother. "For all that wolves can heal, we can't grow back limbs. We lost your leg, Adam. Bay is taking it hard."

Something shattered within him. He'd known he was too late. He'd professed his feelings for her when they'd had nothing to lose, though he'd wanted to do it earlier. She hadn't wanted a full man. Why would she want half a man?

Maddox came up to him and held his hand "Adam, don't think that."

Adam huffed a laugh then grunted in pain. "I thought you couldn't read minds."

Maddox shrugged. "I can't. But I know what you're feeling. Bay loves you. One leg or two. It sucks. You're going to have to live hundreds of years like this, but you're strong. You're the Enforcer. You're going to make it."

Adam wanted to believe him. But in all honesty, what could he do with one leg? He was a fucking werewolf. When he shifted he'd only have three legs. Holy shit.

Everything started to crash down on him, but his wolf growled. Not at the situation, but at him.

*"We are strong. Don't forget that. We lost our Anna, and we almost lost our Bay. We won't lose again. Remember that."*

Adam closed his eyes at his wolf's words. For the past twenty years, he'd ignored and resented his wolf. But he'd been wrong to do that.

*"I've missed you, too."*

Adam let out a rough laugh, and Maddox smiled, the stark contrast between the white jagged scar on his face and his tanned skin deepening.

"You're going to be okay," North added. "We'll fit you with a prosthesis, the best out there. You're tough."

"What about being an Enforcer?" he asked, afraid of the answer.

Ellie shook her head. "You know the Moon Goddess is the one who decides who gets what power and position. If you couldn't do your job, she'd have given it to someone else."

"No, it doesn't work that way. It will go to only Kade's sons."

"If he has them. If not, it will go to a Pack member who can protect their people. I know being a member of my old Pack is a death sentence, but they did have the same powers you did. The same hierarchy. I know what I'm talking about. If the Moon Goddess didn't believe in you, you wouldn't still have your powers."

As Adam could still feel the rest of the Pack and their dangers, he knew he was still the Enforcer. Tension radiated through him.

"What if I can't do it?"

"You will, Adam. I believe in you." Adam turned to the voice at the door and his breath caught.

Bay.

\*\*\*\*

The others quickly filed out the room as she walked toward him, Micah in her arms.

"I believe in you," she repeated.

She looked down at him, her breath coming out in weak pants. He looked so big against the hospital bed, but so weak. He had gashes along his forehead and arms, and bruises in various stages of healing dotted his body. He was shirtless, his ripped muscles still looking sexy, even though he was in pain. Yes, there had to be something wrong with her. Here she was, thinking of all the ways she could lick and rub up against his body like a cat in heat when he was injured.

234

She pointedly looked down his body and rested to where his leg had been.

God, she felt so guilty for leaving his leg in the cave. Though she hadn't had a choice, she still wanted to weep at her failings.

"I know I'm not a full man. You can leave when you want to."

She looked sharply at him and frowned. Micah stirred in her arms, and she patted his little butt to calm him as the tension in the room increased.

"You are everything to me. You are an amazing man. Never sell yourself short. *Never* call yourself anything like that again. You are not half a man. You are *my* man. And *never* downgrade yourself in front of our son. Do you hear me?"

Adam smiled, his green eyes gleaming. "I like it when you get all fiery. Your red curls bounce around your face."

She relaxed and walked to his side. "Hey." Cautiously, she trailed her finger down his arm until she reached his hand. He gripped hers tightly, and the tears she'd held back since she walked in the room slid down her cheeks.

"Aw, baby, don't cry for me." He pulled her closer, and she moved to sit next to him on the bed. She did it carefully, afraid of hurting him.

"I don't want to hurt you," she said on a hiccup.

"You'd only hurt me if you didn't sit by my side, Bay."

She swallowed hard. "I love you."

He smiled, tears forming in his tired-looking eyes. "I love you too."

He held her hand, and she held Micah with her other. "He's okay?" he asked.

"He's perfect." When Adam let out a relived breath, she smiled. "We'll make it work."

He nodded then traced the newly formed tattoos along her arms. "Like Josh?"

She closed her eyes, hoping beyond hope when she opened them the tattoos would be gone. But of course, when she opened them, they hadn't disappeared. They were still as dark and vivid as ever. "Josh and I think it's because I finally let go and let my demon half rule for a bit. It was the only way I could be strong enough to save you."

"You know, at any other time in my life, like ten minutes ago, I would have felt the need to say I could take care of myself. But if it's you saving me, I'm okay. Though I'd rather save you."

"Actually, I wish no one had to save anyone."

He grinned. "But if someone *had* to save someone..."

She smiled. "I love the male mind, so arrogant."

"I can't help it. It's in my genes."

"I don't think these tattoos are going away."

"Good. I think their damned sexy. I can't wait to see what they taste like."

She blushed and was sure her face matched the color of her hair. "Adam, not in front of Micah," she scolded.

"He's going to have to get used to it."

Warmth filled her. Though it was aggravating and sad beyond hell that it had taken a near-death experience for them to actually talk, she would take it. They needed to move on with Micah and with each other.

"I think we can try that."

"Good," he said, smiling, though he still looked so tired. She'd have to let him sleep soon, but she didn't want to leave his side. "Do you know if you have any other new powers?"

She shook her head and cradled Micah closer to her when he fussed. "Not yet. I think only time will tell."

"Then we'll deal with all of that together."

"Adam, are you sure? You're not just reacting to the fact you almost died? You really want us?"

He met her gaze head-on and nodded. "I love you, Bay Jamenson. I love you and our son. I'm sorry I didn't say it before. Nothing can fix what I did before. I know I acted like an ass and treated you horribly. You deserve so much more than me."

"Adam..."

"No, let me finish, please. You came to this Pack for help, and I made you feel like crap, like nothing. No, less than nothing. I was so busy mourning a life I'd lost I couldn't see the life I had and could have. I'm so sorry, baby. But I'll do whatever I can to make it up to you."

Warmth filled her, and she leaned over to kiss him softly. He parted his lips, and she moaned. With great reluctance, she pulled back. "I love you, Adam. You don't need to make anything up to me. You already have by being here now."

Micah let out a cry, and she pulled back so he had more room to move around.

"Let me hold him."

A sweet thrill, a sense of their future, whipped through her, and she carefully placed their son in his arms. He cradled Micah in his large hands, and tears slid down her cheeks.

"Hey, buddy," Adam said, his voice a raspy breath. "Your momma is so brave. I hope you know how special you are. I'm going to do everything in my power to prove to you and her that I can be the best daddy and mate. Okay?"

Bay's body shook as she sobbed with happiness.

"We've been in our heads and haven't been talking. That's why we got to where we were. We were too scared to say what we were feeling, and we almost lost each other. We need to be with each other in actions, not just words."

Adam nodded and lifted his arm so she could settle against his uninjured side. His warmth seeped through to her bones, and she sighed.

"I want to be a family. I'm going to be the Enforcer of our Pack and protect us. But I'm going to need you on my side."

"Yes, always."

"Good, and then we can start making more babies and have Jasper and Kade add on to the house."

Bay laughed softly and played with Micah's little foot as it poked out of his blanket. "You're sure thinking a lot."

"I haven't been living for so long, and I've missed so much. I don't want to miss anything else with you."

She sighed again and smiled. "I like that idea."

"Good, because, Bay Jamenson, you're my mate, and I will do everything to make sure you know that."

"I already do, Adam. I already do."

# CHAPTER 21

B ay knelt in the grass, the cool breeze blowing through her hair. She closed her eyes, letting the early afternoon sun warm her face. Adam knelt beside her and wrapped his hand around her shoulders. They'd left Micah with Cailin so they could make this trip together.

"Hey, Anna, I've brought someone I think you should meet," Adam said as he kissed Bay's forehead.

Though she'd expected to feel a twinge of jealousy for the woman who had, for so long, held Adam's heart, she realized she couldn't possibly feel that. The place radiated warmth and peace, something Anna herself had also done according to everyone else.

"Hi, Anna, it's me, Bay, though I guess you already know that." Bay blushed, feeling awkward. Adam kissed her temple and rubbed her arm.

"You're doing great, Bay. So, Anna, this is my mate, the woman I've told you about."

The fact that he'd already told Anna about her made Bay want to smile and lean into his embrace. So she did.

"I just wanted to let you know I'm going to take care of him, Anna, I promise."

"She has a lot on her plate, I think."

Bay laughed and brushed a speck of dirt off Anna's tombstone. "I'm going to take care of him, don't worry."

They sat and spoke to Anna for a few more minutes until a gentle wind rushed along her face. She could have sworn it was a palm cupping her face.

Anna.

Bay gripped Adam's hand helped him stand and led them back to their home. He was still on crutches and wouldn't be fitted with a prosthesis for a few weeks, but he was getting the hang of it. It made her want to scream in anger when she saw nothing below his knee. They were both angry but moving on. He would learn to walk again, and when needed, he would learn to move on three legs when he shifted. He was stronger than he thought he was. God, she loved him. They still had a lot to talk about, but they were moving in the right direction with even talking at all.

"We have a Pack circle meeting tonight, but we have the afternoon off for just you and me," Adam said as his voice grew lower.

"And Micah is going to be with Aunt Cailin until after the circle." She grinned, and he crutched toward the bedroom.

"Meet me there," he called out.

"Wow, what a come-on. How will I survive?" she teased.

Adam laughed, and she followed him. Once she met him in their bedroom, he looked unsure of himself.

"I'm not sure how to...you know." He gave a weak smile, and her heart broke for him.

She smiled and kissed him, the scent of pine enveloping her. "We'll figure it out. We'll go slow."

He growled. "But what if I don't want to go slow?"

"Then we'll go faster. It's no biggie. As long as I get you, I'm happy."

"Mmm, I like that."

Bay smiled then gripped his shirt. "Sit on the bed."

He raised a brow. "Bossy?"

"Hell yeah, plus, I want to do something we haven't done before."

Adam groaned and hobbled over to the bed.

"No wait! Don't sit yet. Can you stand a bit longer?"

He laughed then nodded. "Come here, Bay."

She walked toward him and wrung her hands. "Sorry."

He rested on his crutches then cupped her face. "Stop being nervous. What is it you want me to do?"

"I want you to strip down and then sit on the bed."

His eyes darkened, and he groaned. "Okay." He gulped, and she kissed his nose.

"I'm going to see you, Adam. *All* of you. Don't be afraid."

"I don't think I could be afraid with you by my side, Bay."

"You say the nicest things."

"Not always, but I will."

He slowly stripped down, and she didn't help him. She knew he needed to do some things on his own and didn't want to make him feel weak. Because no matter what the Centrals had done to him, he would never be weak.

He finally stood on his one leg, naked, and aroused. His long body was tanned, well-muscled, and all hers. His cock stood out, and she licked her lips.

"Fuck, Bay, when you do that I just want to slide my cock down your throat to feel those pretty lips wrapped around it."

"I know. That's one thing we've never done. Now sit down on the edge."

"Yes, ma'am."

"Damn straight." He sat down and put his crutches off to the side, and she stripped down as well.

"I love you naked. Well, I love you every day, but damn, you naked? Hell, yeah. Come here and let me lick those pretty nipples."

Yep, she was pretty sure she almost came from his words alone. As it was, her pussy was so wet she could feel her juices sliding down her inner thigh.

"As much as I want you to do that, I want to taste you first."

"God, I love you."

"Because I want to go down on you?" she teased as she knelt between his legs.

He brushed a hand through her hair and grinned. "Among many things."

"Good." With that, she scored her nails down his thighs, being sure not to mess with the bandage at the end of where the rest of his leg used to be.

He hissed in a breath, and she licked up the vein on the underside of his dick.

"Fuck!"

She grinned then swirled her tongue around the head, licking that little taste of pre-cum. The musky flavor burst on her tongue, and she groaned.

"Mmm." She sucked him down whole, hollowing her cheeks, then looked up at him.

"Holy fuck, Bay." He brushed her cheek, and she bobbed her head, letting her throat relax to take him down farther. "Jesus, I'm going to come before I get in

242

you, baby. With you looking up at me like that when I'm down your throat, I just may die happy."

She licked and sucked him then rolled his balls in her hand. She felt his cock start to twitch as she slowly rubbed the spot behind his balls. He gripped her hair, and she relaxed, letting him set the pace. She widened her mouth as much as possible, and he thrust harder. She hollowed her cheeks again, and he bumped the back of her throat before screaming out, his cum heating her tongue. She swallowed it all then lapped up any she missed.

She looked up at him, her body thrumming with heated energy.

"God, Bay, that was hot."

She grinned then stood on shaky legs before pushing him back on the bed. "Wanna see something hotter?"

"I love you."

"I love you, too." She straddled his still hard cock and smiled. Damn, she loved werewolves and their stamina. "Wait, do we need a condom?" She groaned. She didn't want to have to get up.

"No, if we make another baby, then that's fine. I just want you."

Warmth spread through her, and then she slowly slid down his cock. They both groaned as she sat to adjust to his girth. Her pussy wrapped tight around him, and she squeezed her muscles.

"Holy shit, if you do that again, I'll come, and I don't think I have another one in me, baby."

She laughed then leaned down to kiss him. "Then let's get moving."

He gripped her hips and thrust up, using his leg as leverage. She leaned over him and moved with him, his hips meeting with hers with every thrust. His cock hit that special spot, and her body thrummed, reaching that exact level of tension that said something was going to happen soon. She threw her head back as he licked and bit her nipples.

Just as that tension reached its highest point, she looked into his eyes, which glowed gold with passion. She knew hers would reflect that passion as well. "I love you."

"I love you, Bay Jamenson." He thrust harder, faster, impaling her with his cock, and then they both came, falling, cascading, until they lay panting, out of breath, and sweaty.

"Well, at least we still got it." Adam laughed.

"You know, we may have to try again, just to be sure."

Adam held her close, his cock still deep inside her, and kissed her temple. "Whatever you say. I'm game." He squeezed her ass, and she wiggled down on him, content and happy.

****

Adam traversed the dirt walkway on his crutches, trying not to curse because he just wanted his leg back. Yes, he was okay with what his life was now, but that didn't mean every once in a while he didn't just want things to be easier.

Bay rubbed the small of his back but didn't guide or help him. He loved that she knew he needed to walk in there under his own power—even with crutches. This was a Pack circle, and he needed to be strong, be the Enforcer.

They walked into the circle, the stone stadium seating resonated the deep power of an age-old magic and the passing time filled with rites and tradition.

The other Pack members turned toward him, and he raised his chin. As a group, the Pack member who were not of his family lowered their gazes and bared their throats. Acceptance spread through him.

They wanted him.

But not just him.

He could feel their submission toward Bay as well. They were the Enforcer pair. They, together, would protect the Pack.

He let out a breath, and Bay kissed his shoulder. "Let's go, big boy."

Adam leaned over and kissed her forehead then made his way to where his family was already sitting.

Cailin wasn't there as she was watching the Jamenson children by herself, but he knew she'd find out everything that happened once one of them made it to her. Maddox sat to the side, alone, his gaze resting on Ellie, who sat close to North. It was odd, but Maddox never seemed to want to touch Ellie. Adam didn't understand it, but it wasn't his business. Yet. Ellie leaned over and whispered something in North's ear, and he shook his head. Adam could hear Maddox's growl. When his brother noticed Adam watching, Maddox turned and faced the center of the circle.

To the other side of Ellie and North sat Reed, Hannah, and Josh. Hannah sat between her two men, leaning into Reed's embrace and holding Josh's hand. Adam held back a wince at the scar on Josh's neck. They'd come too close to losing him. There was an air of sadness around the trio, but Adam didn't know what had caused it.

Jasper and Willow sat on the other side of Reed, Willow leaning heavily into Jasper's side. Those two looked like they were in sync in everything they did.

Even though their mating had started out rocky, they were closer now than ever.

Adam and Bay made it to their seats in front of Jasper and Willow and sat. Jasper slapped Adam's back in hello, and Adam raised his head. Kade and Melanie came in last, their steps sure and steady. They were the Heir mated pair and truly were ready to be Alpha. The people in the circle lowered their heads in submission, and Mel and Kade nodded back, a sign of their acceptance and seniority.

Once they sat down, Bay leaned into Adam's side, and they watched as the Alpha, his father, walked up to the podium, his mother standing behind him in support.

The wolves lowered their gazes, their bodies humming with respect, awe, and submission. This was their Alpha, their protector, their leader.

"We're here tonight because we've come to a time when we must take a stand," his father began, his voice low and soothing in that odd sense of an Alpha, the tone that held magic and promise. "The Centrals have gone to the depths of hell and are no longer merely wolves. Their souls are dark and clouded, their bodies mere husks for a much darker power. We, as Redwoods, cannot do what they have done. Nor do we want to.

"They have killed our families and our friends, breached our wards, and come into our homes. This cannot happen again. We will not allow this to happen again."

The circle shouted in response, and the Alpha held out a hand. They quieted at once.

"With each fight they bring us, we have fought back. But we are losing. We are Redwoods. We. Do. Not. Lose."

The shouts returned, and his father let them. The wolves showed their anger toward the Centrals, their solidarity toward their own Pack. This was Pack. This was home. Adam squeezed Bay closer and felt her wolf rise against his. Her wolf was Pack now and didn't want to lose either.

Good.

"When Josh and Hannah came into our Pack, we gained the trinity bond and the ability to block the demon from opening another portal to hell and bring others to his cause. Without that, Caym was cut off from his brethren. That helped because we can fight one demon. We have to. But more than one? An army? No, we don't have to fight that. But we were still losing. Our wards were still being breached. But now, with the addition of a new member, we will have the upper hand on our wards."

Adam stiffened as Bay moved from his side and stood. He raised a brow, and she kissed him softly.

"Don't worry," she whispered as she and Kade made their way to his father's side.

"You all know that Bay is the daughter of our enemy, Caym," his father said, his voice daring anyone to object to her presence.

No one did.

"The blood running through the demon's veins is the reason he, and those he shares a bloodline with, can break our wards. Yet, when Josh was bitten, it wasn't enough. His blood wasn't enough to help us secure the wards. But Bay's blood will be."

Alarm spread through Adam, and he growled. What the fuck were they planning? How much blood did they need? Jasper gripped his shoulder and held him back. Oh, fuck.

His father nodded to Kade and took out a menacing blade. Adam reached for his crutches.

"With her blood, our wards will be strengthened through the Alpha and Heir bonds. She is family, she is Pack, she is ours."

With that, he quickly sliced into his palm and then Bay's. Adam growled again at the sight of her blood. She'd already been brought into the Pack when he'd bit her and marked her, but this was different. Bay hadn't prepared him for this.

"Let it happen; she'll be okay. She's tough," Jasper whispered, but Adam ignored him.

Their Alpha and Bay clasped hands, and Adam felt the magic wash over him and their Pack. It was as if he could feel the strength of her blood in their wards. Kade sliced his palm and Bay's other hand, and Adam growled. Magic washed over them as Kade pressed his hand to Bay's and the three at the podium connected in magic and power.

Bay held up their joined hands, the three of them standing as one, and the circle cheered, the power and strength and togetherness pouring out of all of them. Bay smiled then ran to Adam's side.

"I'm fine, see?" She held out her hand, and Adam kissed the now healed wounds.

"Never do that again."

"That's why I didn't tell you."

"We'll talk about this later," he said as he bit her lip then laved the sting he surely caused. "I love you, Bay."

"I love you, too, my big bad Enforcer. We're going to beat them you know."

"I know; we have to." He held her close and kissed her temple, letting her cool ice-and-berries scent wash over him.

As long as his mate was in his arms and their child was safe, they would be okay. They were Redwoods; they could survive it all.

248

# EPILOGUE

Caym screamed and threw a dagger at a wolf. The wolf yipped then fell to the floor. The fucking Redwoods had changed their wards. They had used his own flesh and blood to do it. He'd kill her. He'd kill them all.

"We'll crush the Redwoods, Caym," Corbin promised as he hugged him from behind. "We have to."

Caym didn't find any comfort in his words or touches. He never did.

"What is your plan then, oh Alpha?" he sneered. "Tell me."

"We'll use Ellie. She'll come back if we force her. If I can't get to her, we'll make her come to us."

Caym turned in Corbin's arms and looked at the man who he called lover.

"What is your plan?"

"Take away the one thing she has. Trust."

Caym nodded. That just might work. They'd use her as their inside track. After all, if they could unleash their horror from the outside, they could use her like a virus from the inside. Between her and his plan with the other, all would be well. They would win, and the Redwoods would crumble.

And if they killed the Central princess in the process, well, that was just the icing on his cake.

## The End

*Coming soon in the Redwood Pack world, a special novella with the triad of the Pack, Hannah, Josh, and Reed, called Blurred Expectations.*
*Then...Maddox.*

# A Note from Carrie Ann

Thank you so much for reading **ENFORCER'S REDEMPTION**. I do hope if you liked this story, that you would please leave a review. Not only does a review spread the word to other readers, they let us authors know if you'd like to see more stories like this from us. I love hearing from readers and talking to them when I can. If you want to make sure you know what's coming next from me, you can sign up for my newsletter at www.CarrieAnnRyan.com; follow me on twitter at @CarrieAnnRyan, or like my Facebook page. I also have a Facebook Fan Club where we have trivia, chats, and other goodies. You guys are the reason I get to do what I do and I thank you.

Make sure you're signed up for my MAILING LIST so you can know when the next releases are available as well as find giveaways and FREE READS.

Adam and Bay's story is only beginning. You'll be able to read more about them in the entire Redwood Pack series. I'm also not leaving this world completely. You've met some of the Talons and because I fell for Gideon the first time he walked on the page to help the Redwoods, I knew I had to tell his story. I also knew I wanted to write some of the Redwood Pack children's stories. Rather than write two full series where I wasn't sure how they would work together, I'm doing one better. The Talon Pack series will be out in early 2015. It is set thirty years in the future and will revolve around the Talon Pack and how they are interacting in the world and with the Redwoods. Because it's set thirty years in the future, I get to write about a few of the Redwood Pack children finding their mates.

The first novel will be about the Talon Alpha Gideon and....Brie, Jasper and Willow's daughter thirty years from now. It's called *Tattered Loyalties*.

If you don't want to wait that long, I also have my Dante's Circle and Montgomery Ink series going in full swing now so there's always a Carrie Ann book on the horizon! Plus coming in 2015, I have the Bad Boys of Haven! Wow, I'm tired just thinking about it but I can't wait.

**Redwood Pack Series:**
Book 1: An Alpha's Path
Book 2: A Taste for a Mate
Book 3: Trinity Bound
Book 3.5: A Night Away
Book 4: Enforcer's Redemption
Book 4.5: Blurred Expectations
Book 4.7: Forgiveness
Book 5: Shattered Emotions
Book 6: Hidden Destiny
Book 6.5: A Beta's Haven
Book 7: Fighting Fate
Book 7.5 Loving the Omega
Book 7.7: The Hunted Heart
Book 8: Wicked Wolf

Want to keep up to date with the next Carrie Ann Ryan Release? Receive Text Alerts easily!
**Text CARRIE to 24587**

# About Carrie Ann and her Books

New York Times and USA Today Bestselling Author Carrie Ann Ryan never thought she'd be a writer. Not really. No, she loved math and science and even went on to graduate school in chemistry. Yes, she read as a kid and devoured teen fiction and Harry Potter, but it wasn't until someone handed her a romance book in her late teens that she realized that there was something out there just for her. When another author suggested she use the voices in her head for good and not evil, The Redwood Pack and all her other stories were born.

Carrie Ann is a bestselling author of over twenty novels and novellas and has so much more on her mind (and on her spreadsheets *grins*) that she isn't planning on giving up her dream anytime soon.

## www.CarrieAnnRyan.com

**Redwood Pack Series:**
Book 1: An Alpha's Path
Book 2: A Taste for a Mate
Book 3: Trinity Bound
Book 3.5: A Night Away
Book 4: Enforcer's Redemption
Book 4.5: Blurred Expectations
Book 4.7: Forgiveness
Book 5: Shattered Emotions
Book 6: Hidden Destiny
Book 6.5: A Beta's Haven
Book 7: Fighting Fate
Book 7.5 Loving the Omega
Book 7.7: The Hunted Heart

Book 8: Wicked Wolf

## The Talon Pack (Following the Redwood Pack Series):
Book 1: Tattered Loyalties
Book 2: An Alpha's Choice
Book 3: Mated in Mist (Coming in 2016)

## The Redwood Pack Volumes:
Redwood Pack Vol 1
Redwood Pack Vol 2
Redwood Pack Vol 3
Redwood Pack Vol 4
Redwood Pack Vol 5
Redwood Pack Vol 6

## Montgomery Ink:
Book 0.5: Ink Inspired
Book 0.6: Ink Reunited
Book 1: Delicate Ink
Book 1.5 Forever Ink
Book 2: Tempting Boundaries
Book 3: Harder than Words
Book 4: Written in Ink (Coming Oct 2015)

## The Branded Pack Series:
## (Written with Alexandra Ivy)
Books 1 & 2: Stolen and Forgiven
Books 3 & 4: Abandoned and Unseen (Coming Sept 2015)

## Dante's Circle Series:
Book 1: Dust of My Wings
Book 2: Her Warriors' Three Wishes
Book 3: An Unlucky Moon
The Dante's Circle Box Set (Contains Books 1-3)

Book 3.5: His Choice
Book 4: Tangled Innocence
Book 5: Fierce Enchantment
Book 6: An Immortal's Song (Coming in 2016)

**Holiday, Montana Series:**
Book 1: Charmed Spirits
Book 2: Santa's Executive
Book 3: Finding Abigail
The Holiday Montana Box Set (Contains Books 1-3)
Book 4: Her Lucky Love
Book 5: Dreams of Ivory

**Tempting Signs Series:**
Finally Found You

# Excerpt: Shattered Emotions

**From the next book in New York Times Bestselling Author Carrie Ann Ryan's Redwood Pack Series**

Maddox Jamenson ran a hand through his too-long hair and looked out onto the land that had for so long called to his family and Pack. The tall trees weren't redwoods, but damn close because they seemingly touched the clouds, reaching for something that he didn't even know if he needed. He looked over his shoulder at the sound of the party he was late to, but ignored it.

They'd just have to wait a bit longer.

The cool October air tickled the back of his neck, sending shivers down his body, though those shivers didn't just come from nature. No, the power he held as the Omega of the Redwood Pack drained then filled him with more emotion than he should have been able to take.

Being the Omega was his job, his destiny. He could feel every emotion from his Pack, every need, want, desire, and heartache. It was up to him to block it all out or take it in and try to help.

One day he'd take a break from it though.

Step away from the Pack and the den, if only for a moment.

If only to breathe.

He held back a laugh. No, that wouldn't be any time soon. Not in a time of war and strife. In a time of loss and new life within his own family.

He was Maddox—he'd stay where he needed to be.

Alone, but surrounded.

He was so freaking tired, and he really didn't know why.

Thoughts of dark eyes and an even darker past flashed through his mind, and he closed his eyes.

Oh, yeah, that's why he was so tired.

"Mad?" Cailin, his baby sister, called as she came up to stand beside him.

Maddox looked down at her striking beauty, her black-blue hair and stunning Jamenson-green eyes. Even though she was only in her twenties, he knew he'd have to start fighting off potential mates soon. No way was he going to let his little sister get hurt.

"What is it, Cai?" he asked as he wrapped his arm around her shoulders. Unlike the rest of his family, he wasn't that comfortable with touching others. He'd held Bay when she'd needed him after the birth of her son, but he didn't like hugging anyone else—except his sister.

And maybe *her*...

No, never *her*...

"Why are you out here standing all alone?" she asked. She leaned into his hold, loneliness, a common emotion with her, leached off her and seeped into his chaotic hold on his own emotions.

He shrugged, not really knowing the answer. He'd always preferred to be alone, especially these days. The feelings that came from being the Omega fell on his shoulders with a heavy still silence that never went away.

Cailin scoffed, and he was pretty sure he could feel her rolling her eyes. She wasn't very subtle.

"You need to stop moping, brother mine."

"I'm not moping," he countered.

"Oh, shut up. You've been moping since you-know-who came you-know-where."

"Oh, my, however shall I figure out that code of yours?" he teased, not liking that she saw right through him.

"Well, I could say her name for you if you're that lost." This time a happier emotion drifted from her. She smiled, and he pinched her arm.

"Hey! I'm going to tell Mom!" She rubbed her arm and stuck her tongue out.

Maddox threw his head back and laughed—something he hadn't done much of lately. "Oh, my God, you're like twelve."

"Am not."

"I'm not going to argue with you."

"Why are we fighting?" she asked and smiled again.

"Because you're a pest and my baby sister."

Cailin let out a breath. "I really wish all of you would stop calling me your *baby* sister. It's not like I'm in diapers anymore. I'm a woman."

Maddox closed his eyes and groaned. "Don't remind me."

"Hey! I don't understand what your problem is. Kade and Jasper went out all the time and found women. Reed found men *and* women. Adam wasn't a monk before Anna. You've had your fair share, even if you're hiding most of it. And, North...well, I don't really want to think about what North's up to."

Maddox shook his head, trying to get the images of North doing whatever the hell he did out of his mind. In fact, he tried to keep his twin out of his mind more often than not, especially lately when the betrayal that was of his own making tasted too fresh. He'd been the one to push them together so he'd be the one to deal with it.

"You're not allowed to date," Maddox ordered, ignoring the pain that came with thinking of North.

Cailin leveled a look at him. "Um, I think I am, and I have been dating if you haven't noticed."

Rage filled him, his fists clenching as his heart raced. "What? Who? What little prick do I have to kill?"

Cailin threw up her arms and stomped away before she turned around, stomped right back, and got in his face.

"You see? This is why I don't mention it. I'm a woman. Not a girl. A woman. I've dated humans and wolves. Not that I'd let you know who. Oh, and I'm not a virgin. Just so you know."

Maddox covered his ears with his hands and hummed.

No, there was no way his baby sister was talking about...well...sex.

No. Freaking. Way.

"Sex. Maddox. Sex. Sex. Sex."

"Stop it, Cailin!"

"Oh, my God! You're such a prude!"

"And you're too young to have sex."

"Oh, shut up. It's not like I'm screwing every man I see."

Maddox closed his eyes again and prayed for patience. "I would hope not. We're already in a war with the Centrals. We don't need to kill our own Pack members."

Cailin rolled her eyes. "You need to grow up. Okay? I'm being safe—with my body and my heart. I haven't found a mate yet, and my wolf is just now starting to want one. When it happens, I don't want my brothers beating him up."

"I'm not making any promises. You have six of us, plus Josh. Not to mention what the women will do. Oh, yeah, and our folks."

"I know, hence why I'm telling you." Acceptance seeped off her, giving him another taste of emotion.

"I don't want to think about you and a man. Okay?"

"Fine, don't think about it. Just don't get in the way. Now, do we want to talk about your mating?"

"No." Hell freaking no.

"No?"

"No. Now, I'm going to go talk to Dad," he said as he brushed by her.

"Maddox Jamenson! Don't you dare tell Daddy what we talked about!"

"You know, you only call him Daddy when you're in trouble."

"Oh, shut up. Don't you dare tell him I had sex."

"You'll have to catch me first." He took off at a run, Cailin chasing behind him at full steam, which was difficult in the dress she wore for the party they were late to.

He wouldn't actually tell his dad. Some things were sacred, though if some bastard thought he could touch Maddox's baby sister, that would be another story. He'd have to do some digging on his own—after the party.

Cailin jumped on his back and wrapped her arms around his neck. "Don't, Maddox!"

He laughed, even though she was blocking his air. She released her hold, and he tossed her to the ground. She glared at him from below him, her dress pooling around her and her eyes glowing gold as her wolf rose to the surface.

"I won't, lady bug butt."

"I hate when you call me that. And you got my dress dirty."

"You're the baby, get over it. They're used to seeing you in mud. You're a tomboy, even if you try to hide it."

"I hate you, Maddox."

"Love you, too, lady bug butt."

Maddox gripped her hand and picked her up off the ground as they both walked toward the den center where Adam and Bay's belated mating ceremony was being held. They'd have to be ready to smile and act like the two of them—Maddox and Cailin—were perfectly happy being the few unmated Jamensons. Even if it was of his own choice in his case.

His baby sister had put a smile on his face, even though she gave him more worries than he needed at his age. Maybe everything would be okay.

He spotted a wisp of dark hair out of the corner of his eye and froze.

Well, hell, maybe not *that* okay.

North, his twin, walked up to him, the object of Maddox's pain on his arm. He and North looked almost identical with the same too-long sandy blond hair, same jade-green eyes, same athletic build.

North, however, was missing the jagged scar on the right side of his face.

Not that Maddox would have ever wanted his brother subjected to that.

Not for anything his twin had done in the past, present, or future.

He still loved the man, even if it hurt to look at him.

"Oh good," North said, "I'm glad we're not the only ones running late. I have a feeling Adam and Bay won't mind since they only have eyes for each other."

Maddox nodded silently and forced his gaze to North's companion.

Ellie Reyes.

His mate.

Or, at least, his could-be mate. Wolves had a few potential mates out there, some more suited than others, so that didn't mean when one found that potential they had to mate.

Maddox *couldn't* mate Ellie. Though the mating urge had reared up and rode him hard, he hadn't marked her, hadn't mated her—despite how desperately he wanted to.

She wasn't to be his.

His wolf nudged along the inside of his skin, whimpering but, as always, didn't say anything.

Ellie stood by North's side, that haunted look in her dark brown eyes reaching out to Maddox. He couldn't feel her emotions though—just as he couldn't feel North's. It could have been considered a blessing, but Maddox was never sure.

He wanted to know what made her tick, what went on in that mind of hers. He wanted to be able to help her, even if he couldn't bear to be near her.

North gave him a bland look, but Maddox could see his twin clench his jaw. Ellie stared at him as if she wanted him to say something, but he had no idea what.

"We're already late, guys. We don't want to be any later," Cailin said over the rising tension.

Maddox shook his head, trying to clear his thoughts of the woman with dark eyes who could have been his and wasn't.

North looked between Maddox and Ellie, a shuttered look on his face, then nodded. "Agreed. I'm not in the mood to deal with the wrath of any of the Jamenson women."

Maddox blinked, tearing his gaze from Ellie. He was only torturing himself.

They made their way to the den center where the mating ceremony between Adam and Bay would take place. Though the couple had been mated for almost two years, they hadn't had the ceremony or celebrated their joining with their family and Pack yet.

Maddox couldn't really blame them for waiting, not when their meeting had been too tumultuous to begin with. Adam had almost lost Bay with his pain—Maddox hid a wince at that.

Goddess, that pain had almost been too much for him to bear—for Adam *and* Maddox. It was little wonder Maddox had tried to put a distance between him and his brother after Adam had repeatedly shaken off his help. There was only so much most Omegas could take before he broke down and sobbed uncontrollably.

Not that he did that.

No, he was stronger than that. He buried it all and worked with what he could. He could shut out the mid-level emotions, the ones that ran through the Pack daily. The high-level happiness was almost too overwhelming sometimes.

He thought back to the time Mel and Kade, his brother and Heir, had announced their pregnancy. The joy in the air had been so thick, so overwhelming, that Maddox had to set himself apart from the celebration.

Like usual.

The elation and cheer sometimes did help tone down the pain and angst within the Pack. For every person within the web who smiled, there was another who cried, and Maddox felt it all.

It was a wonder he didn't go freaking crazy.

"Maddox?"

He started at the sound of Ellie's voice.

Ellie.

Why was she talking to him?

She *never* talked to him.

They had an understanding. He wouldn't talk to her, and she wouldn't talk to him. That way they'd get over each other and their wolves would settle down, while she mated with North and made happy little pups.

It had never been spoken aloud, but damn it, it was their agreement.

Okay, fine Ellie hadn't mentioned it, but he'd live in his own denial and be fine with it.

"Yes?" he asked, his voice gruff.

"You're just standing there watching the Pack. I think it's freaking out the children."

Maddox frowned and looked at the group of pups around them, all standing still, their eyes wide. One of the little girl's lip trembled, and Maddox cursed inwardly. It seemed that his scar and overall attitude scared everyone these days.

"Sorry, just thinking," he mumbled.

"They're about to start," Ellie whispered, then left to stand by North without another word. It was as if standing by him hurt too much to deal with.

Well, it wasn't a fucking picnic for him either.

"Uncle Maddox?" Finn, Mel and Kade's son, asked as he walked toward him.

Maddox grinned at the little boy who would one day be Alpha and had so recently been broken beyond repair—or so most had thought.

He reached down and picked his nephew up, needing the comfort himself. He didn't know why, but Finn settled him more than anyone else. If Maddox didn't know better, he'd say Finn could have been the future Omega, but no, since he was slated to be alpha, it must have been just the strength of his character that shone through.

The little boy would make a great Alpha one day.

"You ready to see Uncle Adam and Aunt Bay kiss?" Maddox asked, and Finn shrugged. At two years old, Finn didn't get the whole idea of cooties yet. It would come.

The rest of the family stood upfront surrounding Bay and Adam as Maddox made his way to stand near them, Finn still in his hold. He moved so he could stand by Mel and Kade, that way they knew their son was safe. He couldn't blame them for the worry seeping off them. After all, they'd almost lost Finn before.

Jasper and Willow stood beside them, their daughter Brie in Jasper's arms. It never failed to amuse Maddox to see the big bad Beta holding the little girl with such reverence. Across from them, Hannah stood between his brother, Reed, and their mate, Josh, each of the men holding one of their twins. Again, the sight of the big men going soft and holding their babies made Maddox think it was all worthwhile. Beside them, Cailin, North, and Ellie stood, though Ellie stood apart from them, as if she didn't want to be there.

After all, because she hadn't officially mated North—or himself, no, don't think about that—she wasn't family, but that didn't stop the Jamensons from wanting her there.

His parents stood at the top of the circle and began the ceremony. Maddox tuned out the words; he had to. The joy was so overwhelming he felt as though he was going to burst. Each of family members seemed to radiate happiness and promises of a future. Sweat rolled down his back as he fought to take it all in.

Sometimes too many good feelings were as bad as the painful ones, but he had to stick through it. He'd scream and curse at the goddess for his powers later.

His gaze met Ellie's, and he froze, all thoughts of happiness fleeing him.

He couldn't tell what she was feeling because even a bond he should have held with her through the Omega was non-existent, but he saw it in her eyes—envy...and pity.

She knew what he was dealing with.

Yet, she wanted what Bay and Adam had.

Maybe North would help with that.

Maddox couldn't do it.

The crowd started to clap, and Finn touched his cheek. He met his nephew's eyes and nodded. Yes, it was time to act like the happy brother, not the angst-filled Omega he seemed to be lately.

Maddox looked at the happy couple as they kissed, Adam picking Bay up easily, as if he hadn't lost his leg in the war with the Centrals. Bay's long red hair framed her face as the wind picked up, blowing strands around both her and Adam, bringing them even closer together.

A child's scream pierced the celebration, and Maddox tensed.

"What the hell?" Kade asked as he took Finn from Maddox's arms and handed him to Mel. "Take Finn. We're going to find out what that was."

Mel clutched Finn close but looked as if she wanted to join them. He pressed a hard kiss to his mate's lips then turned toward Maddox and the rest of his brothers.

Adam growled, a line forming between his brows. He ran a hand up and down his mate's arm as Bay frowned as well. Adam was the Enforcer, meaning he could sense danger and threats from outside forces. "I don't sense anything. It's not from outside the Pack."

Maddox met his brother's gaze, each of them knowing what that meant. If Adam couldn't feel it, that meant it was from *inside* the Pack.

The brothers and other pack members ran in the direction of the scream. Pain, tension, worry, and anger pulsed at Maddox through the bonds, and he had to tamp them down. He couldn't focus on what was in front of him if he worried about what was within him. Another scream echoed amongst the trees, and the sense of dread that had only been a small ball before now grew, tearing at his stomach, sending shivers down his spine.

Gina, the daughter of Mel and Kade's closest friends, Larissa and Neil, ran up to them, tears running down her face, her dress torn and muddy. Her skin was as pale as a ghost, her eyes wide, haunted.

Kade picked her up and held her close. "What is it, baby?"

"Mom..." The little girl hiccupped and buried her head into Kade's neck.

Maddox kept running, reached down, and felt for the thread that connected him to Larissa and Neil. With all the emotions running through the day, he hadn't been able to deal with them all, so he'd blocked down some of them.

He stopped and closed his eyes, searching for the thread but coming up empty.

Oh, no.

No.

Maddox heard Jasper's howl of anguish when he opened his eyes, knowing what he'd find when he stepped closer.

Larissa and Neil lay in a heap of tangled limbs and blood, their eyes vacant, their bodies cooling.

Melanie came running behind him, her scream tearing through him. The emotions of the others—terror, grief, and vengeance—slapped at him.

The scene was out of a horror novel. The scent of death lingered in the air, but that's not what scared him.

No, it was the underlying scent of another that made his body shake as his wolf clawed at his skin. It wasn't a new scent or a wrong scent. No, this one was familiar, almost comforting, and yet it was now all over the dead couple, blending with their fading ones.

It was the spicy scent of the most decadent dessert, the scent that haunted his dreams and, right now, filled him with dread.

Ellie.

Maddox looked over his shoulder as she walked toward him, the scent intensifying as her presence added another layer to the older scent trail. Her eyes were wide, unbelieving.

The others froze. Wolves that were not family growled as she came to his side.

She couldn't have done this.

The evidence was there...wasn't it?

He took her hand, and she gasped at the unfamiliar contact.

Her soft skin yielded under his, and he brought her closer, needing to protect her even though she wasn't his. His wolf needed to do this more than it needed air.

There had to be another explanation because, if there wasn't, the woman he'd hidden from, the woman who could have been his mate, had just signed her own death warrant.

# Dust of My Wings

## From New York Times Bestselling Author Carrie Ann Ryan's Dante's Circle Series

*Humans aren't as alone as they choose to believe. Every human possesses a trait of supernatural that lays dormant within their genetic make-up. Centuries of diluting and breeding have allowed humans to think they are alone and untouched by magic. But what happens when something changes?*

Neat freak lab tech, Lily Banner lives her life as any ordinary human. She's dedicated to her work and loves to hang out with her friends at Dante's Circle, their local bar. When she discovers a strange blue dust at work she meets a handsome stranger holding secrets – and maybe her heart. But after a close call with a thunderstorm, she may not be as ordinary as she thinks.

Shade Griffin is a warrior angel sent to Earth to protect the supernaturals' secrets. One problem, he can't stop leaving dust in odd places around town. Now he has to find every ounce of his dust and keep the presence of the supernatural a secret. But after a close encounter with a sexy lab tech and a lightning quick connection, his millennia old loyalties may shift and he could lose more than just his wings in the chaos.

Warning: Contains a sexy angel with a choice to make and a green-eyed lab tech who dreams of a dark-winged stranger. Oh yeah, and a shocking spark that's sure to leave them begging for more.

# Ink Inspired

## From New York Times Bestselling Author Carrie Ann Ryan's Montgomery Ink Series

Shepard Montgomery loves the feel of a needle in his hands, the ink that he lays on another, and the thrill he gets when his art is finished, appreciated, and loved. At least that's the way it used to be. Now he's struggling to figure out why he's a tattoo artist at all as he wades through the college frat boys and tourists who just want a thrill, not a permanent reminder of their trip. Once he sees the Ice Princess walk through Midnight Ink's doors though, he knows he might just have found the inspiration he needs.

Shea Little has spent her life listening to her family's desires. She went to the best schools, participated in the most proper of social events, and almost married the man her family wanted for her. When she ran from that and found a job she actually likes, she thought she'd rebelled enough. Now though, she wants one more thing—only Shepard stands in the way. She'll not only have to let him learn more about her in order to get inked, but find out what it means to be truly free.

Made in the USA
Lexington, KY
21 April 2016